NIGHTMARE FUEL 2

WOL-VRIEY

NIGHTMARE FUEL 2

WOL-VRIEY

Burning Bulb

PUBLISHING

Nightmare Fuel 2
By **Wol-vriey**

Burning Bulb Publishing
P.O. Box 4721
Bridgeport, WV 26330-4721
United States of America
www.BurningBulbPublishing.com

Cover by Gary Lee Vincent with NightCafe Studio.

First Edition.

Paperback Edition ISBN: 978-1-964172-08-8

CHAPTER 1

Like it generally happens to individuals who've experienced something that everyone else considers impossible, it soon seemed to Dustin Mitchell that he had imagined everything that had recently happened to him.

Three weeks had passed since he'd escaped from the deranged Real Dreams cult and their worm goddess Boku Veeza. And during those three weeks, the very idea that such a group of people (or deity) existed had slowly come to seem more and more absurd to him.

In fact, Dustin would have put everything down to his having suffered a psychotic episode, but for three facts:

Firstly, the house opposite his—the Mills' house—was still empty, with neither of its renters having been seen in the past three weeks.

Secondly, his friend Seth Taylor was officially missing now, also for the past three weeks.

And thirdly, and most impossible to avoid, Dustin's ex-girlfriend Melissa was officially missing too. Along with her new girlfriend Jordan Hayes. Also, for the past three weeks.

The police had visited Dustin twice concerning Melissa Boyd's disappearance. Not to arrest him or because they considered him a suspect, but simply because the circumstances of her and her girlfriend's vanishing made no sense to anyone.

According to the detectives, both young women seemed to "Walked off of the face of the Earth."

Dustin could easily have told the detectives what he knew about Melissa and Jordan's disappearance, along with Seth Taylor's going missing, and also the strange emptiness of his neighbors' house, but if he did that, the police would think he was crazy.

Hell, Dustin hardly believed he'd experienced any of it himself.

A cult that worshipped a giant worm deity that had a woman's face; and that cult having its headquarters somewhere in eastern Massachusetts? Somewhere near Raynham, MA, where Dustin lived?

A cult that was powered by the strange narcotic named *Nif,* or more properly 'Nightmare Fuel?'

No, no one would believe Dustin Mitchell. And he had no proof of anything that had happened either.

So, since escaping from Real Dreams, Dustin had done the only thing he could—drink a lot of beer and continue with his life as if it had never been interrupted by those inexplicable experiences.

And for the past three weeks, this approach had worked very well.

But Dustin Mitchell's life was about to get complicated again. And in ways he couldn't even begin to imagine.

CHAPTER 2

Dustin was having a vivid nightmare. Of course, he didn't know this, everything seemed real as real could be, as many dreams tended to be.

Dustin sat in his living room, drinking beer and watching a TV show. It was late at night and he knew he'd better get to bed.

A realtor by profession, Dustin was showing a house to a couple tomorrow morning and he needed to be fresh for that appointment.

He got up, walked into his bathroom, and like he liked to say nowadays, he 'pissed the heartache away.' This description was apt because many times he drank to forget Melissa Boyd and Jordan Hayes, both of whom he'd had deep feelings for. His heartache for Melissa was understandable as he'd dated her for three years and they'd lived together for two of those. But he'd known Jordan for just one night, and somehow, in that short period, her memory had become indelibly engraved on his soul.

He switched channels on the TV, seeking something to hold his attention. He had the ceiling fan going at full speed; the summer was here now and there were hardly any cool nights anymore. The windows were open and so were the drapes, but he really couldn't see anything outside. The night was a dark presence that seemed to pulse with derision for those who lived their lives in daylight.

Dustin finally found a TV show he liked. 'Paranormal Wives.' It was a ghost-hunting show that was normally packed with busty women, and he settled down for an hour of amusement.

On tonight's show, the Paranormal Wives were chasing a black spiderlike creature that had escaped from Dimension 666 and was threatening to impregnate Earth's woman with horrible satanic versions of itself. Dustin watched in horror as one hapless victim of the spider creature began vomiting up its dripping bulbous eggs.

The woman seemed unable to stop throwing up and when she was done, there was a pile of these nasty throbbing pink orbs on her rug, while she herself had shriveled down to a skeleton covered in skin.

Dustin was horrified by what he was witnessing. And then he was even more horrified. Because, all of a sudden, the giant black spider thing was here in his living room.

However, the monster showed no interest in eating or (thankfully) impregnating Dustin, as he'd twice watched it attempt to do to men on the TV show, since, being a non-sentient alien, it had difficulty telling human genders apart.

And besides, as Dustin quickly noticed, the monster had brought its own dinner along with it. It was dragging a helpless woman—not one of the paranormal beauties—along with it. The woman was screaming entreaties at the alien monstrosity, all of which were unheeded, maybe because her voice was somehow silent.

Dustin wanted to rush to the poor woman's aid, but now there seemed to be a wall between himself and her; a flexible transparent wall that he could push against but not penetrate through. He understood that this wall was also what was blocking off the victim's screams from him.

He got a good look at the bug. It seemed to him the most horrible kind of insect. Totally black in color, its body was that of a giant cockroach, and its head was a giant featureless ball. However, the oddest thing about the monster was that it had lovely female breasts.

But Dustin didn't pay attention to the monster's body for long. The bug was already hanging the woman up on his living room fan. It had wrapped spider-silk from its spinnerets around her neck, knotted it into a noose, and was now tightening the noose around the woman's neck.

Dustin suddenly recognized the black bug's victim. It was Candice Raveling, the woman who'd lived in the house opposite his for several years, before she'd been murdered last spring.

But if she's dead, he thought, *and indeed Candice died by hanging back then, what the hell is she doing alive in my living room now, being hung all over again?*

Then Candice noticed him too and screamed at him.

"Help me, Dustin!" he lipread. "Help me!"

And then the invisible barrier seemed to vanish, because as the bug monster dropped Candice Raveling to dangle from the fan, she let out a final strident scream that Dustin heard loud and clear.

CHAPTER 3

Dustin Mitchell woke up.

For a moment he lay in bed trembling from the nightmare. He was sweating a little, but a slight breeze was coming in through the open window and this cooled him somewhat.

What the hell? Dustin wondered, as the terror the nightmare had filled him with slowly subsided. Since escaping from the Real Dreams organization, he'd had other nightmares that had integrated elements from his experience amongst those crazy worm worshippers, elements like the black insect and his murdered neighbor. But none of those dreams had been as vivid as this one.

Dustin pushed himself up on an elbow and then sat up.

And there was something else.

That scream I heard right at the end of my nightmare. Did I dream that or did I actually hear it?

The terror that had carried over to waking from the dream had all faded now, but the mystery about the source of the sound still disturbed him.

He flicked on the bedside lamp and stared at the clock on the opposite wall. The time was 3.19 a.m.

He stared over at his bedroom windows, both of which were open.

The sound seemed to have come in through the west window, which faced the currently empty (not vacant) Mills house.

It was that detail—that he could actually assign a location to the origin of the noise—that decided Dustin Mitchell. Had he not been able to place the direction that the supposed scream had come from, he'd have written it off as a mere figment of his fantasy. But now, he felt he needed to act, and act quickly.

For a moment, he considered calling the police. But what would he tell the 9-1-1 operator? He couldn't very well say that he'd had a nightmare and then imagined he'd heard a scream.

And yet, that scream! It had an urgency to it—like someone might be in danger. And if someone is in danger in the Mills' house, every second counts. I can get over there long before the police arrive, that's if they come here at all and don't simply dismiss me as a prank caller.

While reasoning this out, Dustin was already getting out of bed and pulling on some clothes. He was propelled by an intense sense of urgency.

That scream! If I actually heard it at all!

After finally pulling on a pair of sneakers, he picked up his cellphone, then grabbed a flashlight from the bottom drawer of the nightstand and hurried out of his bedroom.

His next stop was the kitchen, where he searched out the sharpest knife he could find. He wasn't taking any chances on what he might discover in the house opposite. He'd been thinking of buying a gun for protection, but hadn't gotten around to doing so yet.

He weighed the knife in his hand.

This'll have to do for tonight.

Dustin had gotten his front door open before he remembered that he would need the keys to his neighbor's house to get in.

Even though neither neighbor had been seen for three weeks, a copy of their house keys were in Dustin's possession, because he worked for the realty company that had rented them the building.

Dustin had been meaning to return the house keys to the office ever since tenants had moved in opposite, but he'd never gotten around to doing so, because his life had suddenly become so complicated that he'd forgotten the keys were in his house.

He hurried back now to pick up those spare keys and then ran out of his front door, with that horrible imagined scream propelling him on.

CHAPTER 4

At this time of night, Thiel's Way was silent as an empty grave.

Dustin was of course headed for the house opposite his, the one directly across the road.

The other three houses on the cul de sac began a hundred yards away on his left. Almost all of their interior lights seemed to be turned off.

Dustin crossed the road while a cool breeze blew around him and overhead the thinnest imaginable sliver of moon shone down.

The emptiness and silence of the night made it seem impossible that anything could be wrong so close by. The knife he was gripping tightly suddenly seemed completely unnecessary. He felt almost like he was in the wrong here, going across the street to attack someone.

What if the police suddenly drive past the top of the street and find me like this?

The lights from behind him, from his own house, were turning his shadow into a sinister thing, like a creepy silhouette from an old monster movie. Stretched up like this, the knife in his hand looked long and scary.

Dustin first adjusted his grip on the knife so that its shadow would look less threatening, then, when that didn't really make much of a difference, he moved his knife hand in front of his body so that it no longer cast a shadow beside him.

By now he'd stepped up onto his neighbor's driveway.

What if it's just some hobo squatting in there that just got scared by a rat? Or the scream could've been someone's TV. But, there's no sound from anyone's television. The night is as quiet as if everyone in Raynham has died.

That was a creepy thought, not the sort that Dustin needed when he was possibly entering a dangerous situation.

Anyway, he was about to find out what the true situation of things was. He'd reached his neighbors' front stoop and was now climbing the steps.

A few steps more and he was slipping the key in the front door.

CHAPTER 5

After he got the Mills' front door open, Dustin hesitated for a moment before stepping inside their house. This situation reeked strongly of déjà vu.

This is exactly the same way I found Candice dead. I smelled something like roadkill, crossed the street to investigate, and there she was, already rotting away.

But tonight, there was no smell of rotting flesh in the air. Finding that fact encouraging, Dustin pushed the door fully wide and stepped inside the house.

However, once fully through the front door and shining his flashlight into the darkness ahead, his worries returned.

Dustin knew for a fact that this house he'd just stepped into was haunted.

In fact, if his missing (actually *dead*) friend Seth Taylor was to be believed, this house was an incredibly dangerous place to be in. Talk less of residing in it.

And Doris and Reggie Mills rented this place because they wanted a haunted house to live in. So, I'm not being unreasonable if I expect to find a ghost in their living room now. What if the noise I heard was poltergeist activity? What the hell do I do then?

"Hey, is there anyone in here?" he asked loudly, while remaining in the foyer and playing the light over the closest walls. He now realized how idiotic his coming here was.

What if . . . no, not damn ghosts . . . junkies. What if there's junkies in here shooting up? What the hell do I do then?

He stared down at his knife and then stuck it in his belt. A kitchen knife wasn't likely to frighten drug addicts very much.

"Hey, I'm the realtor for the building," Dustin called out again, this time while aiming the beam of his flashlight into the living room, which he couldn't properly see into from where he stood. "I live across the street and I heard a noise. Is anyone in here? If there is, guys, you're trespassing, and if you don't get out now, I'm gonna call the cops on you."

Once again there was no reply. He thought he heard something though, like a rat that the sound of his voice had frightened away.

Taking courage from the silence, Dustin found the light switch on the wall and turned on the lights.

After snapping off his flashlight, he cautiously walked forward to the living room.

And then he stood there in the living room entrance feeling faint.

"Oh, holy fuck, not again!" he whispered in loud disbelief.

CHAPTER 6

But it appeared that the same evil lightning had struck twice in the same place.

Just like last spring, when he'd discovered the late Candice Raveling hanging from her living room fan, now there was another person dangling from the same fan. Illuminated only by light from the foyer, the body was indistinct.

Dustin quickly located the living room light switch and flicked it on.

Shit!

Just like last time, the victim was a woman. She dangled with her face looking away from Dustin, and he saw that her hands were tied behind her back with zip ties and that . . .

Oh no—they killed a cat again!

But yes, this woman's murderers (whoever they were) had killed another cat. The brown cat was strung up beside the woman, its neck beside hers in the same noose. It was dead, with its little furry form already stiff.

The woman had pissed on the floor beneath her and the cat had pissed down the woman's back, making her dress wet.

Did Real Dreams do this? Are they after me now?

But that didn't make any sense to Dustin.

Why would the Real Dreams organization kill this woman in the house opposite mine, if I'm their intended target?

This was a confusing point, because Dustin doubted that his previous associates had any further interest in him.

And . . . I've never been certain that Real Dreams were the one who killed Candice Raveling in the first place.

As Dustin stared at both corpses, the human and the feline, a feeling of indescribable revulsion settled on him. It felt like Death itself was dressing him in a shroud. In a very short while, the horror Dustin felt was so intense that it seemed like he was choking on it, and he had to step back from the bodies in order to breathe.

He'd stepped away from the body in a different direction to that from which he'd entered the living room, and this enabled him to see the dead woman's face.

Her black hair was in her eyes, so he couldn't tell if he knew her or not, but her face was turned blue, her mouth was partly open, and her tongue protruded.

He managed to overcome the urge to vomit that threatened to overcome him as he stared at her.

Okay, I need to get the police over here ASAP.

Dustin began feeling around in his pocket for his cellphone, seemingly unable to locate it, though he could feel his fingers brushing against its glass display.

Alright, I need to calm down here. So long as I don't see any female shadows flitting across the wall, I think I can manage that. Now I'll just take a deep breath, hold it and release it. Now, take another deep breath . . .

And right then, halfway through the second deep breath that was meant to calm Dustin, was when the supposedly dead woman opened her eyes and gasped at him.

CHAPTER 7

It took Dustin a few seconds to accept that the woman he'd thought was dead was actually still alive, and then he rushed to help her.

Relieved that he'd thought to bring a knife along with him, he pulled it out of his belt and hurried back to the woman's side. To touch her, he had to step in the wet piss-patch underneath her.

When he touched her, she began kicking; weakly, but wildly enough to hinder his attempt to rescue her.

With her hair in her eyes like this, and the dead cat dangling between them, he knew she couldn't see his face, and he suspected she thought that her would-be killers were back to finish the job.

"Calm down, I'm not going to hurt you," he whispered to her, suddenly aware that the individual or individuals who'd strung her up might still be in the house and might rush out at him at any moment.

She kept kicking. Realizing she was locked in her terror and possibly couldn't even hear him, he stuck his knife back into his belt. Then he stepped behind her, grabbed her around the waist, and lifted her up to release the strain on her neck. That worked, but it also meant he couldn't cut the rope away or even loosen it. For that he'd need a second pair of hands.

This position was also very awkward, because when he'd lifted the woman up, the dead cat's rear legs and tail had gotten wedged between them both, and contact with the dead animal was making him feel queasy.

Still holding the woman up, Dustin looked around, trying to figure out what to do, whether to lower her on the rope again and cut away at it, or . . .

Then Dustin hit on the solution.

"Hold on, I'll be right back," he told the woman and then lowered her back down on the noose.

She'd stopped kicking when he'd lifted her, but now she resumed, and so vigorously that he worried that she might inadvertently break her own neck.

Realizing there wasn't time to lose if he really wanted to save her life, he rushed over to fetch an end table from beside the living room couch.

Once back at the woman's side, Dustin arranged the end table near her dangling legs, and then hoisted her up again and set her feet on the table. Once he did this, she collapsed back on him. When she was acceptably balanced on the end table, he reached up and loosened the noose around her throat.

Once he did this, the dead cat fell through the noose. It hung between them for a second, before Dustin swatted it aside.

The noose had left a deep burn in the woman's flesh, in which the spiral grooves of the rope's twists were clearly etched. Made glaringly obvious by its very absence of hurt was the bare patch on the right side of her neck where the dead cat had been. In this case it was almost the devil's signature that something really strange had happened to her. The divisions of the indent looked like she had a fat pink worm wrapped around her neck. Its similarity to a memory filled Dustin with fear.

While the unknown woman gasped for breath, Dustin slipped the noose up over her head.

"Okay, you're free now," he told the woman when the looped rope was dangling safely by her right ear.

She fell backward into his arms then, and he carried her over to the couch.

CHAPTER 8

"Th-thank you! Thank you!" the woman gasped weakly, as Dustin lay her down on the couch.

Strangely enough, she sounded like someone he knew, but her hair was still in her eyes, plastered to her face by her sweat, and for the moment, Dustin ignored her identity.

What was important to him was that she was still alive.

It again occurred to him to call the police, and he even reached for his cellphone so he could do this. But then after an ill-advised glance at the dead cat, which had fallen into the circle of the woman's piss, he decided to instead first free her hands. Then he'd get her out of here, and then he'd call the cops. He couldn't shake the feeling that the killers were still around somewhere in the house.

And also, Dustin had had enough weird paranormal experiences of recent to know that one didn't hang around in a haunted house any longer than one needed to.

"You'll need to turn around so I can cut your hands free," he told the woman.

She did so readily if weakly, and he sawed at the zip ties until they separated.

Then, while she weakly rubbed at her wrists, he pushed the hair back from her eyes to see her face.

And yes, he discovered that he did know her.

CHAPTER 9

This woman whom Dustin had just rescued from death was one of the waitresses at the Real Dreams club.

He struggled to come up with her name. Then finally it came to him.

"Hey, you're Bianca, aren't you?" He didn't know her surname, however.

For a moment, his question seemed to unnerve her, as if she imagined he'd rescued her from one sort of death merely to subject her to another.

But then she nodded and wheezed, "Y-yes, I-I am. How d-d-do you know m-me?" Then she peered closely at him. "D-Dustin? It's y-y-you, isn't it?"

He replied with a nod.

"What are you . . . ?" She fell silent, wincing in pain and tenderly feeling her neck. Speaking appeared to hurt after the throttling the noose had afflicted on her throat, and Dustin waited patiently until she was able to finish her sentence: "Dustin, wh-what are y-y-ou doing here?"

"I live opposite this place," he explained, taking a seat beside her on the couch. "I was asleep, and just as I awoke, I thought heard someone scream. So, I came here to investigate."

She took some time to ponder this, and while she did so, he in turn recalled their previous encounter. Three weeks ago, she'd been walking almost naked through the Real Dreams clubhouse, laughing and serving glasses of *Nif*, the club's trademark drink, to its members.

And she offered me a blowjob, he remembered too. *And we both laughed and she offered me advice about not asking dumb questions.* He sighed, and regarded the angry rope burns around Bianca's neck. *And tonight, someone tried to kill her. Damn, those were happier times for us both.*

"We-we need to-to get out of here f-fast," Bianca told him painfully and slowly. The calm she'd originally shown after recognizing him seemed to vanish into thin air.

15

Dustin looked around and nodded. "Yeah. I was gonna call the police in on this, but . . . did the club do this to you?"

She nodded slowly, her gaze not leaving his.

"Well, I guess there's no point calling the cops then," he said.

She shook her head. "No there isn't. Y-you know wh-what they're c-c-capable of."

He looked around for a moment, and his eyes once more settled on the dead cat, the sight of which made him shudder each time he viewed it, though he didn't really understand why this was.

"Who did this . . . ?" he began asking Bianca, then finished: ". . . I guess you'll tell me the details once were safe in my place."

"Help m-me up, Dustin," Bianca wheezed at him and he bent and did so.

He got her to her feet and would've let go of her, but she was so wobbly that he held on to her.

While steering Bianca towards the light switch to turn off the living room lights, Dustin hoped that none of the neighbors had woken up during the period that he'd been in here, and had noticed that the house lights were on, and had decided to call the cops.

Of course, the probability of this happening was low, as all of the window drapes were shut, but . . .

There'd be no way in hell we'd explain the marks around Bianca's neck to the cops, or the dead cat either.

Then he relaxed. *What am I worrying about? Hardly anyone on our street knows that the Mills haven't been seen for almost a month now. I should be more relieved that since setting foot in here, I haven't encountered any ghosts!*

He flipped off the living room lights and steered Bianca towards the front entrance. She clung to him tightly. He was certain that after all the oxygen deprivation she'd just suffered, the world must be swimming before her eyes.

"H-how'd you g-get the keys t-t-to this place anyway?" Bianca asked slowly when they arrived at the front door. "On the way here, I h-heard that th-th-the house belongs t-t-to Reggie an-and Doris, but *their* k-keys are *still* a-at the clubhouse, i-in Queen Bee's office."

Dustin managed a smile as they stepped outside into the warm welcoming night.

"You may not believe it," he replied, "but my uncle owns the company that leased this house to the Mills."

"Oh, I di-didn't know that." Bianca said.

CHAPTER 10

Outside, the night was as barren of life as before. After considering the distance between the Mills' house and his own, and how long it would take Bianca to walk it even while steadied by him, Dustin decided to carry her.

She seemed relieved when he picked her up, and quickly wrapped her arms around his neck.

She said nothing as he walked down the Mills' driveway, across the intervening road, and up his own driveway.

On his front porch, he set her on her feet and opened his front door.

Once she was lying down on his living room couch, he went back to lock his front door. Then he returned to the living room and sat opposite her.

"So . . . what the hell . . . ?" he prompted, unsure if she was even up to making any dialogue at all. "Hey, maybe it'd be better if I just wait till morning to find out what happened."

But she shook her head. "I-I-I d-don't think tha-tha-that's a good idea." Once again, she tenderly felt the rope burn around her neck. "The way my throat hurts n-now, I doubt I'll b-be able to talk b-by daybreak."

He nodded his understanding. "Okay, but stop whenever you want. So, what the hell happened? Last time we met you were all . . . you know."

She attempted to smile, but the smile became a grimace. "There's not t-t-too much t-t-to t-t-tell. Our great hi-hi-high p-priestess Queen Bee ordered my-my execution."

That information really surprised Dustin. "But . . . but why would she do that? I recall that when we first met, *you* were advising *me* on how to behave at the club."

Bianca rolled her eyes and seemed to slump further down into the couch she was lying on. "The most crazy sh-sh-shit happened to me, tha-that's all. It turns out tha-that my boyfriend Freddy was a damn infidel."

17

"Huh?" Things now began to make sense to Dustin.

Up to this point, Bianca had been speaking slowly and also stuttering, choosing her words with care, as if large phrases might hurt her vocal cords while in transit through them. But now she grew animated and spat out her tale with fluent vehemence.

"I had no idea Freddy was recording our club meetings with a view to making a big media expose about Real Dreams," she went on, her previously pained expression turning angry. "And nobody believes I'm telling the truth that I had nothing to do with it, because Freddy, that asshole, hid all of the videos he'd made in my apartment."

"Shit!" Dustin said.

She frowned at him and sat up on the couch. "Yeah right, shit. Let me explain a little better. I room with Freddy's mother, who runs a boarding house in Attleboro. Mama Madison's a holy roller and I always thought that she and Freddy don't see eye to eye, but now I have the feeling she's the one who put him up to dating me and exposing the club."

Dustin was very aware that in her animated emotional state, Bianca had been doing more talking than was good for her throat. He wasn't in the least bit surprised when she suddenly gasped in pain, fell silent, and then grabbed her neck.

"Shit, I need a drink," she finally told him in a miserable voice, sounding now as if she'd just said everything important about her life that could ever be said. "Hey, you wouldn't happen to have any *Nif* around here, would you?"

CHAPTER 11

Bianca's request shocked Dustin. But of course, it made sense.

Nif (or 'Nightmare Fuel') was the psychological engine of the Real Dreams organization. The delicious rainbow-colored hallucinogenic drink altered the perceptions of its drinkers in very unsubtle ways, permitting them to see black as white and vice versa.

Under *Nif*'s influence, the most despicable and evil actions were regarded simply as 'an alternate way of doing things.' And, just like in a mass hallucination or a hive mind, all *Nif* drinkers shared the same corrupted thought process. Maybe they shared the thoughts of their worm goddess.

The rainbow drink's source? This was something that Dustin Mitchell preferred not to think about.

Dustin felt certain that before being hung in the Mills' living room, Bianca had been doped up with *Nif* to the point where she thought she was doing the cult deity Boku Veeza a favor by dying.

CHAPTER 12

"Shit, Dustin, I could really use some *Nif* right now," Bianca told him, while looking at him expectantly.

"I haven't any at home I'm afraid," he replied her, adding, "you gotta remember I was a newbie," when she gave him a disappointed look. "I hadn't yet begun having a weekly *Nif* supply."

"Yeah, that's right," Bianca grudgingly agreed. Then, all of a sudden, her expression brightened up. "Hey, I know where there's gotta be plenty of *Nif.*"

"Where?" Dustin asked.

Bianca gestured towards the living room windows that faced the street. "Back in the house we just left. Reggie and Doris Mills were the club secretaries and organizers. They've gotta have a ton of *Nif* in their home."

Dustin shook his head at her. "You're not seriously suggesting that we return to the house you just escaped from, the house where you were almost killed, just to fetch a drink."

It didn't seem like she understood the irony in his question.

"No, not both of us," she said weakly. "Just you go. It won't take long. They should have some *Nif* in their fridge."

And there it was, staring him in the face again. Dustin knew there was a decanter of Nightmare Fuel in the Mills' fridge; it had been there the last time he'd been in their kitchen, which had also been on the last day he'd been in their house before he'd 'escaped' from the Real Dreams organization.

Yeah, there's Nif in the fridge of the house opposite mine. And maybe there's a lot more of the stuff in the kitchen cupboards. And all of this while, like a former alcoholic who goes into a bar, orders a drink, but never drinks it . . . all this while I've successfully resisted going over there to have a drink of the stuff. And right now, when I've completely overcome the craving for Nif, when I don't even think about it anymore, I've got a woman in my living room who wants it.

"Maybe you should avoid *Nif* for the time being," Dustin told Bianca seriously. "Look at me. I've been off of *Nif* for weeks now and I'm back to normal."

"I don't want normal!" Bianca growled at him, having clearly once more forgotten how bad her throat hurt. Or maybe, the pain in her throat was part of the reason why she sounded so angry—her voice came out in this raspy tone like she was getting a cold. Meanwhile, the worm-like trench around her neck was bruising up nicely, swelling up fat and plump like a necklace filled with blood.

"I don't want normal," Bianca repeated with a little less fervor. "I just want my good life at Real Dreams back. I'd only worked there a couple months, but I loved being a fulltime Real Dreams employee. I want that life back, with my boyfriend not deceiving me to boot, and all of the *Nif* I can drink."

She stared at Dustin in desperation. Suddenly, tears filled her eyes and she began crying. "I don't think you understand it—but at the moment, I feel like I'm going nuts! I really do. I'm terrified, utterly terrified, and I just know that Tanana is gonna come back and hang me again, and I'm innocent. I'm fucking innocent—I never did anything to deserve being killed." She began tugging on the ends of her black hair. "Dustin, I'm even scared that the cops are gonna arrest me and find me guilty of being innocent."

"So . . . Tanana was the one who hung you?" Dustin said. At her mention of the demon-negresses name, he had instinctively begun looking around, checking the walls and drapes for an insect-limbed spectral female shadow with an immense spherical head. Thankfully, there was no such horror in sight.

Bianca wiped her eyes dry with the back of her hand. "And that clown asshole Malarkey too. Malarkey was holding me up in the air while Tanana was stuffing the cat into the noose, and Malarkey was making jokes, saying stuff like he just knew I'd love being dead, and how I'll be remembered as the woman who had two pussies and . . ."

Bianca broke out into full-blown weeping and Dustin considered the dilemma on his hands.

It's now 4:05 a.m. in the morning, and I have a crying woman in my house, a woman who's just escaped from the same cult I also escaped from and . . .

And then a sobering thought struck him:

This can't be coincidental. Why the hell would the Real Dreams organization murder, or at least attempt to murder, Bianca here in the Mills' house, knowing full well that I live right opposite . . . and that I'm the person most likely to find her corpse in three or four days' time?

A shiver of understanding ran through him.

It's like they're sending me a message. Or a warning. Like they're telling me, 'We know where you are, Dustin. You can run, but you can't hide from us.'

"So, Dustin, please, please, please, will you hurry over to Reggie and Doris's house and fetch me some *Nif?*" Bianca asked in a sad voice. "I really need a drink of that stuff right now."

CHAPTER 13

Dustin shook his head at Bianca. "Sorry, not gonna happen. I'm not for any reason going back over to the Mills' house tonight."

She replied his reply with an angry look and then attempted to get to her feet.

He wagged a finger at her. "And neither are you," he told her.

"But I need some *Nif!*"

"No,' he told her, still wagging that cautionary finger. "What you need to do, lady, is calm down and think clearly." At first, she looked like she would argue with him and attempt to leave the house on her own. If she tried to, she wouldn't make it far. For her own safety, he intended to lock the doors and also tie her up and gag her till morning if he had to. But he hoped it wouldn't come to that.

She stared at him and he stared back at her, until she hissed and settled back down on the couch again.

"Why fucking not?" she asked meekly.

"Use your head. Fifteen minutes ago, you were urging me to get you out of that house as fast as I could, and now you're urging me to go back there? You know as well as I do that Tanana and Malarkey aren't human. They could be back there right now, waiting for you . . . with another cat to kill alongside you. Or maybe even a puppy this time."

The mention of her recent narrow escape finally seemed to calm Bianca. The aggression in her eyes turned to worry and fear. All of a sudden, she was trembling with fright.

"Okay, you've convinced me not to visit there tonight. But how about in the morning? Will you fetch me some *Nif* then?"

Dustin shrugged. "Yeah, maybe; we'll see. Even demons need to sleep sometime." Then he frowned. "Hey, what is it with the pet deaths? Is that some sort of demonic edgelord thing?"

She waved the question aside. "Later, man, when you've gotten me some *Nif*, so that the craziness of my explanation makes sense to me."

Dustin let it go. At least, he wasn't going to have to restrain her.

He pointed to the clock beside the living room TV and then got up to his feet. "Okay, time to go to bed." He gestured to her to get up also.

Once upright, Bianca was still wobbling, which made Dustin hurry over to catch her before she collapsed onto the couch again. He smiled.

How the hell was she planning to make it over to the Mills' house anyway? On her hands and knees?

"I need to take a shower," she said as he escorted her along the hallway to one of the guest bedrooms. "I've sweat myself half to death and I've pissed all over myself, and it smells like the cat pissed on me too."

He pointed out the hallway bathroom to her. "I'll fetch you a fresh towel once I show you your room. Everything else you need is available in there."

She smiled. "You're a really nice guy, Dustin."

"You know what they say—nice guys finish last. Of recent, that's been my lot. I've been finishing last in lots of things, and I didn't even sign up for any of those races."

She looked to reply to that, but once again choked up from the pain in her neck. At least the corpse look was all gone from her face now.

"I think you've overshot your quota of words for tonight," Dustin told her as he opened the bedroom door for her.

She nodded mutely back at him and then yawned.

"Okay, so here you are," he told her, with an answering yawn of his own. "Hold on while I fetch you a towel. Then, have a shower and get some sleep. I'll very likely be gone from the house by the time you wake up, so you'll have to look after yourself; make yourself breakfast and all that. But I'll try to get home early, so we can work out what you're gonna do now."

Once more yawning, she nodded her assent.

He helped Bianca sit on the bed and then left to fetch the towel for her. Along with a tube of toothpaste and a spare toothbrush.

He'd also realized that she'd need a change of clothes. He recalled seeing some of his ex-girlfriend's pants somewhere in his bedroom a few days back, and Bianca could easily wear one of his tee shirts until she washed her own clothes.

Searching for the clothes however delayed him for longer than he'd intended. So much so in fact, that when he arrived back at the guestroom with everything, Bianca was fast asleep.

Dustin stared down at her slumbering form for a while, wincing again at the purple swelling that looped around her neck and at the corrugated indents the zip-ties had left on her wrists.

Deciding there was no point waking Bianca now, he left the things he'd brought her on the reading table in the guestroom and quietly closed the door on her.

Before going to bed himself, Dustin double-checked that all of the house doors that led outside were locked. Then he double-checked that his home security system was active. And then he took the keys out of their locks and carried them all to his bedroom.

No point tempting fate. True, Bianca was fast asleep now, but he wasn't taking the risk of her waking up and sneaking out of his house to attempt to break into the Mills' house.

CHAPTER 14

Friday morning.

Dustin's alarm clock woke him up at 6:30.

After peeing and brushing his teeth, he went to check on Bianca.

Bianca was still asleep, although now she was dressed in the clothes he'd brought her, meaning that she'd gotten up sometime before morning and cleaned herself up.

After once more grimacing at the rope burn around her neck, Dustin shut the door on her and went to brew himself some coffee. He felt groggy after the night's activities and needed to perk himself up. He needed to be in the office in two hours.

Once his coffee was ready, Dustin returned to his living room to think.

Bianca's presence here raised some bothering questions.

First of all, how the hell had she gotten to the Mills' house? Dustin had neither heard a car arriving nor departing. Even if he'd missed their arrival due to his being asleep, the latter noise would have been unavoidable if Tanana and Malarkey had brought her to the Mills' house using a vehicle, as they could only have left the neighborhood *after* she'd screamed (by which time he was awake again) and not before she'd done so, as she'd have been incapable of screaming once they'd tightened the noose around her neck.

But why fool myself? Dustin asked himself while sipping his coffee and trying to decide whether or not he wanted to catch the early morning news on the television. *I already know Bianca didn't arrive here either by a car or a van. They brought her here using the house as a supernatural portal from wherever the Real Dreams club is actually located. She herself said that Reggie and Doris's house keys are still in Queen Bee's office!*

His second question was one he was scared to attempt to answer. And the first second question triggered off a flow of follow-up inquiries in his mind:

And . . . why the hell did they attempt to kill Bianca in the Mills' house anyway? Why not do it elsewhere? And what the hell is this deal with stringing cats up with these women? Are the deaths meant to be sacrifices to their goddess

Boku Veeza? But if they're sacrificing women to Boku Veeza, why not do it in their temple at the Real Dreams club? Why the hell would they hang a second woman in this same house sixteen months after Candice Raveling's murder, when they know the cops will start looking for them once her death is discovered?

Too many unanswerable questions. Dustin turned on the TV and stared at the news anchorman, and considered Bianca's request that he fetch her some *Nif*.

He frowned, realizing that if he drank Nightmare Fuel, all of these illogical actions of the Real Dreams cult would immediately make perfect sense to him.

He shook off the temptation to hurry over to the empty house and raid its kitchen fridge of *Nif*.

I may have to do so anyway if Bianca proves unreasonable on waking up. And of course, once I've gotten the stuff for her, she'll only become a lot more unreasonable than before and will then likely then insist on heading home or to wherever it was that she was abducted from in the first place.

But as for Dustin, he'd resolved he wasn't touching that Nightmare Fuel drink ever again, not even with a fifty-foot straw.

Hell no, I'm not!

CHAPTER 15

Dustin's life hadn't exactly been static in those three intervening weeks.

He'd been to church twice.

The first of these had been when, along with his parents, he'd attended a cousin's wedding.

The second visit to God's house had been on Dustin's own initiative. He'd driven up to the Calvary Chapel church on upper Broadway on a Sunday morning and sat in with the congregation. He'd gone there seeking peace and answers to his questions, but had left unsatisfied and with even more questions.

God (the way Christians generally presented Him at least), was supposedly a kind and benevolent supreme being, never mind all the wars fought in his name and atrocities committed by overzealous followership.

Despite these perceived shortcomings of the Christian deity, Dustin would very much have liked to believe in Him. He just seemed so far away, not to mention completely uninterested in human affairs.

Because I've been in the presence of a deity, a goddess from the pit of nightmares, who isn't the least bit benevolent, a deity who seems to feed and thrive on the suffering of her worshippers.

If Boku Veeza is so easy to find, how come the kind and benevolent Christian heavenly father isn't?

Dustin had left the church resolving to come back at some point to speak to the pastor, and maybe even tell him what he'd experienced.

But he doubted very much that the preacher would believe the tale he'd tell.

CHAPTER 16

This Friday morning again.

Dustin was dressed and ready for work when Bianca emerged from the guestroom. He asked her to join him at the breakfast table and she did.

For a while, they ate in silence, with Bianca grunting in pain each time she swallowed.

Dustin studied her neck. It was much less swollen now. Its skin was peeled however, and she'd have some scars there.

This morning, Bianca was calmer. Now she seemed more like the attractive Latina he'd encountered at the Real Dreams club. While she forced her meal down her throat Dustin wondered if she'd still ask him to get her some Nightmare Fuel from opposite.

At the moment she seemed too composed to make such a silly request, but all it might take to make the craving return would be one moment of terror when *Nif* seemed the only way to steady her emotions.

Finally, with a grunt of disgust, Bianca gave up eating and just drank her coffee. Dustin chose this moment to open a conversation with her.

"What's your surname?" he asked her. "I keep reminding myself that I don't know."

"Sanchez."

He nodded.

She nodded back, drank her coffee, and looked around.

"So, what do we do now?" he asked after eating some more of his own breakfast. "Do you have somewhere safe where you can hide up for a while?"

"I've thought about that," she replied slowly, setting her coffee mug down. "I want you to hide me here for a few days." After saying this, she grimaced like her throat hurt badly.

"Yeah, that may be the best thing," Dustin agreed. "When Candice was murdered, I didn't discover her body for three days, not till she was going rotten over there. And so . . . assuming that no one comes back to the house to confirm that you're really dead—and I don't see why anyone would—you've got at least that long before Queen Bee and her demonic goons start looking for you." Then he frowned. "But where will you hide afterwards? Because, once the Real Dreams high priestess discovers you aren't dead, my house will be the first place she'll have checked for you. You'll need someone reliable to go to before then."

"That part is simple," Bianca replied with a cold smile. "I'll go back home. Freddy's mama is sure to know somewhere safe. Anyhow, all of my ID is at her house, so even if I want to leave town, I have to stop by there first." Bianca suddenly looked pissed off, and tapped the tabletop impatiently. "Hey, is it okay that I use your landline to call people? For obvious reasons, I don't have my cellphone with me."

He shrugged. "Be my guest. But be careful who you call. Don't call anyone who works at Real Dreams."

"Yeah, I won't. I don't wanna wind up like Freddy."

Dustin stared a question at her and she explained further:

"The club have Freddy captive now. They're gonna punish him at the next meeting. Dammit, how the hell could Freddy have been so dumb? He knew what would happen if he got caught!"

While saying this, she looked very upset. Her emotions were clearly torn, because even though Freddy had gotten her into trouble with the club, he was still her boyfriend, and she was very worried about what they would do to him.

Dustin realistically held out no hope for Freddy's survival. He'd witnessed several 'punishments' that Real Dreams had meted out to 'infidel spies' and all had been brutal and conclusive.

CHAPTER 17

The rest of Friday went as planned.

Dustin showed houses to two couples, rented one out to an Englishman on vacation, and then had lunch with his Uncle Rich.

Richmond Mitchell was a large man with an equally large voice. He had balding blond hair and a whitening mustache and beard. He was a shrewd businessman and Dustin was his favorite nephew.

The pair of them sat in the restaurant and ordered burgers and fries.

"Hey, have you heard from Seth yet?" Uncle Rich asked Dustin when they were halfway through their meal.

Dustin shook his head. "No, I haven't."

Uncle Rich paused before biting into his burger. "Strange, real damn strange."

"What's so strange, Uncle Rich?"

His uncle looked confused. "I'm talkin' 'bout the way, he and Amy just up and disappeared. I want them to handle another jinxed house for me—you know, check if it's haunted and all that stuff?" The older man bit into his burger, chewed a while, drank some of his Dr. Pepper, and then nodded again. "So strange, son. Even Woody don't know their whereabouts."

Woody Taylor was Seth's younger brother. Along with Jimmy Fisher and Jen Carlson, the three of them rounded out Seth's paranormal investigations crew GROW, aka the Ghost Research Outfit Worldwide.

Woody had called Dustin too, asking if he knew anything about Seth and Amy's whereabouts.

Dustin, who knew that Seth and Amy were both dead—murdered by Real Dreams—had simply lied that he'd not heard from them. There was no point in saying anything else.

"Yeah, it's really odd," he told his uncle now. "Normally, you'd expect Seth would take the others into his confidence if he and Amy were onto something big. Well, I'd expect him to tell Woody at least."

Uncle Rich nodded and looked disturbed. "Your neighbors the Mills, they back from their vacation yet?"

Dustin shook his head. "Not yet. Doris called me from Oregon yesterday. Said she and Reggie were enjoying themselves so much they might never come back east." He laughed. "I doubt that tho'."

This supposed trip to Peoria, Oregon, was Dustin's explanation to his uncle of the Mills' 'disappearance.' Not like Uncle Rich knew that Doris and Reggie Mills had been gone from their home for three weeks and wouldn't ever be returning, but Dustin had thought it wise to come up with a story anyway, just in case anyone asked how his new neighbors were getting along in their new home.

Uncle Rich was just finishing up his burger. "Oh, they'd better come back to Massachusetts. If they don't, I'm gonna be back to square one with that crappy house of theirs. I don't think there's anyone else in this state that I can con into renting or buying it."

Dustin waved his cup of Coke at his uncle. "Why not? It isn't like their house is haunted, is it? Seth and GROW confirmed to you that the building is ghost-free."

Uncle Rich frowned and his mouth twisted up like he'd just smelled some roadkill. "Son, just finish up your damn lunch and let's get back to the damn office. We've got ourselves some damn houses to sell."

Dustin kept his amusement to himself as they left the restaurant.

Before driving home that evening, he called his house phone and spoke to Bianca, who told him that no one had driven into the cul de sac all day and then gave him a list of groceries to buy for dinner.

Relieved that she was fine, he drove to a grocery store, bought what she'd requested, and then drove home to spend the evening with her.

Dustin had initially planned to ask Bianca why Real Dreams had strung up a cat along with her (and earlier, with Candice Raveling also), but she was still wincing while speaking, so he put off his questions until tomorrow.

All-in-all it had been a pleasant day.

Except of course, for his constant worry that a storm of shit was about to fall on his head.

CHAPTER 18

Shortly after he'd woken up the next morning, Dustin Mitchell heard the sound of a vehicle parking in the street outside his house.

Oops, here arrives trouble, he thought. *I'm not expecting anyone today and I don't think that empty house is either.*

He was in his living room and quickly walked over to look out through the windows.

A young woman was getting out of a red Honda Civic. Dustin studied her as she shut the driver's door.

She was very good-looking. That much he could tell even from twenty yards away. She was dressed casually in dark clothes and he wondered who she was and what she could possibly want here. The mystery deepened even more when she began staring at the Mills' house.

"Who the hell's that?" Bianca asked, arriving behind Dustin at that moment from the hallway. Bianca, who had a look of intense fright on her face, made no attempt to peek out of the window.

"No idea. Just some young woman."

"Well, go find out who she is, wilya? Her presence here bothers me, and if she bothers me enough, I'll start bothering you again to fetch me some *Nif.*"

"I need no further encouragement," Dustin told her truthfully, and headed for the front door. He'd already decided to go find out what the hot young woman wanted, not just because she was standing outside his house, but also because he wanted to experience her beauty at close range.

He was out the front door and heading for her car in no time. The morning sky was cloudy with the promise of rain to follow shortly. The weatherman had promised rain in the afternoon.

The woman smiled when she saw him approaching.

"Hello, you must be Dustin Mitchell," she said. "I'm Faith Mills, Reggie Mills' niece."

Up close like this, the young woman was utterly gorgeous, all beauty and alluring curves. She was a brunette and seemed to be in her late twenties.

What struck Dustin most about her were her blue eyes; eyes like ocean water.

She was wearing a black jacket over a frilly cream top, black leather pants, and black boots.

Dustin had a moment's fantasy that he was once more in the presence of a goddess, a gentle one this time.

"Oh yes, of course," he replied. "Your uncle and aunt aren't home at the moment. They're vacationing in Peoria, Oregon."

Faith Mills grinned at Dustin, who had already checked her left hand for a wedding ring and found none. Fantastic.

"Yes, I know," Faith replied him. "That's the reason why I'm here. Uncle Reggie called me up on Wednesday and asked me to housesit for him and Aunt Doris while they're away."

She flashed a set of keys at Dustin. "Keys to their house. They were delivered by courier yesterday."

She gestured over at the Mills' empty residence. "Uncle Reggie said they were gonna call you themselves, but they'd lost your cellphone number."

Dustin nodded inanely. He was stumped by her statement and also trapped in his own lie. Reggie was dead and Doris was . . . The point was that neither husband nor wife could've sent her those keys. But because Dustin had told everyone that they were vacationing, he was unable now to challenge Faith Mills' statement to that effect.

And besides, she'd come with the keys to their house.

He glanced back over at his house, making sure Bianca was keeping out of sight. She was, and so he turned back to his gorgeous new neighbor.

"Well then, you're welcome to the neighborhood," he told her. Then he gestured at her car, the backseat of which was loaded with luggage. "Why don't you drive up the driveway and I'll come give you a hand with carrying your stuff into the house?"

"That would be great," Faith replied him. "The reason I stopped out here was to introduce myself to you, so you wouldn't wonder who'd moved in opposite. From what I heard, you're the realtor who found them this house."

Dustin smiled. This was becoming more surreal by the moment. "So, just drive on up to the garage and I'll be over there in five—I need to pick up my cellphone in case there's any phone calls while I'm not home."

She nodded and walked back over to her car. Dustin hurried back inside his house.

What the hell?

CHAPTER 19

What was that about?" Bianca Sanchez asked Dustin when he stepped back into his house. "You look both completely baffled and worried to boot."

"I'm about to have a new neighbor," Dustin told her and then filled her in on what Faith Mills had just told him.

"But that's crazy," Bianca agreed with him. "Reggie's dead and Doris is in never-never-land. . . you know like I do that Doris won't ever be making any cellphone calls again in her life. Even if she wants to, she doesn't have any hands anymore."

"Yeah," Dustin agreed. "So, who the hell called up Faith Mills and asked her to temporarily take up residence opposite me?"

Bianca smirked. "One group of psychos readily comes to my mind."

Dustin had just picked up his cellphone from the coffee table in the living room. "The Real Dreams club? Stop being paranoid." He however liked the fact that she was referring to the Real Dreams members as 'psychos.' It meant that the *Nif* drink was losing its psychological hold on her.

"I'm not being paranoid. Also, my being paranoid doesn't mean they *aren't* after me. And, hey—you're not really listening to me."

While replying, her previous statement, Dustin had been staring out through the living room windows. Faith Mills was just putting the Mills' garage shutters up.

"Hey, I gotta go," he told Bianca, and then hurried back to the front door again.

"Hey, wait, you're forgetting something!" Bianca called after him, just as he got the front door open.

"I can't wait; I promised to help her unpack," Dustin explained. "We can discuss her in more detail later, once I get back."

Bianca shook her head at him. "Oh, but it's not little Miss Mystery over there that I'm thinking about. Well, not really. I just remembered that the noose used to hang me is still dangling from the living room fan, and that the dead cat is still lying in the piss-patch I made."

Dustin made a horrified face. "Oh, shit. We forgot to clean up the mess."

She shrugged at him. "Well, yeah? On the positive side of things tho', the cat won't be smelling yet, and my pee would've dried up by now." She grinned and made a thumbs-up gesture. "Score one for me."

"You're nasty," Dustin said and hurried out the front door again.

CHAPTER 20

By the time Dustin reached the Mills' garage, Faith was emerging from the garage's connecting door to the kitchen.

She was beaming and seemed very pleased.

If there's a dead cat and a noose in her living room, she hasn't noticed it yet. That just means she hasn't looked into the living room yet. Alright, so Bianca was right and the cat hasn't begun smelling yet. But how about the piss smell from the rug? That should be obvious.

"Sorry I took so long getting back here," he said.

From its previous state of extreme congestion, all that remained on the backseat of her car were several large shopping bags.

She waved his apology away. "I've not even begun unpacking yet. You should see all the stuff I've got in the trunk."

She leaned into the backseat and began handing grocery bags to Dustin. "All of these find their destiny in the kitchen, please," she told him. "You can just place them on the counter and I'll unpack them later."

Laden high and low with bags, Dustin hurried off into the kitchen. He planned to quickly place the grocery bags in the kitchen and then dash into the living room to retrieve the cat corpse at least. He doubted he'd have sufficient time to also loosen the noose from the fan before Faith brought the next set of bags in.

However, once the dead cat was hidden, the urine patch in the living room could possibly be blamed on vagrants.

But, once through the kitchen door, Dustin smelled a pleasant lavender fragrance coming from the living room that definitely hadn't been there last night.

Surprised by this, he peeked out of the kitchen into the living room. An armchair blocked off his view of the portion of the floor beneath the fan, but there was no noose dangling from the fan either.

Dustin felt a sudden thrill of fear. *Who cleaned up this place?*

"Some folks are just nasty," Faith told Dustin, her voice so unexpected and so close to his ear that he almost yelped in fright.

He spun around. She was standing behind him with two large suitcases.

"You should've left those for me to handle," he told her.

"Gladly," she said and put them down so he could pick them up.

Dustin picked up both suitcases. They were quite heavy. "Where do these go?" he asked. Though he'd been in here quite a lot when her uncle and aunt lived here, his many visits had never taken him beyond the kitchen, the living room, and the bathroom in the hallway.

"Follow me," Faith said brightly, and led him out of the kitchen.

As they walked through the living room towards the hallway, Dustin confirmed that neither dead cat nor noose were still in there. The piss-patch still was though.

Then a thought struck Dustin:

"You were saying some people are just nasty," he prompted Faith. "What did you mean by that?"

She was in front of him. She turned around and her face twisted up in disgust and she shivered. "Ugh! You can smell the Lysol in here, right? You're lucky you didn't come in here earlier. There was a dead cat on the rug over there. Some Satanist sickos must have hanged it in here. The noose was hanging from the fan."

Dustin, who felt relieved that her finding the cat hadn't prompted a feminine freak-out, feigned surprise. "That's just sick. What did you do with the cat?"

"It's out back," she told him. "I wrapped it in several garbage bags along with the rope and dumped it out back."

Then she grinned at him. "Hey, can you help me bury it?"

"No problem," Dustin said. "But first, where do you want these suitcases? My arms are starting to ache."

She laughed. "Follow me, those go in the bedroom."

CHAPTER 21

After bringing all of Faith's stuff into the house, Dustin found a spade in the garage and went round the back to bury the dead cat.

The layout of the Mills' backyard was much the same as his: thirty or so yards to a tree border, through which he could vaguely view one of the houses along the next street.

Faith had left the dead animal on her back stoop. Dustin stared at the small bundle she'd made of it in disgust. She'd had the presence of mind to wrap the cat in layers of dark plastic bag, and also to spray the package with lavender Lysol, but that did little to ease the disquiet that the animal's death created in Dustin's mind.

"Why the hell would Tanana and Malarkey hang this cat up alongside Bianca?" he asked himself aloud while picking up the dark package. "It makes no sense. And why did they also kill Candice Raveling the same way last year?"

Just as he was stepping back from the porch, Faith pushed the back door open.

"You okay out there, Dustin?" she asked.

He nodded and waved the pack of cat at her. "More or less. Gimme a few moments and I'll have it disposed of for you."

Faith made a face. "Okay, I'll be waiting."

"Hey," he asked as she was about vanishing inside again, "any particular place that you'd like it buried?"

She made a face again and her brow also wrinkled up. "I don't really care," she said finally. "So long as it's not in the house with me. Ugh!"

She backed away from the door and he was left outside with the cat.

He did some thinking and finally decided to bury the animal in one of the flower beds near the back porch.

That'll be like giving the poor creature a memorial wreath of flowers, he thought as his spade turned up the layers of dark earth.

CHAPTER 22

While burying the cat, Dustin's mind kept straying to another detail of the weirdness that had been happening around him. This one concerning the 'vanished' Mills.

He knew that Reggie and Doris had a daughter, Jessica. The teenager attended a private school in Worcester.

And as far as I can tell, that young lady is likely still unaware that her parents are both . . .

He sighed and tamped down the replaced soil with the flat of the spade.

"Bye, cat, hope you enjoy yourself in cat heaven," he said by way of making a prayer for the animal. Then he burst into laughter, wondering why he was being so sentimental about an animal that he'd not given much thought to since encountering Bianca in here.

Maybe it's because pets are less complicated than people. I've got one woman in my house who shouldn't be there, and now, I've got a new neighbor, another woman who shouldn't be here either. I'm starting to have the feeling that all this is leading up to something . . . something I might hate if I knew exactly what it was.

He climbed up the back porch, wiped his shoes clean on the doormat, and reentered the house.

As he approached the living room, he heard Faith Mills in her kitchen putting things on shelves. That was a nice sound, the comforting sound of a woman making a home out this place again.

But then, as Dustin reached the living room, his feeling of apprehension peaked. He knew it was the house affecting him.

Dammit! I need to grow a pair! I keep expecting ghosts to jump out and haunt me at any moment.

Maybe Dustin Mitchell was superstitious (admittedly a bad trait in a realtor), but this particular building really did creep him out.

But then, maybe it isn't the building affecting me, but what it represents.

CHAPTER 23

"I used to work at a high school in Middleborough," Faith told Dustin when they were both seated in her living room. "But the principal hated me and I got fired. I was about to start sending out job applications when Uncle Reggie asked me to housesit for him."

Dustin nodded. It was so comfortable listening to her speak, even if she was lying.

But is she lying? Maybe she isn't. More likely, someone posing as her dead uncle did contact her and ask her to housesit this place. And the only other people who know where her uncle and aunt actually are at the moment are the Real Dreams club members.

And then it hit him:

Oh no! They're setting her up as a sacrifice. The cultists know their sacrifice of Bianca didn't work, and now they've got a new candidate to kill.

But that didn't make sense.

Faith found the dead cat in here on her arrival. Meaning that the Real Dreams organization aren't yet aware that Bianca survived.

"Hey, are you Okay?" Faith asked him.

He replied her with a blank stare. "Huh?"

"All of a sudden, you seemed to have zoned out. Hey, am I boring you?"

Dustin shook his head. "Nah, not at all. I was just wondering who could've killed that cat in here, and for what nasty purpose."

"Oh, forget them. It doesn't bother me any. I'm a very resilient woman."

She was smiling at him, and he nodded easily, almost tranquilized by her beauty, sucked into her dreamy blue eyes.

"So, like I was saying," she went on. "Jobless like I was, I would've turned down my uncle and aunt's housesitting offer, but they're paying me to live here."

"Huh?"

She nodded. "It's true. I get five hundred bucks a week to live here till they come back from Oregon. That's seventy bucks a day."

"That's wonderful," Dustin replied, though inside he now felt very frightened for her, because he now understood that yes, she really was simply a lamb being readied for sacrificial slaughter.

Why else would her imaginary uncle and aunt be willing to pay her so much to live here?

"Yeah, it really is wonderful," Faith told him. "And it's put me off looking for a new job for a while. Which is great, cuz I really need a rest after dealing with all of that high school politics." Then she giggled. "You know, I'm not sure why I'm telling you all of this stuff. But somehow, I feel like you're a nice person. I've known you all of one hour and you make me feel really comfortable."

Dustin nodded. He too had wondered why she'd been so open with him about all of this. But like she said, he also felt a connection with her.

Love at first sight? I doubt that. More likely, I just want into her pants already because she's so gorgeous.

But seeing how beautiful Faith Mills was also put a damper on his desire for her.

Of course, a woman this beautiful will have a hundred suitors banging on her door. And I'm sure to meet most of them in the coming days.

Well, at least it had been a nice thought. Dustin resumed smiling at Faith.

"Do you have any brothers or sisters?" Faith asked him.

He shook his head. "I'm an only child."

"I've an older sister," she told him. "She's . . ." Then she stopped speaking and looked sad and pensive.

"What's wrong?" Dustin asked after a while of her saying nothing.

Faith shook her head. "Grace—that's my sister's name—Grace. She was in a bad car accident a while ago, and she got disfigured."

Dustin was shocked. "Oh, that's just horrible."

Faith nodded and looked even sadder. "Yes, it is. We were out in a car together and this truck reversed into the road out of nowhere and backed into us. The driver was drunk. The truck had a load of steel girders. One of the girders shook loose and crashed through our windshield. I was driving at the time. The girder missed me but it tore off half of Grace's face."

Dustin felt sickened by the imagery her description created in his mind. "Oh, that's just horrible," he found himself repeating. "How is your sister now?"

Faith managed to smile. "Oh, she's much better now. The construction company the truck driver worked for paid for plastic surgery to fix her face." She sighed. "Of course, she's nowhere near as pretty as before, but she's not an eyesore either."

Dustin couldn't think of anything to say to this, except "Hmmm."

Faith looked around for her cellphone and when she found it, showed Dustin a picture.

"Here's the two of us a couple years back," she said, walking over to sit on the arm of his chair. "See how pretty Grace was back then?"

Dustin studied the picture. The picture was a selfie taken inside a car. Grace was driving and Faith was leaning towards her to catch them both in the shot. Grace wasn't as beautiful as Faith was, but she had the same incredible blue eyes as her younger sister.

"She's really cute," Dustin said honestly. "I'm so, so sorry that she had to have such bad luck like that."

Faith seemed recovered by now. She shrugged. "Sadly, we're no longer as close as we used to be. Grace blames me for causing the crash, and also, I think she's a little jealous of me now. I mean, she still looks pretty good herself, but not as hot as before."

Dustin was intrigued. "Do you have any pictures of her after she had surgery?"

Faith shook her head at him. "No, she won't let herself be photographed anymore. If anyone points a camera or a phone at her, she performs a perfect freakout. She's also become something of a recluse." Faith sighed. "Of course, Grace can afford to act like a diva because of the huge settlement the construction company paid her for the accident."

Dustin smiled. "Now you sound a little jealous of her."

Faith grinned back. "Really? No, I'm not jealous of Grace." Then she laughed. "Alright, maybe I am, just a wee bit. My big sis may have lost some of her pretty, but she gets to laze around now, while I still have to go out and work—" she gestured around the living room, "— or housesit for dollars."

CHAPTER 24

During a short lull in the conversation, Faith Mills said: "Oh, I really should be a better hostess. How about I fetch you a drink?"

Dustin laughed. "Oh, I'm fine." He made a gesture back in the direction of his house. "I really should be getting back to my place; got some housecleaning to do."

"Not yet," Faith said and got to her feet.

And it was now, when Faith no longer distracted him, that Dustin re-noticed the painting on the wall.

Just like the first time he'd visited Faith's aunt Doris, he'd been sitting with his back to the painting. He also attributed his not noticing it earlier to his mind blanking it out—he had that much of a desire (both conscious and subconscious) to completely forget his crazy and surreal experiences at the Real Dreams club.

But now, he turned and stared with intense fear and loathing at the painting of the worm goddess Boku Veeza's human grove, that impossibly gruesome depiction of the five kneeling and armless people with trees planted in their head.

Then Dustin got up from his chair and walked over to stand by the painting.

Looking at the painting now, Dustin felt disoriented. Once again, he felt—no, he knew—that something was different about the painting.

But what can that be? There's the five worshippers, and the three lizard-human guardians, and the watching background of human and nonhuman eyes. Hey, why does the pentagram look different? Oh shit, it's not a pentagram anymore—it's a sexagram now! Doris Mills is now included in the painting! But how can that possibly be? No one's been in here since . . . No, I don't know that for sure. It's quite possible that someone—maybe even that murdering demon pair—brought a replacement picture in here, maybe when they tried to kill Bianca.

And so, he remembered Bianca, and wondered what she was up to at the moment. On waking up, she'd told him his place was a mess, and said she'd clean it up this morning. But now, with him suddenly having an unexpected neighbor, Dustin didn't think Bianca would want the noise of the vacuum cleaner carrying across the street, because if the new neighbor happened to be nosy (or suspicious), Dustin might then need to answer some tricky questions about whom he had at home with him.

He put his mind off of Bianca. His thoughts switched to Faith instead, who was out of his range of vision, but who he could hear bustling about in the kitchen. He heard her open and shut the fridge.

He turned his attention back to the picture. His dread subsided somewhat now that the surprise had become familiar.

Yes, Doris was definitely included in the painting now. There were now *six* worshippers with trees growing in their heads, not five like he'd initially thought. Of course, Doris's face wasn't clearly delineated, but she had to be the woman with the smallest tree in her brain, the half-sized one.

His thoughts drifted back to how the painting had achieved the change. Because, everything else in it was exactly the way he remembered it. Except that, where previously he'd always imagined he could see Reggie's and Doris's eyes as part of the dark and smeared background of watchers, now those spots were vacant.

Well, one possibility I refuse to consider is that this horrible painting updates itself at will. Because that is simply crazy. But Real Dreams is both the definition and the acme of crazy. So . . .

"Hey, I'm back," Faith said and then headed over to his side, where she stood looking quizzically at the image. "So, I'll admit it, Dustin, Uncle Reggie and Aunt Doris definitely have some really weird tastes."

"This is probably the most gruesome painting I've ever had to look at in my life," Dustin said, gratefully turning away from it to stare at his beautiful companion instead.

Okay, this isn't really déjà vu, but I do recall being in a similar situation with her beautiful aunt. Only difference is, she's not making any attempt to seduce me.

"Your drink," Faith said, holding out a glass to him.

Oh, hell no! Dustin thought in horror when he saw the glass of *Nif* she was offering him. He stared at the rainbow-hued drink in horror. Then he hurriedly stepped away from Faith, like she was holding a snake.

What the . . . ! Hell no!

Faith saw the startled and dismayed look on his face. "What's the matter?" She laughed as he shrank back from her. "Yeah, I know it's a funny-looking drink, but it tastes absolutely rave."

"It looks like something brewed by Elton John, Jodie Foster, and Lil Nas X."

Faith laughed. "Yeah, it really does. You know, I thought I'd brought some beer along with me, or at least a bottle of wine. But I forgot them at my place. This stuff is all they've got in the fridge. Drink up, drink up, there's lots more where this came from."

"I think I'll pass," Dustin protested. Now he felt in control of himself again, it seemed absurd that he'd been so scared of a drink. But he knew this was no mere drink. This was . . .

"Oh, come on," Faith urged him after taking a sip from her glass. "It's utterly delicious." She turned to the painting beside them, and added, "and it gives one a new perspective on things." She nodded. "Yeah, this stuff really gives you a clearer perspective."

Dustin shook his head. "That's exactly what I'm afraid of." He smiled. "Please don't be offended, but not today. Maybe next time I visit you."

Faith shrugged. "Sure, but it's your loss though."

Dustin was relieved that she wasn't insisting that he drink along with her. Even though his desire for *Nif* had faded away over the past weeks, the sight of the shimmering and swirling liquid rainbow was fast reawakening a craving for it.

He also felt bothered by how much he liked Faith. Outside of work, he'd hardly spoken to a woman for three weeks, and suddenly being confronted with Faith's beauty like this was having a devastating effect on him.

I need to get away from her before I say something foolish, he thought.

"Well, I really do need to head back home," he told her. "I'd love to stay—"

"Oh, please do. I don't intend to do much today where the house is concerned."

"—but I need to clean my place. I can't even invite you over there, it's a total pigsty."

Her disappointment was obvious. Then she smiled. "Okay, but you're free tomorrow, Sunday, right?"

He nodded. "Yeah, I'm free tomorrow."

"Okay, so how about if we spend tomorrow together then? I know it sounds a bit odd cuz we just met, but I really don't have anything planned for this weekend . . . except if you do?"

He shook his head. "I've nothing planned. I've been drifting for weeks now, since—"

He stopped himself just in time. He realized he'd been about telling her the story of his recent strange experiences. That was the dangerous effect a beautiful woman had on a man.

And I didn't even need Nif to loosen my tongue.

"Since . . . what?" she asked.

He waved her question off. "Best to just forget it. Just some weird stuff that recently happened to me that I'm doing my best to leave in the past." He pointed to her half-filled glass of *Nif*. "Seeing the weird colors of that just seemed to fill my head with those crazy memories again."

She nodded and then laughed, but it wasn't a mocking laugh. "I think I understand. Trust me, I've had some really weird experiences too. Maybe, when we get to know each other better, we can swap creepy life stories."

He laughed too at the blasé way she'd said it.

After she'd placed the drink she'd brought for him on the coffee table, they walked together to her front door.

"Well, it's been great meeting you," Dustin told her. "Welcome to the neighborhood and see you tomorrow. How's noon for you?"

"Noon's perfect. I'm sure I'll have woken up by then. I'll cook us lunch and then we can watch TV and chill, or drive out somewhere if you prefer."

"Staying in will be fine. I'll get us something to drink. Would you prefer beer or should I buy us some wine?"

She shook her head and lifted her glass of *Nif*. "I'll stick with this rainbow stuff for the time being. I'm starting to like it, and there's alcohol in it too. Man, you really should try some."

"Maybe tomorrow," Dustin said, shaking his head while unconsciously stepping back, which made Faith laugh again.

CHAPTER 25

Once Dustin was home again, he felt relieved. He felt like he'd just escaped from a dragon's lair.

For a moment back there, I almost gave in to my memories and accepted that glass of Nif from her.

All of a sudden, Dustin noticed that his house felt eerily quiet. He sensed a subtle shift in the ambience of the place. When he'd left home an hour and a half ago, his house had radiated a feeling of a womanly presence. But now the house felt empty, as if the pleasant female vibe that had previously coated its walls with warmth had been drained from it.

Where's Bianca? He wondered.

"Bianca!" he called out. "Hey, Bianca, are you okay?"

When she didn't reply, he went looking for her.

She wasn't in the kitchen or in her bedroom or in the guest bathroom. The back door was unlocked, but Bianca wasn't out on the back porch or in the backyard.

Feeling very alarmed now, Dustin retraced his steps. And it was only now, on reentering his living room, that he caught sight of the strange bottle on his coffee table.

Oh no! he thought on seeing it, as there was no mistaking what it was or who had put it there.

The bottle was a crystal decanter. It was shaped like a coiled worm with a woman's head as its stopper. This transparent figurine of the worm goddess Boku Veeza was a very ugly thing and was filled to the brim with sparkling rainbow-tinted *Nif*, the very same drink that Dustin had just turned down drinking with his new neighbor.

He'd seen this sort of bottle before—the Mills had one in their fridge. Faith may even have poured their drinks from it.

Oh shit! Real Dreams have visited here and abducted Bianca! But when? It has to be when I was burying the cat out back. That's the only time I wouldn't have noticed them arriving and leaving. But even then, I should've heard some—

This was when Dustin spotted the note on the coffee table, held in place by the bottom of the worm-woman decanter.

A closer look revealed that the note was lying on top of a second sheet of paper, this one folded over in half. This folded page was clearly intended for his attention also.

Dustin pried the two sheets loose from the base of the decanter with trembling fingers. He read the note first.

The note was written on lined yellow paper and smelled of nice female perfume.

It read:

Hello Dustin,

So lovely that you've kept quiet about us all this while, darling. You truly are one of us. Our Goddess sends her loving regards. Have a drink of *Nif,* and my itching asshole will visit your tongue soon.

Yours,
Queen Bee.

P.S. That infidel bitch Bianca somehow escaped us, but we'll soon have her again. No one fucks with Boku Veeza. QB

Well at least Bianca got away from them, Dustin thought. *I don't have to worry about her.*

He now unfolded the second sheet of paper. This turned out to be a photocopy of a document, reduced to half-size.

As he read the document, Dustin felt the color draining from his face:

"I, Dustin Mitchell, do now pledge my endless loyalty to the glorious goddess Boku Veeza. As of this moment and henceforth, I, Dustin Mitchell, agree that, body and soul and forever and forever, I truly belong to Boku Veeza, the Almighty and all-powerful one. I, Dustin Mitchell, acknowledge Boku Veeza as my maker and vow that I will never love another god or goddess nor desert or forsake Boku Veeza for any other and that . . .'

There was a lot more of this ramble, but Dustin's gaze swept down the document to its bottom, where he'd affixed his signature above a dotted line.

He stood there in the middle of his living room, staring from hellish contract to liquor-filled decanter with dread.

And yet, mingled in with the dread, Dustin also felt a terrible longing. A longing for a resolution.

Most of his time since 'escaping' from the worshippers of the worm goddess had been spent in a kind of limbo; in a psychic inertia. He'd felt helpless to do anything other than nothing. So, he'd done his realtor work, drank lots of beer to drown his heartache, and in between, thought about nothing and done nothing.

But nothing had its limits.

Seeing this drink in front of him was a prodding to act in a certain direction.

It really seems like I'm damned if I do and damned too if I don't. Real Dreams clearly aren't finished with me yet.

Dustin shrugged. Seeing as it looked like the crazy was reinserting itself into his life, he might as well go with the flow.

At first, he considered getting a glass from his kitchen, but then he decided 'why bother?' and simply picked up the decanter, pulled off its woman-head stopper, and tilted the neck of the bottle to his lips.

Back down the wormhole.

And then Dustin drank deep of the *Nif.* He drank very deep indeed.

CHAPTER 26

After three long swallows of Nightmare Fuel, Dustin lowered the wormlike decanter and sat on his couch.

He knew what was about to happen and both dreaded and welcomed it.

The change began slowly. At first, he imagined visual distortion at the corners of his eyes. It didn't matter which way he turned his head; things looked odd at the outer angles, like there were two versions of reality fighting for dominance and prominence.

I've never had this kind of reaction while drinking Nif before, he thought in some alarm. *This must be a product of my long abstinence.*

The visual distortion at the periphery of Dustin's vision speedily moved inward towards his nose, so that reality was contained in a shrinking tube before his eyes, while all that existed to either side— most of what he saw—was a jarring hellish chaos of planes and angles that would terrify even the most avant-garde of painters or architects.

And then the shrinking tube vanished and Dustin was back 'in the real' again.

But of course, this wasn't the real world everyone experienced. But the real world as revealed by *Nif,* a distortion of everything that only the worshippers of the worm goddess Boku Veeza could ever experience, like seeing the human universe in goddess-vision.

Yep, I'm messed up again, Dustin thought with that blasé unconcern that was the signature characteristic of a *Nif* drinker, a person who could view the greatest obscenity or brutality with the greatest calm.

He didn't regard Nif drinkers as 'addicts,' because the drink wasn't addictive in any normal sense. The craving for it was purely psychological. Just like he'd done, you could easily leave Nightmare Fuel behind, but life seemed a whole lot more interesting when you indulged in the rainbow liquor that wiped your inhibitions away more efficiently than a carwash cleaned his Ford F-150.

Dustin smiled to himself. Without understanding what he himself meant by this, he felt that *everything* now made sense to him.

There were no longer any mysteries that were too strange to be understood.

There were no mysteries, period.

All is revealed by Nif. All glory to Boku Veeza. She is one in all and all in one.

CHAPTER 27

And then after a few more gulps of *Nif*, because the incredible drink seemed to fill him with the understanding that it was the right thing to do, Dustin got up and left his house, and crossed the road to go visit Faith Mills again.

Most likely because of his long layoff from *Nif*, the neighborhood looked a little odd at first, like it had two separate versions that were doing their best to appear as one.

"I've been expecting you back," Faith whispered throatily on opening her front door, naked except for her slippers. "I don't know what the hell is in that rainbow drink my uncle and aunt left in their fridge, but right now I'm hornier than ten porn stars."

Standing on Faith's threshold, Dustin admired her body. However, it seemed he spent too in long doing so, because Faith suddenly grabbed him by the collar of his shirt.

"Come right on in and fuck me," Faith whispered in Dustin's ear as she pulled him into the house. "Come on in, realtor, and make yourself at home in my pussy."

CHAPTER 28

Too much in a hurry to reach the bedroom, they made love down on the living room carpet.

"Let's keep away from that damp patch where the cat was," Faith told him. "It smells like someone pissed on the poor animal."

Her body wasn't perfect, but it was perfect for him.

Afterwards, they talked about their lives.

"I've lived all of my life here in Raynham," Dustin told her with a laugh. "The only time I ever leave this small town is when my uncle gets hold of a property in one of the nearby towns, usually Attleboro, Halifax, or Westport, and I'm handling the sale or rental for him. Or when I go visit my mom and dad at their beachfront home in Plymouth."

"I've travelled a little bit," Faith told him. "My father was an actor, and during the school vacations, me, my mother, and my sister went places with him. My plan in life was to be an actor too, but that didn't work out."

She sat up so that her back was against an armchair and grinned down at him. "Before we make love again, I think I'll have another drink of that rainbow stuff in the fridge. And . . . you promised you'd try some next time you visited me. Well, this is the next time."

He ran a finger between her breasts. "Pour me a glass too."

He wondered if Faith had any idea of what the 'rainbow stuff' she was drinking was, of its origins.

Of course not. She can't possibly be aware that that stuff is the elixir of the worm goddess Boku Veeza, or of all that it opens one's mind too.

Watching Faith's hips sway as she walked towards the kitchen, Dustin felt satisfied.

Then Dustin laughed. Everything was wrong in his life again, and that was fine with him.

CHAPTER 29

Faith waved her glass of *Nif* at Dustin. "You know, I really like what this rainbow stuff does to you," she said, tapping the glass with a finger for emphasis. Her tap made its contents swirl like a fluorescent neon jelly.

"It's called *Nif*, which is short for Nightmare Fuel," Dustin felt obliged to enlighten her.

She frowned at him. "That's a really weird name."

"But as far as I can tell, a well-deserved one," Dustin said. He felt like saying more—he wanted to explain about the cult of the goddess Boku Veeza, but he didn't want to alarm Faith. "At least that's what your aunt and uncle called it."

"You've drank it before then?"

"More than once when I visited them."

"And . . .?" she asked.

"And *what?*"

"And, what do you think of its effect? How do you rate the way this so-called Nightmare Fuel makes you feel? I mean compared to other drugs?"

Dustin sipped from his own Nightmare Fuel. "I'm no expert on drug usage. I generally stick to beer or whiskey. My entire experience with narcotics is doing marijuana at uni . . . and later, I occasionally did coke with a girlfriend who was a total snow bunny. But nothing since then. So maybe I'm the wrong person to ask. I don't even recall how it felt to get high. I'm not sure how weed rates compared to getting drunk."

She shook her head. "Baby, I think you prefer alcohol to weed."

He gave her a puzzled look. "What makes you say that?"

"People generally stick to what pleasures them the most, and in this case, also what they feel more in control of. You're scared that you'll become addicted to drugs, so you drink instead." She frowned. "But forget that. Compare this rainbow—*Nif*, right?—compare this *Nif* drink to booze."

"Okay, I'll try." He drank some more *Nif* and tried to compose the many layers of understanding *Nif* had gifted him into words. It seemed an impossible task.

And anyhow, Dustin was very aware that Faith was merely sporting with him. She already knew what his reply would be, but wanted to hear him say it.

He felt amused also.

With the way she's going, not taking it easy on how many drinks she's having, by tomorrow she'll be living on Mars, so far as hallucinations are concerned.

"It's sort of like this," he said. "When you drink beer or any other sort of alcoholic beverage, at first it helps relax you—I mean, you lose your inhibitions and your stress level is much lowered because things don't seem as important as they are anymore. But then, after a certain point—a point that varies according to individual tolerance, of course—after that point, the alcohol becomes more of a hindrance than a help. You start losing control, until you're literally out of your mind. You know what I mean: that friend of yours who drinks so much, she doesn't even remember who fucked her that night. Taken to extremes, you black out and can't remember a thing the next morning."

"And this stuff?" Faith asked, holding out her glass to him. "How does this make you feel?" While speaking, she'd trailed her fingers into his crotch and begun playing with his penis, which had instantly responded.

"No, let me ask you that question," Dustin told her. "How does this *Nif* make *you* feel?"

Still fondling his cock, which was now hard and jerking, she squeezed up her features in thought.

"Hmm, that's a good one," she replied after a few moments. "O.K., lemme try to put it in words. The feeling I'm getting starts off just like how you described for alcohol: I feel more confident and lose both my worries and my inhibitions. For instance, under normal circumstances, I'd never had met you naked at my front door and brazenly propositioned you for sex like I did. Normally, I take my time with relationship stuff, but,"—she lifted her almost-empty glass and stared at it wondrously—"but after drinking this stuff, that initial dating period seemed to be totally irrelevant, and all I could think was how I needed you right now . . . and there seemed to be no reason not to have you right now either." She frowned. "You know, the even weirder thing about this is that somehow I knew you wanted to fuck me too and that you'd soon be coming over to do exactly that."

Dustin nodded. He felt like getting between her legs and eating her pussy, but she clearly had more to say about the wonders of *Nif*, and he knew from experience that young women found it difficult to carry on conversations when their clitoris was being sucked on. He imagined that older women, being more experienced in receiving cunnilingus, could very likely carry on phone conversations or even make posts on Facebook while being pleasured. And long-time lesbians shouldn't have any problems either.

Of course, if Faith kept on stroking his erection like she was doing, he might ejaculate before she finished telling him how great *Nif* was.

He pointed this out to her.

"Come if you have to," she replied while keeping up the firm motion of hand on penis. "Don't try to hold back. I like how your dick feels in my hand. The way it's throbbing and jerking, it feels like I'm holding a small animal, something like a hamster."

Dustin relaxed and let her manipulate him.

"And yeah, there's more," Faith said. "The thing about *Nif* is, at no point do I feel like I'm losing control of myself. Instead of that happening, my mind—my brain, my reasoning power—seems to amplify. And the more *Nif* I drink, the greater this increase." She paused stroking and speaking so she could spit in her palm and lubricate his penis with the spit.

"In fact," she went on as she resumed stroking him, "in fact, now I think I understand things that don't make any sense to me. And that worries me a little."

"W-what are-are-are y-y-you t-talking a-ab-a-about?" Dustin asked her in short gasps as he felt himself coming to a climax.

"Well, take for instance that painting over there. The human something or other, you called it."

"The-the H-hu-human Grove. Wha-wha-what about it?"

She turned from the painting and laughed at the tormented expression on his face. "You're about to come, aren't you?"

He wasn't able to reply. He merely nodded back.

She stopped stroking his erection. "We'd better take care of that first then, so you'll understand what I'm talking about," she told him, and then she ducked her mouth down onto his penis. The sensation of her lips sliding down his erection, lips that she'd instinctively tightened into a ring to give him the best sensation, immediately pushed him over the edge. She'd forced her mouth down on him as far as it could go. Feeling his penis brush somewhere deep inside of her head, Dustin ejaculated, while Faith fondled his balls as if encouraging the sperm cells in there to depart from him en-masse.

Afterwards, while Dustin caught his breath, Faith wiped her lips with her hand.

"Come tastes nowhere as good as *Nif*, that's for sure," she said. Then she frowned. "And that's more about the 'losing inhibitions' part of this. Normally, I don't swallow. Nor would I normally have sex without a condom."

"Thanks for swallowing today," Dustin said with all honesty. "I really needed you to."

Faith nodded seriously. "Now that you're calm again, let's talk about the painting on the wall, shall we?"

CHAPTER 30

What do you see in it?" Dustin asked her when they'd walked hand-in-hand over to the wall and stood, naked as Adam and Even in the Garden of Eden, staring at the painting of the six suffering worshippers with trees planted in their heads.

She shook her head. "It's not so much *what* I see in it anymore, but *how* I see it. Now, this wonderful painting seems different than earlier. And the more I drink, the more wonderful it seems and the more different."

Dustin laughed. "Alcohol does that too. Everyone knows the joke about a man in a bar who's sitting beside a woman he finds totally unattractive, but who, twelve drinks later he thinks is Marilyn Monroe."

She frowned. "Be serious. This is very different."

"I'm only joking," he replied. "I know what you mean. When I'm not drinking *Nif*, I hate this painting. It's the most gruesome thing in the world." He frowned. "But now . . ."

"Yes?" she prompted. "And now . . . ? How does it seem to you?"

"You're the one supposed to be explaining," Dustin said.

She shook her head at him again. "Uh uh, baby. Those thirty million sperm cells you just fed me have given me a sore throat. So, you explain for me, and then you can feed me another thirty million sperm cells for dinner."

"Well, it's like you say. I don't see any difference in the painting, but now there seems to be more there than previously, if that makes any sense."

He hoped she got what he meant.

"Oh, it does, it does," she gushed at him. "It's such a subtle thing. And it's somehow three-dimensional too, like its coming out of itself into this living room." She leaned over and kissed Dustin. He smelt his come on her lips. "Does that make sense to you, baby?"

"It does; it does!"

She touched the painting, running slim fingers down the trunks of two of the depicted trees, both times ending the motion of her fingertips at the point where the fat tree roots sank into human brains, where blood welled from the tormented pale human flesh to dribble down the faces of those delighted sufferers.

"I feel tactile sensations now, like the texture of the tree bark," she described dreamily. "I can feel the blood bubbling from their heads onto their bodies, almost. Wow, I can smell the fruit growing in the trees in this human orchard. They're tantalizingly ripe now, juicy enough to pick and eat."

Dustin drank some *Nif* and smiled. His fingers unconsciously extended and touched one of the painted lizard-like guardians. He felt the painting in the same way as Faith. The contact with the female guardian was strange; he knew he felt the scales on her orange body.

"I feel as if this painting holds the secret of eternal life," Faith said.

"You know, Doris used to say that also."

Faith turned from the painting to study him with interest. "Oh, did she?"

He nodded. "Yeah, she did. Searching for the secret in this painting almost drove your aunt crazy."

Faith sighed. "It's not bad to be crazy. You live in a world of your own making; a world you have total control over; which is what all of us are seeking for in the everyday rat race. The mad are the kings and queens we all wish we were. Which makes ironic sense, I guess, seeing as historically, so many kings and queens acted like mad people." She swayed on her feet like she was tipsy. "So, madness just may be the ultimate form of sanity. And, in your state of madness, you know things no one else does." She began laughing like she was crazy.

"O.K., we've stared at this painting long enough," Dustin told her. "Let's finish our *Nif* and make love again. Or do it the other way around." He linked his arm in hers again and pointed her back toward the furniture. "What do you say to that?"

"You owe me cunnilingus for the blowjob I gave you," she told him and began laughing again.

CHAPTER 31

Dustin spent the rest of Saturday with Faith. They made love and talked and watched TV and ate and made love and talked some more.

And of course, they drank lots of Nightmare Fuel.

Twice, Dustin's phone rang. The first time, it was his Uncle Rich calling to ask a family-related question. A distant relative of theirs had died and Uncle Rich was traveling southwest to Utah for the funeral. Dustin's parents couldn't make the trip, so he wondered if Dustin wanted to come along in their stead.

Dustin said he'd think about it.

The second call was from Woody Taylor, Seth Taylor's younger brother. Woody was of course, a member of Seth's paranormal crew, the Ghost Research Outfit Worldwide (GROW, for short).

"Aren't you gonna answer that one too?" Faith asked when Dustin dropped the still-ringing phone back on the chair it had been lying on.

Dustin waved it off. "I'm not in the mood to talk to the guy. He can leave a voicemail and I'll get back to him later."

Dustin knew what Woody would want to talk about. Woody could only be calling him to ask if he'd heard from Seth yet. At the moment Dustin wasn't in the mood to discuss Seth Taylor.

Faith pressed her left index finger into the left side of her lips, which she'd pouted. "You know, if you don't answer it, he'll likely call back right when one of us is about to come."

"You're right." Dustin picked up his phone and silenced it.

After that, Dustin paid no more attention to his phone or the outside world. Here, in Faith's house, was where he wanted to be, consuming her beauty and being in turn swallowed up by the sea in her eyes.

Dustin had thought that at some point they'd run out of *Nif*, but then Faith discovered three small casks of the rainbow liquor in the store.

"I wonder where they buy it from," she told Dustin as they stared together at the brown wooden containers.

"Doris said a friend of hers brews the stuff," Dustin replied.

So far, he'd not mentioned her aunt's involvement with the worship of Boku Veeza.

The information was constantly on the tip of his tongue, and it took all of his self-restraint not to spill those beans. High on *Nif* like Faith was, like he was too, he knew she'd believe him if he told her.

And then he'd be able to explain to her that that crazy painting on her wall depicted a real circle of armless, tree-headed people, that that unbelievable Human Grove actually existed in real life.

He would explain to her what *Nif* was and where it actually came from.

He knew that if he told her this, she would believe him. She would understand too, how great the worm goddess was, and how it was right to worship her, though she was an insatiable evil.

And of course, then Dustin would of necessity have to inform Faith that her aunt Doris whom she believed to be in Peoria, Oregon, was actually the sixth member of that human grove—that in fact, Doris Mills was the worshipper with the young, half-grown tree in her head.

And he'd need to tell Faith about her uncle Reginald's death . . .

And then, he'd have to explain to Faith Mills, that whomever had invited her to housesit this house was an impostor who had extremely bad intentions toward her. He'd need to tell her about the woman/cat sacrifices, and how he believed the plan now was to make her one of them.

In her case there'll be no need to abduct her. Just like Candice Raveling, she's already here.

And of course, because she was under the influence of the goddess Boku Veeza's elixir, Faith would accept all of this unquestioningly. It would all make perfect sense to her. She would likely ask Dustin to sponsor her to be a member of Real Dreams and say she'd love to meet Queen Bee and everyone else there.

Dustin felt great pressure to confess what he knew to Faith. But he managed to control himself.

"We need to regulate our consumption of this stuff," Dustin told Faith after they'd refilled the worm-shaped decanter in the kitchen from one of the casks of *Nif.* "I don't believe you can overdose on it, but what if it pickles the liver like booze?"

Faith nodded her agreement. "Yeah, you're right. And there's an even more valid reason: we'd better not drink it all up before I find out where to buy more."

"Tell me: you're not seeing any weird shit, are you?"

She shook her head. "Nah, though sometimes it's like I've got three nipples on each breast and you've got three dicks or four hands. But other than that, I'm fine. Why'd you ask? Are you seeing weird things?"

"The walls keep shaking like tissue paper, that's all."

"You're okay too then. Hey, yeah—one more thing. Last orgasm I had, I had something like a vision of a dead woman hanging from the fan. She was all rotted up and . . ." Faith began giggling like mad. "And . . . you're not gonna believe this. Oh, you really won't . . ."

"Not believe *what?*"

"There was a cat hung up beside her; its neck in the same noose as hers." Faith nodded. "Yeah, it was so crazy." She pointed. "The dead woman was hanging right there, over that patch on the floor; both she and the poor cat were both rotted away and coated with flies. I was horrified and scared, but you were making love to me, so I knew things were actually fine, and I was having a fantastic orgasm. And then I blinked my eyes and she was gone."

She sighed at him and raised her glass of *Nif* to her lips. "But other than that, everything is peachy. I've never felt better in my whole life."

"Yeah," Dustin agreed, wrapping his arm around her. "I feel wonderful too. But I'm gonna stop drinking *Nif* for the rest of today so the walls of the house stop shaking. Oh, and that includes the ceiling and the floor also."

CHAPTER 32

Sunday morning came and went in a pleasant blur. Dustin had spent the night at Faith's house but gone home in the morning, with the promise to come back in the afternoon.

Being at home gave him time to catch up with his emails and messages.

He still hadn't decided whether or not he'd travel west with Uncle Rich. He vaguely remembered the old man who'd passed on, but wasn't sure if that memory warranted him making a trip out of state. Dustin also didn't want to discuss this with his parents, as they might ask him to make the journey in their place merely to keep up appearances with the rest of the family.

Then he remembered Woody Taylor's phone call. Checking through his phone log, Dustin saw that Woody had called him a total of thirteen times yesterday. And had left him four voicemails.

He played the voicemails. They were all similar:

"Hey, Dustin, call me back once you get this! It's fucking urgent that I speak to you ASAP!"

Dustin wondered what the matter was. A feeling of dread slowly grew in his mind that Woody and GROW may have gotten themselves in trouble again.

It must be something real important for him to keep calling back like that. Maybe I should've called him yesterday.

He called Woody, but now proved to be Woody's own turn to go into voicemail. After five attempts at getting through, Dustin gave up. After leaving a voicemail of his own, he turned on the TV and started channel surfing.

Time passed.

At around noon, Dustin remembered that he'd initially planned to visit a church this Sunday morning.

He'd had no specific church in mind; he'd just have driven around till he found one and entered to listen to the preacher.

So far, he'd considered this as part of his therapy, his paranormal debriefing so to speak. Now that he'd discovered that the supernatural really did exist, he couldn't behave like an atheist and say it didn't. But what he *could* do, was replace one belief system with another. He could purge the memory of what he'd seen and experienced amongst the worshippers of Boku Veeza from his soul with the more traditional belief in Jehovah.

Of course, Dustin could just have dialed up a televangelist and watched them at home, but that didn't compare to sitting down among people who believed in God and Jesus and the Saints, and listening to the preacher affirm that Almighty God was good and that evil came from the devil.

And yes, those previous two times that Dustin had visited churches, he'd come away feeling cleansed of the evil terrors of Boku Veeza.

But unfortunately, this purged feeling never lasted. By Tuesday or Wednesday latest he was back in a pseudo-nervy condition.

It occurred to him that he could simply have committed to attending a church regularly, but he wasn't a Christian, and had no honest intention of becoming one. He'd just wanted something to comfort him after the real-life nightmares he'd had, and possibly, to also absolve him of any subconscious guilt he felt over his participation in the rituals and orgies to worship the evil worm goddess.

But now . . .

The woman-worm decanter still sat atop Dustin's coffee table and beside it lay both the contract he'd signed with Boku Veeza and her high priestess's teasing note to him.

He shook his head at the decanter.

And now, I'm back in the goddess's evil fold whether I like it or not. And now that I've Nif to drink again, I'm fine with that.

However, the *Nif* hadn't really gotten a hold of him yet. He'd not yet reached that stabilizing point where things were entirely abnormal yet normal, where evil and good weren't merely the flip side of one coin, but the alloy from which the coin itself was fabricated; where actions in themselves had no inherent good or evil nature; where the interpretation of everything depended entirely on one's personal feelings at the time things occurred.

And now that Dustin wasn't drinking the worm goddess's rainbow milk, he did feel some apprehension. The walls still trembled vaguely around him, and that made him imagine he was in a room of contracting dimensions, with its sides pressing in on him till they would surely meet at the point where he stood and crush him to death, leaving his blood to dribble away . . .

To the glory of Boku Veeza, of course.

Also, for the moment, Dustin felt very concerned that innocent and trusting Faith Mills not end up as Real Dreams' next sacrifice.

And he also wondered what it was that Seth's brother Woody was so desperate to speak to him about.

And, now that for the moment his thoughts were uncluttered by the strange glories that *Nif* gifted its drinkers, Dustin found himself wondering why he hadn't yet heard from Bianca Sanchez.

Alright, she might not have called me because she's worried that Real Dreams may trace the call. Or, they may have already recaptured her. As entwined into their affairs as she was, there has to be a limited number of places she can safely flee to.

After a while Dustin felt too worried. He needed to calm down. To achieve this, he poured himself a glass of *Nif* from the decanter on his coffee table and drank up.

And of course, once he'd gotten the *Nif* down his throat, he began wondering what he'd been worried about to begin with.

Nif was quite the drug. It really was.

It was the ultimate Kool-Aid trip.

CHAPTER 33

Yesterday, Faith had been boisterous and chatty. This afternoon, she seemed strangely subdued. (Dustin was to discover that she was inconsistent like this.)

They were in her kitchen and she was making them lunch. Faith prepared their meal mostly in silence, though she regularly looked over at Dustin and smiled.

"Okay, you can have some *Nif* if it'll cheer you up," Dustin joked after a while. You look like you need a shot of something. Clearly, your morning coffee didn't perk you up enough."

She smiled coolly back at him. "I'm not unhappy. Not at all. I guess one can't always be bubbly."

Dustin decided she was premenstrual. He hoped she'd not start bitching at him or run him out of her house.

"But, oh yes, I do feel like having a drink of *Nif*," Faith said. "If it isn't too early in the day for it." She looked worried when she said this. "Yesterday, we drank about the equivalent of three wine bottles of the stuff."

"Oh, it's never too early for *Nif*."

"Maybe I shouldn't tho'. I'm still seeing weird shit, like additional frypans on this range."

"Your uncle taught me that the cure for that is to drink more *Nif*. After a while it goes away."

He poured their drinks while she cooked. Once she'd had a few swallows of *Nif* she brightened up.

They ate their lunch and afterwards made love. The sex was just as great as yesterday's. It was more kinky though. Today, just as Dustin was about going down on Faith, she restrained him with a hand on his head.

"Hold on," she gasped at him. Then she reached over and picked up her glass of *Nif* from the end table it stood on.

Once again, they were lying on the living room rug. Dustin waited to see what she would do.

Faith dipped her fingers into the *Nif* and smeared it over her clitoris and the lips of her sex. Then, she wet her fingers again, and slipped them into her vagina. She did this several times, till there was a wet rainbow trail running down to her anus.

Dustin stared at her vagina like he was under a spell. The rainbow-coating made the hole look magical, a mine of wonders inviting him to descend into it, seeking the gold in its depths.

"Okay, lick me now," she told him.

Dustin dipped down and lapped at her sex. After sucking on her clitoris for a while, he licked downward to her vagina. Here he was in for a surprise: the mingling of the *Nif* with her vaginal wetness made her hole taste strange, unlike any vagina he'd ever experienced before. He stuck his tongue deep inside of her and swirled it around, seeking to lick and suck all of the captivating taste out of her. The desire to empty her this way consumed him like a fever and he went on sucking and licking her pussy for ages.

In between his frenzied examination of her sexual passage, he was vaguely aware of Faith pouring more *Nif* over her fingers and smearing the iridescent liquid over her clitoris and down into herself, refilling her vacancy. Acting on pure instinct, Dustin backed off each time her rainbow-dripping fingers appeared before his eyes and then ducked back down once they vanished from view.

"Fuck, I'm gonna . . . yes, I'm gonna . . . co-c-coooome!" was the soft announcement Faith gave him that her pleasure had peaked.

She lay gasping with her eyes closed, not saying a thing, so he took the initiative and slipped his manhood deep inside of her. Now she seemed to wake up again. She moved with him slowly to get him off too, and even kissed him a few times, but her mind seemed to be elsewhere, lost somewhere deep inside of herself, in that well of internal pleasure the *Nif* had helped her tap into.

He came quickly, his progress to orgasm accelerated by the *Nif* in her vagina, and the orgasm was exquisite, one of his most sensitive ever. His cock felt as if it had suddenly developed additional nerve endings.

"Holy fuck!" he gasped.

Then he rolled off to her left. She sat up and reached for her glass of *Nif*.

"I want to be a worm," she told him all of a sudden.

When Dustin looked at her after she said this, she was trembling a little and had a little smile on her face.

"Why would you want that?" he asked, while she sipped some *Nif* and smiled beatifically.

"I . . . I d-don't know. No, I do; really, I do. Just now, when we were making love, I could feel you moving inside of me, deep and then deeper, so nice and warm. I imagined I was Mother Earth and you were a worm burrowing deep inside of me. And I knew that right then you were feeling nothing but pleasure, pure pleasure until you came inside of me. And that's why I know I want that; I want to be just like that, deep down inside Mother Earth, blind as a penis, tunneling my simple way through the dark and moist center of things, filled with endless, mindless pleasure until my journey ends and my end begins."

"You make being a worm sound so profound," Dustin said. "Now I almost want to be one myself."

"Then let's be worms together," Faith told him.

"Oh, baby, I wish it were as simple as that."

"It may be. We may just have to find the key that unlocks the puzzle."

CHAPTER 34

Dustin's phone beeped for an incoming text message.

Sky-high on Nightmare Fuel and sexual gratification and not really welcoming any disturbance to his current state of euphoric contemplation of Faith's hot body, Dustin ignored the beep.

But just as he was relaxing again, the phone beeped again, and then a third time.

"Maybe you should answer it," Faith told him. "Might be that guy from yesterday who's texting you now. Did you call him back?"

"I tried, but I couldn't get through to him," Dustin said and reached out a languid hand to pick up the cellphone.

"You're right, it is him," he announced a moment later. "Hold on a moment while I see what he wants."

Woody's text was simple and to the exclamation point: 'DUDE, SKYPE ME RIGHT NOW!!!!!!!!!!!!!!!!!!!!!!!!!!!!!!!!!!!!'

That was the content of all three texts that Woody had sent him.

Something about Woody's request, maybe the eternity of exclamation points after each one, got through to Dustin.

He fired off a reply of, 'Gimme five minutes.'

"Excuse me for a little while; I gotta get home," he told Faith. "I'll be back in a jiffy."

She was as high on *Nif* as he was. She accepted his leaving as grandly as a queen would have. "Is it something serious?" she asked in a regal voice, as he got to his feet and began dressing.

"It may be. The guy seems to think so. Me, I'm not sure."

She blew him a kiss. "Okay, but hurry back, baby, and let's resume our discussion about becoming worms."

Dustin caught the kiss and hurried off.

CHAPTER 35

Back home again, Dustin got his laptop out of its bag, and clipped a webcam to it. He carried the laptop out to the living room and sat on the couch with it on his lap.

What the hell does Woody want to say that can't be discussed on the phone? he wondered while the laptop powered up.

At this point he accepted the fact that he was once more fully under the influence of *Nif.* Everything was crystal-clear again. The walls no longer shifted like laundry blown by wind; and while he'd been crossing the road, the neighborhood no longer had the aspect of a 3-D movie.

So yeah, alright. Dunno if this is good or bad tho'.

He got Skype up and running. He'd expected to vidcall with just Woody, but Jimmy Fisher and Jen Carlson, the two other 'surviving' GROW members (though of course they still didn't know this), were there with Woody.

Just like Dustin, Woody was seated on a living room couch, Jen was seated next to Woody, while Jimmy was leaning over the back of the couch.

All three of them looked very nervous. In fact, they looked frightened.

"Hey, guys!" Dustin greeted the trio of paranormal researchers. "Sorry, I couldn't get back to you yesterday. What the hell is so urgent? Have you news of Seth and Amy's whereabouts?"

Woody Taylor was a shorter, thinner, and more worried-looking version of his older brother. He shook his head. "Yeah, and no." Then Woody frowned. "Hey, Dustin, are you alright?"

"Me?" Dustin frowned back. "Yeah, I'm good. Why?"

"You seem a little off," Woody explained. "Like you're hungover or some—"

"Forget that and tell him what we've discovered," Jen interrupted. Jen was a short-haired blonde, small and bespectacled. Dustin wasn't sure if she and Jimmy were still dating or not.

"Hey, hey," Woody replied Jen testily. "I'm just asking 'bout the guy's health. He looks somewhat—"

"It's not *his* health we're concerned about now. It's *ours*," Jen said impatiently.

"Yeah, dude, tell him what we found out," Jimmy agreed. "We don't know how long it'll be before those psychos come looking for us."

Jimmy was their camera guy. He was tall and rugged looking, with black hair and a few tattoos.

"Okay, so what have you discovered?" Dustin asked. "Like Jen says, don't worry about me, I'm fine—for now at least."

Woody made a face. He was clearly trying not to show how worried he was, but was having a hard time of it. "Okay, I'll try to start from the beginning. How much do you know about what Seth and Amy were investigating when they went missing?"

Dustin knew just about everything about that, but of course, he couldn't say so. So, he replied. "Well, last time I saw Amy was when she met me at Rudy's Truck Stop, on the Wednesday before they went missing. She wouldn't say much, said it was way too dangerous. However, she did mention a cult of some sort."

"That cult is what we want to talk to you about," Woody said. "They're called Real Dreams and apparently worship a worm goddess of some kind."

"She's called Boku Veeza," Jen added with a disgusted twist of her lips.

"Never heard of her before," Dustin lied.

"Nor had we, until Seth's girlfriend Tanana told us—him, really—about her," Woody went on. "Anyway, Tanana got both Seth and Amy invites to join the Real Dreams club. Tanana did warn them that they couldn't take any cameras and stuff along, but we—"

"Tanana's a strange name," Dustin interrupted. "Is she like, Eskimo or something?"

"She's black. Tanana Reeves. Very easy on the eyes too."

"Seth met her on Tinder," Jimmy added. "It was sheer coincidence that she happened to be a member of a cult of worm worshippers."

"Anyway, to get back to our story," Woody went on. "That Friday night, Tanana arrives here to collect Seth and Amy, she blindfolds them, and that was the last we saw of either of them."

"How come you didn't tell me any of this earlier?" Dustin asked. "Or the cops, for that matter? For the past three weeks, all you've told me is that Seth was investigating something."

Woody sighed. "Man, we weren't intentionally deceiving you. We honestly believed that Seth and Amy were still alive. Cuz, see, all that while we'd not heard from Tanana either."

"She contacted us yesterday morning," Jen said, adjusting her spectacles on the bridge of her nose. "And she sent us some photos."

"That's why I called you," Woody went on. "Hold on a moment while I send the pictures over to your phone."

Woody picked his cellphone up from the couch and unlocked it. While he searched for the images he wanted, Jimmy leaned further forward over the back of the couch and wagged a finger at the laptop webcam.

"You're not gonna like these pics, bro," he told Dustin. "They're badly fucked-up shit."

"We think Seth and Amy are both dead," Jen added, tucking her short blonde hair behind her right ear with a finger. She shivered like the room around her was cold. Jimmy planted a kiss on her cheek and then leaned back to his initial position behind the couch, though now holding one of Jen's hands in his.

"Are you saying that Seth and Amy are both dead?" Dustin asked.

Woody looked up from his cellphone. "Judge for yourself. Either these snaps are real, or those Real Dreams jerks have one hell of a special effects team working for them."

Dustin picked up his own cellphone from beside him and swiped it open. Woody had sent him about ten pictures on WhatsApp.

Dustin looked through them. Four of the pictures were stills from Tanana's video of herself killing Seth. Four others were stills of Malarkey murdering Amy. The last two stills were photographs of Boku Veeza.

No one had spoken at all while Dustin examined the pictures.

Now he looked up and saw that the three webcammed people were staring curiously at him.

"What the hell do you make of those!?" Woody demanded of Dustin. "Real or fakes?"

Dustin shook his head. "These have got to be fakes," he said calmly. "Not because . . . I mean . . . the black woman—Tanana?—

she looks like she's become a bug, and the clown guy has horns and metal claws."

"I think they're demons," Jen said in a scared voice.

Jimmy looked like he was about saying something comforting to Jen, but before he could speak, Jen jumped on the couch like something had startled her.

Dustin couldn't see anything outside of the rectangle framed by his laptop screen, but he'd heard a muffled 'Bump!' sort of sound too.

"It's gotta be them," Jen said nervously. "Guys, remember that Tanana said they'll be coming to visit us too!"

"What's going on over there?" Dustin asked. In all honesty, he didn't really care. Woody, Jen, and Jimmy were all infidels who'd tried to expose the glorious goddess Boku Veeza. And all three of them deserved what was going to happen to them.

"All hail Boku Veeza," he murmured softly.

On his laptop screen, Jimmy walked out of view.

"Where are you going, baby?" Jen called after him.

"I think someone's in our bedroom," Dustin heard Jimmy reply.

"That's impossible," Woody replied him. "We checked earlier. We're the only ones in the apartment."

"But are we really?" Jen asked nervously. Now she was visibly trembling. She had beads of sweat on her forehead. Jen looked like she wanted to run for her life, but wasn't sure what direction was safe.

"Guys, what's going on over there?" Dustin asked.

But none of them replied him. They were caught up in the grip of an unknown and unseen terror.

CHAPTER 36

Woody had now abandoned the laptop on the coffee table.

Dustin had the perspective of looking at Woody's 'Planet Hollywood' tee shirt for a few seconds, and then Woody's scared face filled the screen.

"Hey, man, I think they're here . . . Tanana and—"

Then he stepped out of view of the webcam and Dustin could see clearly again. The angle of the laptop's placement on the coffee table gave Dustin a good view of the farther half of the living room and of the hallway entrance.

Jen had frozen up where she was on the couch. She was trembling and moaning to herself, like a small baby.

Behind her, her boyfriend Jimmy was running out of the hallway, with a look of horror on his face. Jimmy almost made it out into the living room, when Malarkey caught up with him.

The demon clown wore a blue costume patterned with white and red polka dots, topped off by a green hat with orange feathers. As usual, one side of his face was painted white, the other black.

In true demon form, giant horns sprouted from the clown's forehead.

This time, Malarkey's left hand was a giant shiny knife.

"Run! Run!" Jimmy yelled at the others, with one hand outstretched as if urging them to flee. "Go, go, G—!"

It was now that Malarkey shoved the blade of the giant knife all the way through Jimmy's body, so that it burst out close to his heart.

Jimmy let out a loud gasp of pain. A few moments later, blood began bubbling from his lips. He remained jerking like that. Propped up on his killer's knife. Almost dead, not far from it at all.

His torment finally broke Jen out of her daze. She got to her feet and began walking towards Woody, who'd once more appeared in the camera frame. Woody was holding a gun, which he pointed at Malarkey.

Woody fired twice. Both bullets seemed to hit the clown in his left ear, because Malarkey's head snapped suddenly to the right, but then

Dustin saw a decorative plate on the far wall shatter into pieces and he realized that the bullets had simply gone through Malarkey's head, which remained unharmed and popped back upright again.

"Fools, you can't kill us!" Tanana said, stepping briskly into view. Then she grabbed hold of Jen, who had noticed her coming and had been attempting to flee the other way.

The demoness was wearing a cream-colored pantsuit. She looked like a congresswoman.

"Let me go!" Jen screamed, but instead of doing so, Tanana punched her in the face. Jen's head snapped back and she collapsed unconscious onto the couch.

Woody hadn't fired again. Dustin took this to mean that he'd given up the attempt as useless. Woody had however stepped out of view again. Dustin imagined he heard a door slam, but he couldn't be sure of this.

His gruesome death captured by the webcam, Jimmy had just expired on Malarkey's knife hand. With a loud giggle, Malarkey jerked the blade out of Jimmy's back, letting the dead man fall to the ground.

Tanana was looking down at Jen with amusement on her dusky face.

"Why the hell don't these motherfuckers ever learn?" she asked Malarkey. "We keep killing 'em, but they repopulate like grubs."

Malarkey laughed. "So, we'll keep killin' 'em, girl. More fun that way. Gives us something fun to do."

"What about the one that got away?" Tanana asked him. "He's the leader now that his brother is dead."

"You know he won't get far. No one runs beyond the reach of Boku Veeza."

The clown wiped his knife-hand clean on the couch and then shaped it back into a regular hand. He walked around the side of the couch and stood beside Tanana, also staring down at Jen.

"What'll we do with her?" Tanana asked. "Fuck her up too, or . . . ?"

"We'll take her back to Queen Bee and let her decide. At the very least, she'll provide some entertainment for the club members."

And then both of them turned and stared at the laptop.

"Oh, hi, Dustin," Tanana waved cheerily at him. "Long time, no see."

"You look like a congresswoman out campaigning for votes," Dustin told her.

She smirked. "Ha ha, you overlooked the fuck-me heels," she said, lifting a leg so he could see that her pink high heels were at least a foot high. "However, if by 'congress' you mean fucking, then I'm game."

"How's it hangin', bro?" Malarkey asked.

"Same old, same old," Dustin replied. "My love life went to shit after the girls died, but life is making amends now. Got little to complain about."

"Glad to hear it," the clown replied. "Delete all records of this conversation, wilya?"

"Yeah, sure."

"See you around, honey," Tanana said. "You look good enough to eat."

Dustin waved to the onscreen pair. "Yeah, you devils take care now. Don't get into any trouble."

Dustin's statement cracked Malarkey up. "Bro, I already told ya, that realtor job of yours ain't your calling in life. You should be a clown too. Sometimes you're so funny, I almost piss myself listening to ya." He nudged his black companion. "Ain't that right?"

Tanana smiled coolly. "The dude sure is funny when he puts his mind to it."

Then the two of them turned away from Dustin. Tanana picked up Jen's body and slung it over her shoulder. Meanwhile, Malarkey had walked back around the couch and had picked up Jimmy's corpse.

What the hell do you want with Jimmy's body? Dustin almost shouted at them through the webcam as they walked off down the hallway.

But then he calmed down and smiled. He knew the answer to that one: Boku Veeza.

Oh yes, our worm goddess just LOVES the taste of infidel flesh.

Dustin got up and poured himself a glass of *Nif* from the worm-shaped decanter on his coffee table.

CHAPTER 37

Dustin enjoyed how *Nif* gave you a 'corrected' perspective of things.

Now that he was once more in 'the *Nif* grove,' he understood clearly the necessity of destroying the remnants of the Ghost Research Outfit Worldwide.

Either we strike with a hot iron or they'll expose the goddess's religion to the world before we're ready to do so ourselves.

Nor did he find it in any way odd that subconsciously, he'd already reenrolled himself as part of Boku Veeza's cult.

Thank God, no . . . thank Goddess for Nif, which helps us faithful view things in the bright light of her dark wisdom.

While thinking all of this, Dustin had been staring at the screen of his laptop, which was still a window into Woody's empty living room.

I like how Tanana and Malarkey are so effective at their jobs. Sorta like a spiritual USMC. Okay, but they do leave gaps and shit. They asked me to wipe records of our conversation, but they left Woody's own laptop undestroyed. I guess no one can think of everything.

He finished his glass of *Nif* and considered pouring himself another.

Then he shook his head. *I promised Faith I'd be back quickly.*

He got up from the couch and walked back into his bedroom to pick up his house keys.

And waiting in his bedroom, stark naked in his bed in all of her big-breasted glory, there lay Queen Bee, high priestess of the Real Dreams organization.

CHAPTER 38

"Hello, honey," the old brunette said on seeing him. "It seems like forever since I last saw you."

"How . . . how did you get in here?" Dustin managed to ask. As far as he knew, all the doors of his house were locked and she'd not been in the bedroom when he'd come in here earlier to fetch his laptop.

"Does it matter?" she asked back, cupping her mammoth breasts and squeezing them at him. "Don't tell me you aren't pleased to see me. I hope you enjoyed the *Nif* I left for you yesterday."

"Yeah, thanks for that," he said.

She smiled coyly. "It's been so long since I've taken my ass to the doctor for close examination. So, I decided today, I'm going to see my doctor . . . I'm going to see my doctor."

Dustin nodded. "Oh, so you're here just so I can suck on your . . . ?"

His mouth felt dry. Her breasts always had that effect on him. Stacked on her almost skeletal granny body like that, they were the epitome of decadent-sex fantasy.

Of course, Queen Bee's face was youngish. Her plumped-up lips were those of a teenager, while her eyes clearly belonged to that teenager's grandmother. She seemed assembled from both a younger and an older version of herself, as if her face, her chest, and arguably her crotch, were still trapped in the nineties when she'd been a porno actress, and were yet to catch up with the rest of her aging self.

Queen Bee flashed her pearl-white teeth at Dustin and coyly replied, "Why no, of course not, hon. I'm not just here so you can tend to my anal vineyard. I've other things to discuss with you. But we both know I'll feel more relaxed after I've had some of your excellent treatment."

She gestured him closer. "Come to bed, honey. I don't bite."

Dustin thought of Faith. *She's expecting me back over there. She's gonna be pissed if I'm not back over there soon.*

Queen Bee sat up in bed and then turned around, so that she was down on her hands and knees with her ass facing him. Then, as if to emphasize what she wanted from Dustin, the old lady rested her head on a big and soft pillow so that she could reach back and spread the cheeks of her ass wide.

Dustin stared at her anus, with its cluster of purple 'grapes.' The high priestess's hemorrhoids seemed to have grown larger since their last meeting.

I'm doing this for Faith's sake too, Dustin told himself as he knelt on the bed and lowered his head towards the high priestess's asshole. *One thing I don't want happening is our high priestess taking out her sexual frustrations on my new girlfriend.*

"Oh, honey," Queen Bee moaned when he began sucking on her piles. "You've no idea how much I've missed this."

He sucked on and then reached a hand under her to rub her clitoris. In response to this, she reached a hand further back to grab his hair and pull him even deeper into her ass crack.

"Just keep sucking like that!" she groaned. "Yes, like that! Oh shit! I'm gonna come any moment now!"

CHAPTER 39

"Take your pants off," Queen Bee told Dustin after she'd fully trembled through her orgasm. She was now lying on her back with her arms stretched out sideways. "Let your cock breathe."

Dustin shook his head at her. "Not now. I've got a new neighbor now. She's expecting me back at her place."

Queen Bee raised her eyebrows to question his answer. "New neighbor? In the Mills' house?"

Dustin explained about Faith Mills.

"Funny. I don't recall either Reggie or Doris mentioning any favored nieces of theirs."

Dustin shrugged. "You can't expect to know every member of their family."

Queen Bee nodded to that, but looked unconvinced. "Still . . . are you certain she's legit?"

"I wasn't certain at first, but she arrived with the house keys in hand and . . ."

He let his answer fade out. He wasn't about explaining that he'd been so mesmerized by Faith's beauty that he'd not really wanted to challenge her occupancy of the neighboring house.

Queen Bee mused over this for a few moments. "Anyway, even if she isn't legit, she's a fine cover for their disappearance. Works for me."

Dustin remained kneeling beside her. Her globular breasts looked like planets, they magnetized him the way the Earth magnetizes the Moon.

"Boy, take your pants off," Queen Bee told him. "You've got wood from sucking me off. Come fuck my cleavage."

Her sultry voice made his wood even harder. Dustin stared down at those incredible breasts. "I'm . . . I'm . . ."

She pouted her tomato lips at him. "Oh, don't make me beg. Okay, if you insist on me begging, I will . . . Dustin, honey, please, please, please, come here and fuck me hard between my titties."

He began laughing. She was so comical. And the way she looked while pouting, with her pearly teeth flashing between her heart-shaped lips . . .

"Okay, but I'll need to run afterwards."

"You can't run anywhere, anytime soon. You and I have someplace to visit together. That's really why I'm here."

Hearing that, Dustin gave in. One didn't argue with the high priestess of one's religion.

We're going somewhere together? Where? I guess it doesn't matter.

Dustin took his clothes off.

All of a sudden, he felt strange while undressing. In a weird way, staring at her aged face, her grayed brunette hair and her pale eyes, Queen Bee seemed extremely familiar to him. This was indeed an odd feeling, as he was already extremely familiar with her.

At first Dustin was unable to make either head or tail of this feeling. But then he realized it was merely an additional layer of empathy that *Nif* had just granted him.

Maybe the meaning is completely meaningless in actuality, but that's Nif for you. The meaningless meaning that means more than everything.

"Hold on while I lube up," Queen Bee told him once he was naked. Then she sat up and reached over to his nightstand, where a half-empty glass of *Nif* was propping up her handbag. She dipped two fingers into the rainbow liquid and smeared the stuff liberally in her cleavage.

"There," she said with a wink, after sucking the remnant off of her fingers. "My wedding aisle is ready for your bridegroom."

After crooking an inviting finger at him, she squeezed her breasts together. Dustin knelt over her and slid his erection between her mammary hemispheres. Her breasts were so big that they served as bumpers, preventing him from getting as deep between them as he'd have liked. But then he understood how to do this. He treated her breasts like they were the cheeks of her ass in doggy-style position, squeezing hard on them and thrusting downward and inwards.

It feels so good. Her body felt like . . .

"Give me your love milk!" She was smiling up at him. She grabbed the cheeks of his ass and squeezed them as hard as he was doing to her breasts.

Dustin suddenly found himself gasping for breath.

"I'm coming!" he moaned, as the semen shot from him.

He forced himself as deep into her clamped cleavage as the curvature of her breasts would allow. He watched his semen squirt out from the other side of the flesh tunnel and coat her neck.

He remained there atop her, pressing her breasts together and bracing himself on their soft strength, until his own strength gave out and he collapsed sideways onto the bed.

"You look pooped out," Queen Bee said with a gentle laugh.

She reached sideways for the glass of *Nif* again. "And now, boy, we both have somewhere to be."

"Oh, and I forgot to mention," Dustin said in a tired voice while she drank. "Tanana and Malarkey just killed at least one of my friends, and abducted at least one other. You know, Seth and Amy's paranormal guys?"

"Mission accomplished," Queen Bee said, with a cold, cold smile tightening her lips. "Those GROW assholes were becoming a pain in *my* asshole." She smiled sweetly at him. "The sort of pain you can't deal with, honey."

CHAPTER 40

When Dustin and Queen Bee stepped outside of his house, he was shocked to see her car—a silver Audi SUV—parked in his driveway, behind his own F-150.

He was about asking her how she'd managed to drive here without him hearing her . . . and more worryingly, if she'd been in his house *before* he'd returned from Faith's place, as that would mean that he'd walked past her car and not noticed it.

Oh, screw the questions. The answer is obvious: Right now, I'm high on Nif, and Nif skews perceptions. And besides, Queen Bee is good with magic too. She may have made her car both silent and invisible.

He gestured over at the Mills' place. "Gimme a minute to go tell Faith that I'm going somewhere with you."

She nodded. "Okay, but hurry it up."

He hurried across the road to ring Faith's doorbell. He was surprised that when she opened her front door, she was dressed to go out also.

"What kept you?" she asked before he could say what he had come to say. "You said you'd be back in a jiffy."

"I'll explain later," he told her, noting how lovely she looked all dressed up like this. "Where you heading anyway? You didn't mention you'd be going out later."

She shook her head. "I wasn't planning on going anywhere. My sister Grace called and said we needed to meet up. So now, I'm going to her house." Then she glanced over at Queen Bee's car, which was now reversed out of Dustin's driveway and aimed towards the entrance to Thiel's Way. "Who's the old lady?"

"My aunt. My dad's oldest sister."

"Wow! With those huge jugs? She looks like a retired porn star."

"She is. Listen, I came to tell you that she's come to take me somewhere."

As if sensing that she was being discussed by the two young people, Queen Bee honked the horn of her car.

Dustin leaned forward and hurriedly kissed Faith. "Okay, I'll see you once I get back here. Call me if you need anything."

He turned and ran down the driveway to Queen Bee's car.

CHAPTER 41

"I'm taking you to the Real Dreams clubhouse," Queen Bee informed Dustin as she drove up Broadway.

"In the daytime? And . . . and I'm not blindfolded."

Queen Bee laughed. "Concerning blindfolds, I don't think we need bother with those anymore where you're concerned. Don't you agree?"

Dustin nodded. "Yeah, I guess you're right. I'm not gonna blow the whistle on the club."

Queen Bee took her eyes off the road for a moment to smile at him. "You're one-in-a-million, Dustin. I'm so proud of you."

Dustin didn't know what she meant by that. He let it slide. "I thought the club held its meetings at night. Why are we going there in the daytime?"

They'd now reached the north part of town and Queen Bee turned her car right, off of Broadway and onto I-495. "Oh, I've something I want to show you first," she told him as they headed southeast down the interstate. "Something you need to see to understand our organization better."

Dustin nodded. "I'm intrigued. Something like what?"

"Haven't you ever wondered how you escaped from us the last time? How you opened the club's back door and found yourself outside of Reggie and Doris's home?"

"I've been wondering about that for three weeks straight. Half of the time I conclude it didn't happen that way."

Queen Bee laughed loudly at that reply. She didn't speak again for a while. They'd arrived at the cloverleaf highway interchange on the northeast side of Raynham and she concentrated on looping north again onto Route 24.

Only after she'd turned off of Route 24, northeast onto Route 104, and Dustin had realized that they were headed for the town of Bridgewater, did Queen Bee speak again.

"Oh, it definitely did happen that way, honey," she told Dustin with a laugh. "And now I'm about to reveal just how and why that was."

"I can't wait," was his honest reply.

Dustin's assumption that they were headed for Bridgewater proved to be wrong. He sighed as the silver SUV rolled through that town, next stop apparently Halifax.

Yep, definitely Halifax, Dustin concluded when they reached the Plymouth Road junction and Route 104 became Route 106.

Dustin was very familiar with this route because Rich Properties Inc. managed several properties in Halifax.

On the outskirts of Halifax, however, near Robbin's Pond, Queen Bee made a sharp right turn onto a one-lane road that crept through the woods as sluggishly as a starved snake.

Dustin made no comment now. He knew exactly where they were, and knew that there was nothing at the end of this road except several abandoned buildings with a creepy history that kept folks away from the property.

According to the news, the entire family that owned the lots—a middle-aged reverend, his three sons and daughter, and his elderly sister-in-law and her two children—all of them had vanished one cold winter night three years ago, and hadn't been seen since.

I wonder where the hell they could've gone?

Dustin mused on that question while Queen Bee pulled up to the old house.

"Well, here we are," Queen Bee announced as they drove through the front gates of the property.

"This place seems very well kept," Dustin observed as Queen Bee parked her Audi SUV at the side of the main building, a two-story mini mansion.

"We rent it from your Uncle Richmond," Queen Bee told Dustin. "He's actually got this place up for sale, but we bribe him not to sell it to anyone, as it's so useful to us."

Dustin stared at her in surprise. "Uncle Rich, but . . . I've never even heard that we're the ones managing this place." Then a thought rose in his mind. "Hey, is my uncle part of Real Dreams?"

"Richie?" Queen Bee laughed and patted Dustin's crotch. "Oh, hell no. Richie would have a seizure if he knew what I was doing with this place. But your uncle loves money—"

"You got that bit right."

"—And so, we made a deal with him. We contacted him after the Smith family vanished . . ." Then she gave a loud laugh. "No, actually we contacted him *before* the Smiths all went missing."

That sounded really odd to Dustin, and he looked at her sharply. "Are you saying that Real Dreams was responsible for the family's disappearance? You killed them all?"

The high priestess's playful mood turned serious. "Well, you know how we are about discipline. We don't play around when there's any kind of a threat to the worship of Boku Veeza. And the good Reverend Smith was becoming quite a nuisance to us." She sighed. "Most Christians aren't worth the air that they breathe. They're more concerned with the cares and worries of this life—amassing all the wealth they can and building their televangelist-preached John 3:16 version of the American Dream—than with following their supposed savior Jesus. But find one Christian who really knows how to pray and—" she clapped her hands "—'Boom!' you have a ready-made spiritual crisis waiting to happen to us witches."

She laughed coldly. "Unfortunately for himself and his family, Reverend Paul Smith was one of those serious types. He took his demon-chasing duties a little too seriously, and pissed us off."

"And so, you killed his entire family. The cops reported eight people missing. Three adults and five kids, I think. The reverend was reportedly a widower so there was no wife to kidnap also. You . . . I mean, Real Dreams did that?"

Queen Bee nodded. "Yeah, sort of." She gestured at the house. "Unknown to us, Madison Smith, the reverend's widowed sister-in-law wasn't home that night. She and her son had gone out visiting friends."

"That would make six, not eight," Dustin pointed out.

"Madison and Frederic arrived back home and saw us taking the others away," Queen Bee explained. "She turned the car around and sped off and was never seen again." Queen Bee laughed. "But of course, the cops counted her as missing also. And naturally, they blamed her disappearance on the same people who'd abducted the rest of her family."

Even with the *Nif* adjusting his POV, this info made Dustin feel queasy. After all, five children, three of them below the age of ten (if he remembered correctly), had been abducted by the Real Dreams organization on that day.

"What did you do with the kids?" he asked in a soft voice. Evening was just settling in now and its somber shade matched his thoughts when he considered the sort of horrible depravities that Real Dreams might have subjected the children to.

All to the glory of Boku Veeza, of course.

Queen Bee studied the worried expression on his face for a few moments, then she burst into loud laughter.

"Come on and I'll show you what we did with the kids," she said, pushing the driver's door open. Before getting out of the car, she grinned back at Dustin. "Oh, we didn't use them for sex, if that's what's bothering you. We found a much more practical use for them pesky young Christians."

Seriously bemused as to what she meant by 'more practical use,' Dustin opened the car door on his side and got out also.

As Dustin accompanied Queen Bee around the side of the house, he wondered what life was like when you had breasts that were as large as hers, as it surely meant that, no matter where she went, she was always the center of attention, except if she was visiting a film convention for equally busty adult movie stars.

Of course, she likes the attention. God didn't give her this chest; she bought big boobs because she wanted big boobs. The lady wanted a particular sort of life, the kind of lifestyle that having giant jugs would fetch her. She wanted men salivating over her and masturbating to her.

While walking beneath several trees, they turned the rear corner of the building, and Queen Bee said to Dustin, "Of course, you already realize that these buildings aren't the Real Dreams clubhouse that you've been visiting."

He nodded back. "Yes, I figured that you get there from here using everyday places as magical portals. What I don't understand is how you *open* up those paranormal doors."

"Well, honey, now you're about to find out."

CHAPTER 42

Their destination was a much smaller building at the rear of the main house. This was a single-story stone house with maybe just two rooms in it.

Queen Bee turned the handle of the building's front door. It opened easily.

"Doesn't anyone live here?" Dustin asked her as she pushed the door wide open. "How do you keep the place secure?"

She shook her head. "No one ever comes near. Everyone's afraid of being abducted like the reverend's family were."

"Oh . . ."

He followed Queen Bee into the building. The front room was nondescript. It seemed to have been the late preacher's counseling room. The cross that hung on the far wall had been turned upside down.

"We're expected in the basement," Queen Bee told Dustin. After patting him on the buttocks, she walked through the door at the far end of the front room, turned left, and descended a set of stairs.

The stairs led down to what must have originally been Reverend Smith's library, evidenced by the many bookcases in evidence.

But none of this at first caught Dustin's attention, because standing tied up in the middle of the basement was Bianca Sanchez, whom he'd recently saved from being hung in the Mills' home.

Bianca's mouth was gagged and she was bleeding from lots of little cuts on her arms and belly. A few spots of blood dotted the stone floor around her bare feet. Her wounds had clearly been inflicted by Tanana and Malarkey, both of whom were sitting in chairs near the bound woman and appraising her like she was the turkey that they intended to roast for Thanksgiving.

"Sorry we're a bit late," Queen Bee saluted the two seated demons. "I had to get my ass doctored first."

Hearing this, Tanana smirked at Dustin. Sitting legs crossed, she still had on her congresswoman's suit and pink stripper high heels.

Staring at her, Dustin wondered how the devil could be so fucking beautiful.

For the captive Bianca, Dustin felt nothing but disgust. His former interest in helping her escape was gone now, dissolved away by *Nif's* rainbow truths.

Infidels . . . infidels everywhere I look. It makes me sick!

He felt certain he was right about this, and felt he'd feel even more certain he was right once he had some more *Nif* to drink.

But for the moment, there was no *Nif* in sight. There was just Bianca, who stared at him with pleading eyes; eyes that begged him to help her escape again.

Dustin knew he would need to be content with getting high on what was going to be done to her.

But her fate was very obvious. Like lightning was about striking thrice in the same place, once Dustin stepped further into the basement library, he saw the noose hanging behind Bianca, about a foot above her head. The noose dangled from a hook set into the ceiling directly above her.

"Okay, let's open the club door," Queen Bee told Tanana and Malarkey. "I promised Dustin I'd show him how that works. Hey, what did you do with his three friends?"

The demon clown literally grinned ear-to-ear, and counted off on his fingers. "One's dead, one's in storage for later . . . and one of 'em got away from us."

"Motherfucker won't get far, that's for sure," Tanana added, like she was worried Queen Bee might blame her for Woody's escape.

"I have the utmost confidence that you'll soon find and dispatch him too," Queen Bee told them both. Then she looked at the black demoness. "Have you the key on you?"

"Yeah."

Dustin sighed when Tanana pulled a kitten out of . . . somewhere. Dustin didn't see where she got the pet from. Just like he'd seen happen with her before, her hands simply moved near her body and 'Abracadabra!' there was a kitten in them.

The young cat was brown and extremely cute. It snuggled up nicely against the black woman, unaware that it would never become a full-grown member of its species. It yawned and licked itself and Tanana's hands. She stroked it like she really liked it. Maybe she did like it.

"Let's do it," Malarkey said, getting up and stepping over to Bianca's side.

On seeing him approach, Bianca of course tried to get away. With her hands zip-tied behind her and her ankles bound too, there was little she could do, except hop away. And after two hops, she felt over. Then she tried rolling away from the demon clown, but Queen Bee was standing in the way.

Queen Bee laughed down at Bianca.

"You infidel slut," she gloated. "And to think I trusted you! Bitch, I'll show you what I think of you and that dumb boyfriend of yours."

And then the high priestess kicked Bianca in the side, kicked her so violently that Dustin heard Bianca's ribs loudly crack. Previously, Bianca had looked frightened, but now her face twisted up in agony, particularly so when Queen Bee kicked her again, harder this second time than the first. Now Bianca's eyes rolled up in her head. She wasn't dead, but the pain seemed to have transported her to another plane of existence.

Dustin greatly approved.

Boku Veeza is the leech that sucks pain from her enemies as nourishment. All glory to the goddess worm.

"String the bitch up before I shit on her, and then unlock her with the key!" Queen Bee instructed the two demons.

Then she managed to calm herself and smile at Dustin.

"Excuse me," she apologized to him. "I just can't stand it when people betray my trust like that."

She reached out a hand and pulled him down onto the chairs that Malarkey and Tanana had just vacated. "Let's have a seat and watch them," she told him. "I think you'll enjoy seeing this. Like I was saying outside, this is what we used the reverend's children for. Not him, tho'. We fed Reverend Smith directly to Boku Veeza."

"Of course, we cut his tongue out first so he couldn't pray or curse us in his God's name," Tanana added.

Tanana was waiting by the noose with the kitten, which had fallen asleep from her stroking it.

Malarky had just picked up Bianca and was carrying her over. Once he reached the noose, he lifted Bianca up and slipped the looped rope around her neck. Blood from where Bianca's busted ribs had punched through her skin was slowly seeping through her top.

Then Tanana gently placed the kitten on Bianca's right shoulder. The little cat slept on, unaware that its short life was at its end. Tanana slipped the kitten's head through and above the noose, and then she nodded to Malarkey, who now lowered Bianca so that the noose slowly tightened around both she and the kitten's neck.

Last of all, Malarkey peeled the tape gag off of Bianca's mouth.

"Alright, Queenie, the door and the key are both in place," he said. "You can cast the spell now."

By right now, both Bianca and the kitten had revived and begun kicking furiously. Tanana and Malarkey stepped back and watched them. Tanana looked indifferent to the pair's suffering, while Malarkey had a broad clown grin on his face.

The spell that Queen Bee recited made little sense to Dustin. Part of it sounded like some old east-European language and some like Native American lingo. A lot of it sounded like what he thought Boku Veeza herself might say if she spoke in her native tongue, that was if she had one.

Dustin watched to see what was about to happen here.

CHAPTER 43

All of a sudden, Bianca and the cat weren't there in the basement room anymore.

Well, actually the pair were still there, but they weren't—they'd become transparent-like. Dustin could see through them both as they kicked their lives away.

He blinked several times and then wiped his eyes.

Queen Bee stopped chanting and nudged Dustin with her elbow. "Weird, huh?" she asked.

"Oh yes," he replied. It truly was weird. Right at the point where Bianca seemed to be suspended in the air, a door had opened in the center of the room. The door seemed solid enough, except that at first it flickered every few seconds like it would vanish. Finally, it stabilized in place, and one could see a ghostly Bianca gasping away her life in the middle of it. The kitten had already expired.

The door was red in color and about seven feet high and three feet wide. When Dustin stared really hard at its edges, its frame appeared to be set in dark red brickwork which somehow existed out of the range of human vision. The upper half of the door's surface was inscribed with a black pentagram.

Malarkey grabbed the black doorknob and opened the door.

Dustin found himself staring down an extensive cream-colored corridor that was lined with doors, some of which were open, some of which were closed.

The corridor's familiarity chilled him to the bone.

"Hey, isn't this the . . . ?" he asked no one in particular.

"Yeah, honey," Queen Bee replied him while squeezing his arm, "this is the same exit through which you left the club on your last visit."

Dustin mused on this. The basement was now a work of cubist art, something that Picasso might have painted.

There was the room; there was the door within the room; there was the dying woman inside the door, or maybe the door was inside the dangling woman; there was the corridor that was visible through the door, but somehow seemed to be located inside of the dying woman also.

And I can see Tanana standing on the other side of the door; sort of visible and invisible at the same time, though not because she's transparent like Bianca is.

And of course, the door would only exist in one plane. To confirm this, Dustin got to his feet and walked around to Tanana's side behind the magical opening. It was just as he thought: both from the door's 'side' and from behind it, all he could see was a normal room, with Queen Bee sitting in a chair. He couldn't even see Bianca anymore.

He looked up. The noose was still there, but the spread loop of rope contained nothing. No Bianca Sanchez; no brown cat either.

How did Queen Bee just describe the relationship of Bianca to the kitten: the 'door' and the 'key?' That fits perfectly. Wow, I wish we had some Nif handy, so I can properly appreciate what I'm seeing. This is some crazy stuff.

"Okay . . . so . . . how come it's here now?" Dustin asked, skirting Malarkey to complete his circuit around the door. "I mean, the corridor the door opens into? Isn't it permanently linked to the Mills' house?"

"Not at all, Dude," Malarkey replied him. "We can open it wherever we want."

Dustin looked to Queen Bee for confirmation of this. She nodded back at him.

"Yes, that's right, hon. Actually—all glory to Boku Veeza—we can do a hell of a lot more than this. There are actually eighteen of these portals located across the state."

"Six plus six plus six is our lucky number!" Malarkey said with two happy thumbs-ups.

"Activating any one of them activates them all," Tanana added, now stepping out from behind the door to join in the conversation."

"But why so many?" Dustin asked. "Aren't you considering the risk of detection?"

Queen Bee shook her head. "That's the very reason why there's so many, hon."

"Imagine you're the po-po," Tanana explained. "What're you gonna think if you're gettin' constant reports of a hundred or more cars constantly being parked at an out-of-the-way house?" She smirked and her huge lips made a purple heart. "Of course, you're gonna get suspicious and investigate. But how we've got things set up? No fear of that happening. If twenty of so folks—in four or six cars—

meet up at a friend's place for dinner once a week, no one gives a shit what else they're up to in there."

"It's a sweet setup," Malarkey concluded.

"Yes, sounds like it," Dustin agreed. He nodded down at Queen Bee and then bent to lift her to her feet. Doing so brought his crotch into contact with her nipples.

"Let's go," he whispered to her, as he began getting an erection. "I need to drink some *Nif* to process all of this stuff."

"But, of course," she giggled back at him and rubbed her breasts against him, erecting him even more.

Dustin stepped through the door. For a second, he felt doubly odd. He'd walked through the ghostly projection of Bianca, and for the period of transition had felt himself passing through a liquid object like water. But the horrifying thing was that the liquid seemed alive.

Alive with hurt, alive with pain and fear.

"See you later," Tanana called from outside the human-opening. "We're off to go find Woody Taylor."

"Fuck him to death for me when you find him!" Queen Bee called back at them.

Tanana laughed. "What a sweet idea. I just might do that."

"How long do the doors remain open for?" Dustin asked Queen Bee as they walked down the corridors.

"Oh, it varies," the high priestess replied airily. "Sometimes a week, sometimes a month, sometimes merely a few hours. Then we feed the corpse to Boku Veeza to dispose of the evidence and sacrifice some other infidel . . . and their pet." She giggled. "Oh, you can imagine how delighted we were back then when we got the whole of the preacher's family at one shot—well, that bitch Madison did escape us—but like I just showed you, we sure put the rest of their nasty bible-thumping clan to good use. All hail Boku Veeza."

"All hail Boku Veeza," Dustin dutifully chimed in response. Killing all those kids still seemed distasteful to him, but what Boku Veeza wanted, Boku Veeza got.

They'd just walked past the connecting corridor that led to the worm goddess's lair. Dustin felt relieved that Queen Bee hadn't decided to detour that way.

He didn't feel up to seeing the creature he'd unwittingly signed a contract to worship just yet.

CHAPTER 44

By whatever differential/demonic space-time equations ordained after passing through hung-human/hung-cat doors, the time was much later in clubland than it had been outside of it.

By the time Dustin and Queen Bee reached the main clubroom, the place was already filling up with members who'd come for that night's meeting.

That means it's already nine or ten at night. But we just left . . . it was daylight—midafternoon—ten minutes ago!

He turned to ask the high priestess about the time inequality, but someone had already clapped him on the shoulder and spun him round.

"Glad to see you're back!" a tall and bearded man he didn't recognize greeted him. The man was naked except for thong underpants and a bowtie and was holding two glasses of *Nif.* "We were all concerned after you vanished from the temple like that the other day. Hey, here . . ."

He held out one of the drinks to Dustin. "I got it for my girlfriend, but . . . Anyway, how've you been doing since? Queenie said you needed to get your soul together. Must've been really rough for you after the tragedy of what happened to Mel and Jordy."

Dustin looked around for Queen Bee, but she'd vanished into the press of people. "I'm still getting over it," he replied the familiar stranger.

The man nodded understandingly. He was about to say more, but then a woman in a red fishnet bodysuit appeared at his shoulder.

"Baby, where's my drink?" she queried petulantly.

The man winked at Dustin and then pulled his girlfriend away.

Dustin drank from his glass of Nightmare Fuel and relaxed. It had been an unexpected conversation. He made his way through the club, seeking a familiar face as he approached the stage. He hardly recognized anyone in here, but they all seemed to know who he was. Women blew kisses at him and men either nodded sagely at him or gave him a thumbs up.

"Hey, that's Dustin," he heard a man whisper behind him.

"Are you sure?" a woman answered. "I thought Dustin was taller and more muscular, like Vin Diesel."

A passing naked waitress stared at him in clear adoration and pumped her tongue inside of her cheek at him in simulation of a blowjob.

"Later, maybe, baby," he told her and smacked her ass as she walked past.

Seems like I'm some kinda celebrity here now, Dustin thought with a smile as he found a vacant table near the center stage and sat down.

He sipped his drink and his eyes roved this surreal world that the Real Dreams organization had created *somewhere.*

Yes, *somewhere.*

From what he'd seen and from what Queen Bee and the two demons had said, he now felt certain that this clubhouse was located somewhere far from everyday life.

Boku Veeza is a goddess. Are we in her version of heaven, or are we resident in her private hell, playthings to serve her whims?

Around him, varied club activities went on. Soft jazz music filtered down from immense speakers. People sat and talked or walked around greeting friends. The club was only about a quarter full; people kept streaming in through the exits, coming (Dustin knew now) from all of those eighteen hell-gates that had been unlocked by sacrificing Bianca.

Some people (not too many as of yet) were already having sex on the assorted furniture placed near the walls for the purpose.

Dustin wondered about Bianca Sanchez.

Is she still alive, dying a pinch at a time in her transparent limbo?

Malarkey and Tanana had hung the woman carefully, not dropping her abruptly (so the fall would break her neck and speed her departure to the afterlife), but letting her dangle and choke.

Boku Veeza is a sadistic goddess who thrives on the admission of pain to her most beloved worshippers—

He recalled the suffering and horror that he'd sensed from Bianca's liquified shadow when he'd he walked through it.

—Therefore, our goddess will prolong Bianca's suffering for days or weeks . . . until she ceases to find her entertaining.

The thought of time reminded Dustin of the puzzling time differential he'd noticed on arrival here.

He had his cellphone on him, so it would be easy to work out how far forward in time passing through the Bianca-door had shifted he and Queen Bee.

But allowing me in here with my cellphone was clearly an oversight by Queen Bee. Either that, or she's testing me to see how loyal I really am. Because I know that cellphones aren't permitted here in Boku Veeza's world. Getting mine out in here will attract unwanted attention to me. I might even be accused of being an infidel. And that's the last thing anyone wants happening to them.

So, Dustin wisely left his cellphone in his pocket.

Dustin drank and stared around at the ten or so giant ceiling-high murals that depicted the worship of his goddess.

Just like in Faith Mills' living room, here too the painting of the Human Grove had been updated. Doris Mills was now included amongst those armless holiest worshippers, and they knelt around a sexagram, rather than the original pentagram that the mural had depicted when the number of holiest worshippers had been five in number.

Great is Boku Veeza, Dustin agreed. He realized that the painting had upgraded itself. No painter, either human or demon, had touched it.

The evil glory of our goddess is sufficient to make the painting—to make reality even—adjust itself to conform with Her truths.

Dustin drank and smiled and felt good. It felt like he'd last been inside here yesterday. He felt he was back home again.

The intervening time seemed to compress, to collapse till it was paper-thin. He was once more in the heart of things.

All hail Boku Veeza!

CHAPTER 45

After a while, a hush spread through the assembled crowd. Microphone in hand, Queen Bee climbed the steps to the stage.

In true nymphomaniac fashion, the Real Dreams high priestess had changed from her previous street clothes into a clinging cobwebby gown that left absolutely nothing to the imagination of her congregation.

"Well, I'd like to welcome everyone here to another fun night in honor of our goddess Boku Veeza," she said.

Dustin hoped that she would not go so far as to welcome him back to the club. That would have been so embarrassing.

Thankfully, the high priestess had other things on her mind.

"Now, just like moi, I know the rest of you here enjoy a good punishment," she said. Then, raising her voice theatrically, she added: "Particularly when we're punishing infidels!"

At this statement, loud applause rang through the club.

Queen Bee let the applause and excitement run on for a while before raising her hands to calm her audience again.

"And, just like me, I'm sure you all know that there are no worse infidels in existence than those who attempt to supposedly *expose* our glorious goddess Boku Veeza."

"Oh fuck, not those assholes again," a man at the next table to Dustin's said. "How the hell is it, we never seem to run out of them?"

"Infidels are like cockroaches," Queen Bee said as if she had read the man's mind. "It's crazy. You kill ten roaches and by the next day there's twenty more in your kitchen, as if you're breeding the damn things."

"Damn right, Queenie!" a woman yelled from a distance.

Queen Bee laughed loudly, her voice booming far and wide through the speakers. "Relax, Melanie, you know that Boku Veeza has the best bug spray in existence for killing infidel roaches."

"Fuck yeah, she do!" an obese black man shouted.

"Hold your horses, Randy. We'll get to the fucking part a bit later on in our program."

This provoked quite a bit of laughter.

When everyone had calmed down again, Queen Bee said, "Alright, folks, let's get on with it."

A hush at first fell over the gathering as Malarkey shoved a mostly unclothed young man up onto the stage. Then the crowd recognized who the accused was and began hissing and cursing him.

"Yeah, we was fully disappointed too," Tanana said when she climbed up the stage behind the two of them." Still dressed in her business pantsuit, she really did look like a politician when she turned to face the bound man and asked him, "Freddy, my man, what the hell got into you, to think you could betray us and get away with it? Like Boku Veeza was ever gonna let you get away with that dumb shit."

Freddy could not answer her question because his mouth was taped over. For the most part, however, he seemed unharmed.

Dustin, who hadn't recognized the victim, now understood who he was:

Oh, this guy is Freddy Reid. This is Bianca's infidel boyfriend!

It seemed fitting to Dustin that while Bianca (who maintained her innocence) had met her own end outside the club, her boyfriend (who was guilty beyond any shadow of a doubt) would be getting his just desserts inside the club.

Now was when Dustin first paid attention to four steel posts that had slowly been rising up through the floor of the stage for two minutes now. The posts all rose to the same height of about six feet. What actually called Dustin's attention to them was the loud click they all made, all four at the same time, as they locked into position.

The last time that Dustin had witnessed equipment rising through the Real Dreams stage, it has been a prelude to a brutal ax execution. He wondered what he was going to see tonight.

Ah, her aging loveliness Queen Bee didn't prepare me for any show tonight. I'd better drink some Nif to properly understand this.

His glass was empty, so he signaled to a black waiter who came over quickly.

"Hey, you're Dustin, ain't you?" the waiter said on reaching him. "So sorry, brotha, 'bout what happened to your two ladies last time. Hope you have better luck in future."

"Thanks, bro," Dustin told the man, who served him his drink and left.

He must have been in the temple too that sad morning, Dustin thought.

Now that he was properly beneath *Nif*'s mental influence again, Dustin was uncertain of which tragedy he was sadder about: whether the fact that Melissa and Jordan had died on that fateful morning, or the fact that their death had screwed up his chance of becoming one of the guardians of Boku Veeza's Human Grove.

Looking back up to the stage, he realized that he'd missed something during the interlude during which he had been occupied with the negro waiter.

Up on the stage, a group of eight demon-masked men were busily attaching four long silvery chains, each one quite thick, to Freddy Reid's wrists and ankles.

Interestingly, the other end of each silver chain entered a hole in the middle of one of the four steel posts.

This connection made Dustin pay proper attention to the design of the silver poles. He noticed now that each one of them had a crank handle situated opposite the hole from which the chain emerged.

"Alright, y'all, thanks; now get the fuck off of our motherfuckin' stage," Tanana laughingly told the men who'd fixed the chains to Freddy's limbs, with a shooing gesture. "Y'all motherfuckers taking too much time with getting him ready. We're here to kill the sonofabitch, not save his damn life."

The audience burst out laughing.

"All right, settle down everyone," Queen Bee told the audience after the laughter had gone on for a while. When the noise had subsided sufficiently, she said: "Now we need four volunteers. Your race, age, size, height, sexual orientation doesn't matter at all, so long as you hate infidels. O.K., show of hands. First come, first served, and no bitching if I don't pick you."

"Or we'll kill you along with him," Malarkey added with a laugh.

Queen Bee was already selecting volunteers, while walking around the stage and squinting from one side of the hall to the other.

"You, sir, in the front row, with no clothes on. Yeah, you with the erection. Get your dick up here fast, and don't take so much Viagra next time. And, uh okay, the lady over there. Yeah . . . with the bunny ears. No, not you, Penny, I mean the woman behind you, the blonde with small tits and *wearing* bunny ears. Penny, you know I'm never going to pick you. Why? Are you really asking me why? Bitch, your damn breasts are even bigger than mine and I don't want Dustin getting an eyeful of you up here and preferring sucking your piles to mine."

When the laughter over this comment had subsided, Queen Bee picked two more people: "Okay, Jimmy, you didn't put up your hand in time, but I know you've been dying to kill someone for ages, so here's your chance. Get your ass up on the stage too."

While the three persons she had already chosen made their way towards and up onto the stage, the high priestess looked around the club eagle-eyed, skimming over the sea of upraised hands for that elusive final person to complete her macabre quartet.

"Yes, *you*, the young woman in the red dress sitting next to the young woman wearing that crappy blue and red warpaint. No, not you on her right; *you*, on her left side. Shit, you're both wearing red dresses. Don't you young sluts have any sense of fashionable nudity? Yes, yes, yes *you*. Get up, young lady, and come up here. You're our number four."

Selections one, two, and three had all been on the other sides of the stage and Dustin had only seen who they were when they got to the stage.

But this final selection was only a few tables away from him and so he saw the person clearly.

Dustin was shocked to discover that the young woman in the red dress who was approaching the stage (her 'dress' was really a long red tee shirt with the chest cut out so that her bare breasts were on display) was none other than his new neighbor and new girlfriend Faith Mills.

"All hail the greatness of Boku Veeza," Dustin thought aloud. "For only she, in her infinite wickedness, could fuck up my existence so perfectly."

And then he drank a whole lot of *Nif* to help him process and understand what was going on here.

CHAPTER 46

"Okay, everyone, here's what you gonna do," Tanana instructed the four people who'd come up on the stage. "There's four of you, so it should already be obvious that each of you are going to one of these metal posts that came out of the floor of the stage." She looked from face to face and they all nodded back at her.

"Good," she went on with an evil smile on her large lips. "O.K., now it's also gotta be obvious that you're each gonna crank the cranks attached to the poles."

After the two men and two women nodded their understanding of this also, Tanana stepped slightly back from them and addressed everyone in the clubroom, her amplified voice sweet and seductive in the club loudspeakers.

"What ain't so obvious," she told her audience, "is *why* they're going to be turning those cranks and what's going to happen to our snitch friend Freddy here when they fucking do."

Freddy was shaking and looked understandably horrified. But what could the guy do? There was no way for him to escape and he knew it. He simply had to take what was coming to him.

Tanana nodded to Queen Bee. "Time for the history lesson, ma'am."

Queen Bee took centerstage again and said, "Well, back in old times, and by that I mean really ancient times like the days of the Roman Empire, and long before that, criminals who committed particularly horrible crimes, like traitors and such like, were executed by quartering." The high priestess laughed. "You've all seen it before in the movies, I know."

"This is that Braveheart or Gladiator sorta shit," Malarkey the clown interjected. "Old-school death dialed up to eleven."

"Yeah," Queen Bee went on with a laugh. "So, back then, some murderers or kidnappers . . . or whoever was having a bad luck day at the time would wind up in deep shit. Hey, cuz let's face it, folks, back in those times the legal system wasn't like what we enjoy now . . . maybe all you did was simply look at the queen's fat ass in a way that the king didn't like . . . Anyhow, the guy winds up with his arms and legs tied to four horses, and then the horses are whipped into motion and as they run away, they pull the guy into pieces. Four quarters normally, hence the name 'quartering.' "

The high priestess nodded to Tanana, who now stepped forward again and mock-curtsied to the audience.

"Well, my lords and ladies, we ain't got no horses here tonight," she said, handling her microphone like she was rapping. "But these four poles will do just as good. Consider 'em as something like horse-powered, like in power steering. Haha. Each pole contains an engine that's gonna increase the force applied to the crank by a whole lot. So, our four volunteers will turn the cranks to tighten the chains and the pole will augment their efforts. The results should be fun to witness. Of course, Freddy ain't gonna like the shit one bit."

CHAPTER 47

"O.K., ladies and gentlemen," the black demoness gleefully told the four volunteers, "each of you go stand by a pole and prepare to crank dat shit up!"

Now that he'd heard how Freddy Reid was doomed to die, Dustin almost felt sorry for the poor bastard.

Still, I don't get it. Why take the risk? According to what Bianca told me, Freddy was a very trusted member of this organization. What possessed the dude to throw all of that away? What could his motivation possibly be?

Dustin figured he'd never find out and settled back to view the macabre show.

The four volunteers were already behind their poles, and looked raring to go.

Dustin was dismayed by how eager Faith in particular seemed to be to get started. Her hand rested on the crank and was rolling it back and forth, without applying any real pressure to the death lever.

To facilitate an uninterrupted view of activities, Queen Bee and Malarkey had stepped down from the stage, leaving Tanana as the sole Mistress of Ceremonies.

"And now, guys, let's all tear this chump to pieces, shall we?" Tanana said with a loud witch's cackle. "On your fucking marks, get set, crank!"

The cranking began. At first, it was a sedate, rather boring affair. But it quickly picked up steam.

Freddy was still standing on his feet and there was quite a bit of slack on the chains binding him. To get the job done right, his arms had been left to dangle free at his sides, and as such, one of Freddy's first actions was to try and undo his gag, possibly so that he could plead for mercy.

However, he was unable to do this. The gag was tied in place by cords knotted behind his head, and before Freddy could undo the knots, the cranked chains were pulling his wrists outward, away from his body.

"Sorry, baby, but you don't get to beg for mercy," Tanana laughed as Freddy's hands were wrenched well beyond reach of his head.

Up until now, Freddy had managed to remain upright, albeit with an effort, as the chains slowly pulled his legs farther apart.

But suddenly, either Faith or the guy with the boner (the pair were situated at diagonally opposite poles, both of which were attached to Freddy's leg restraints), one or both of them worked their cranks exceptionally violently, and a long length of chain was pulled outward and Freddy was jerked up off the ground and was suddenly hanging in midair.

Everyone gasped and laughed. Because, either by accident or design, the other pair of chains (those attached to Freddy's wrists) had gotten tangled up, meaning that Freddy wasn't pulled up into the air in a spread-eagled position like everyone had expected, but was rather twisted up like a pretzel. His legs were separated in a wide 'V' that hurt Dustin to look at and his left arm was looped down between them, while the right one was stretched straight out from his shoulder.

Freddy hung there with his eyes full of inexpressible pain.

Tanana whistled at the spectacle. "Damn! How the hell did we accomplish this? Any more cranking and his ass is gonna be right next to his head." She laughed. "Okay, guys, give it your best shot."

The cranking resumed. And now, with the physical limits of Freddy's body reached, physical damage began happening to him.

The first evidence of this was the loud popping and ripping noise that echoed through the auditorium as Freddy's legs were pulled out into a straight line. Everyone clearly heard the ligaments that connected his thigh bones to his hips tearing up. And his arms were suffering too. The arm that wasn't twisted up beneath him was getting longer by the moment.

There was no sound in the clubroom; everyone was entranced by the violence. It was a strange way to watch someone die. Violence was usually visible on the surface of the body. But in this case, no blood had so far been seen, the audience were simply being treated to the visual music of the internal damage that Freddy's skin concealed.

But of course, breaking point came soon. The people turning the cranks could smell blood in the air. They had their victim and their *Nif*-addled brains encouraged them to the ultimate bloodletting.

First to rip free was Freddy's right arm. It seemed to peel off of him like a wing of fried chicken. Suddenly it hung free in the air, separate from its owner, and then it plopped wetly to the floor.

"HOLY SHIT! HOLY SHIT!" folks exclaimed in awe.

The woman working the crank that had achieved this feat of human deconstruction seemed entranced. She kept working the crank until its chain had hauled the severed arm right beside her.

Freddy was literally splitting apart now. Now connected to just three cranks, his body turned like it was on a spit.

Of course, Freddy was very close to death's door now. As his body twisted around, his right shoulder rotated like a malfunctioning shower faucet, blowing blood down on the stage and then up into the air in crazy red jets.

Then finally, he was suddenly stretched out in midair, spreadeagled with an arm missing.

Seeing this, Faith and the sexually aroused man began both turning their cranks for all they were worth, with the result that Freddy now began ripping up between the legs like someone was sawing him open there.

The noise as his pelvis separated was atrocious, a horrible wet ripping sound that made Dustin cringe even before the bleeding started. As Freddy's legs separated further, his intestines began slipping out of the red tear that extended up through his crotch into his lower abdomen.

By this point, Freddy was clearly dead. A few more cranks and Faith got Freddy's left leg completely off of him. Along with most of his belly, the leg and hip ripped off somewhere below the rib cage.

With that gone, the dead man plopped to the floor and what was inside of him all spilled out.

Well, Freddy may have been dead by now, but the cranking continued nonetheless. With both female 'crankers' out of the picture, the men continued the mechanized tug of war. There still remained the contest between the 'right leg' and 'left arm' crankers to resolve.

Yes, Freddy's body had fallen in the middle of the stage when Faith had gotten his left leg off, but the slack that had resulted from this was quickly taken up by both cranking men, who wound up with what remained of his body, dangling between their two posts on the side of the stage across from Dustin.

Everyone laughed at the sight of the corpse stretched out like that. It looked like a thick red blanket hung out to dry.

"Alright, boys," Tanana yelled, "show Freddy that even his motherfuckin' corpse ain't safe from us!"

Both men quickly got to cranking again. A few seconds later, Jimmy, the guy whom Queen Bee had tagged as desperate to kill someone, got Freddy's arm off. Or maybe the guy with the erection pulled his leg off. Same difference; the stage was covered with blood, intestines and four pieces of Freddy.

Everyone applauded. The volunteers who'd worked the cranks all began bowing, laughing, and giving each other thumbs-up gestures.

Faith noticed Dustin then and ran down off the stage to hug him. Her face was flushed with excitement. Her nipples, exposed by the slit front of her tee shirt, were stiff against his body.

"Wow, fancy meeting you here!" she told him once they'd separated.

He frowned when they separated and handed her his glass of *Nif*.

"So, everything was a charade?" he asked her while she took a drink from the glass.

She swallowed, then shrugged back at him. "Are you upset that I deceived you?"

"Not at all," Dustin replied honestly. "But I don't see why you had to."

"It seemed a lot more fun to string you along like that," she replied with an impish smile. "It was fun for me anyhow."

He pulled her close and kissed her. He didn't know why, but he felt even closer to her now.

Up on the stage, Tanana was now inspecting Freddy's remains.

"Wow, I'm fucking impressed," she said, walking quickly around the stage to each of the four main separated parts of Freddy's body and holding each one up in turn for the audience to appreciate.

Needless to say, her congresswoman suit was soon covered in gore.

As the demoness traipsed around the stage, Dustin noted that the hexagram carved into the stage had also 'updated itself' into a sexagram.

Boku Veeza is truly marvelous!

Finally, Tanana threw down the last severed bloody chunk of Freddy Reid and grinned at the audience. "Ladies and gents, now *this* is what I call a successful quartering. I don't know 'bout you motherfuckers, but I ain't got no complaints whatsoever 'bout how this infidel shithead just died."

Everyone began laughing again.

"All hail Boku Veeza!' Tanana said, looking crazy beautiful in her bloodied-up pantsuit and crazily high pink heels.

"ALL HAIL BOKU VEEZA!" the audience thundered back at her.

Then Tanana gestured across the stage, to the eight demon-masked men who'd chained Freddy up. "Okay, boys, come clean up the mess and feed him to our loving goddess."

As the men ascended the steps, Tanana bowed to the audience. "Okay, folks, now here's Queenie for y'all again."

CHAPTER 48

"No, no, guys," Queen Bee instructed the cleanup crew when she was back up on the stage. "Don't mop up the blood yet, we're about to spill some more right now."

For some reason she was barefoot, and was stepping delicately, trying not to step into any of the grooves of the giant sexagram carved into the stage.

Queen Bee wasn't equally particular about getting her feet bloody though.

"Just pack the pieces of his body into one of those tubs," she told the workers. "My main concern right now is that we don't slip on a shred of his guts."

Then, once satisfied that her instructions were being properly carried out, Queen Bee returned her attention to the audience. "Well, ladies and gents, I just know you totally enjoyed that punishment." She looked back at the stage and whistled into her microphone. "It's been ages since I last saw so much bad blood spilled for such a good reason."

When the laughter caused by her comment had subsided, she said, "All right now, you know that where entertainment is concerned, our goddess Boku Veeza always delivers. She is the darkness that leads us through the darkness into even greater darkness, the darkness that scares the darkness away and replaces it, the darkness that feeds on the darkness and then shits out more darkness." After laughing to herself for a few moments, the high priestess concluded: "Okay, people, it's time for the Nugget Auction."

"What the hell is a 'Nugget Auction?' " Dustin asked Faith, as everyone around them began murmuring this same question confusedly to themselves.

Faith shrugged back at him. "Baby, I'm as confused as you are."

"I guess we'll just have to wait and find out," Dustin said.

Faith nodded. "But, before they're ready, let's go join my sister Grace. She's dying to meet you."

CHAPTER 49

"Hey there," Grace Mills said over the buzz of the crowd. "I've been dying to meeting you."

She extended a delicate hand and Dustin shook it.

Wow! Faith wasn't joking when she said Grace has identity issues now.

Grace Mills had painted her face in zig-zagging red and blue stripes. If the basic shape of her face bore a resemblance to her sister's, the stripes had eliminated the details for comparison.

In addition, her dark hair hung in her eyes, so that while he could see that her eyes were the same perfect blue as her sister's, he got no clear impression of their size or shape. Her lips were included in the colored zig-zag; they seemed to exist only when Grace opened her mouth.

The third woman at their table had left now, but her chair was right up by a support pillar, and getting to it would have been awkward for Dustin, so Grace moved over to it. To do so, she had to get up, and this allowed Dustin compare her figure to her sister's.

Grace Mills was about the same height as Faith. He couldn't be certain though as Grace was wearing high heels and Faith wasn't.

It was something he always wondered about: the relative heights of women: because of their heels, one day they were one height and the next, another. Particularly in groups of five or more women, except they were clear vertical distinctions between them, he found it hard to determine who was taller or shorter.

He laughed. *About the only way you can really be certain what height a woman is, is when you fuck her: all women are the same height in bed.*

"Grace is jealous that I'm dating you," Faith told him once they were all seated with glasses of *Nif* facing them. "I'm very pleased that she's jealous of me."

Dustin looked at Grace.

She nodded back. The painted face and forward-brushed dark hair made her look creepy.

"It's true," Grace Mills admitted. "You're famous here now." Her voice was several degrees lower than her sister's. Though it was indeed pleasant, it also had something artificial about it, as if it was another side-effect of her accident. He wondered how much scarring her garish zig-zagging makeup hid from the world.

"Yeah, everyone here seems to know who I am now," he admitted to both sisters.

"It's more than that, Dustin," Grace told him seriously. (Unlike her sister, it seemed she always spoke seriously.) "Apparently, Boku Veeza likes you too."

Dustin stared curiously at her. "What's this about?"

Faith replied him: "How you got out of here that last time? Well, it's never happened before. No 'intruder' ever goes into the worm goddess's lair and lives to describe her. Grace and I were both present in the temple that morning when the transformation ritual failed, and . . ." She waved her next comments away as if they didn't matter. "So, anyway, Malarkey later came back to the temple and told Queen Bee that the goddess herself had permitted you to leave. And, with that being the case, who was he to argue with her?"

"So, lots of the women here have a thing for you now," Grace finished. "Myself included." She laughed coldly. "Maybe I'll come visit you at the house when li'l sis is out. Or maybe I'll just fuck you here tonight."

"Don't you dare," Faith told her. "He's mine and mine alone."

Grace laughed some more. "Not here, he ain't, li'l sister. You know the rules like I do: here at the club, we can all sleep with anyone we like."

"So, you'd have sex with my boyfriend?" Faith asked heatedly. Then she turned to stare angrily at Dustin. "Hey, do you want to have sex with Ms. Faceless here?"

"Ms. Faceless? Ouch, that really hurts," Grace replied, in an amused tone of voice that assured Dustin that it didn't.

"Answer me, baby," Faith insisted. "Do you want to sleep with my older sister tonight?"

"Stop fighting over me," he told them both. "At club meetings I'm reserved for the high priestess's use alone. You'd think I studied wine production at uni."

Both sisters stared at him in confusion for a moment, then broke into simultaneous laughter.

"But seriously," Grace asked in that serious way of speaking that she had, "what does the old girl's ass taste like?"

"Oops, you're gonna have to wait for that answer," Dustin replied them. "I'm expected somewhere already."

"You need to go to the bathroom?" Grace asked. "I'll come with you. I need to go too."

He shook his head and pushed his seat back. "No, no. This is more serious. The goddess is calling me. She says I'm to come right away."

He left both sisters staring at him in surprise and hurried off.

CHAPTER 50

Dustin hadn't lied. He could sense Boku Veeza summoning him.

"Dustin, come to me!" Her voice filled his skull like he had no brain in there anymore. It was all he could hear.

Walking beside the stage to reach the corridor that led to the goddess's chamber, he was aware of people coming back up onstage, but he paid them no attention. Similarly, Dustin was aware of people trying to catch his attention and commenting about him, but he paid them no heed either.

His eyes were glazed over and Boku Veeza was all he could think of. His exit from the club hall and walk down the corridor were elements of a dream.

Not until he was standing in the goddess's lair and staring directly up at her from a few yards away, did the haze evaporate from his brain.

"Hello, Dustin," Boku Veeza said, with her voice echoing through his mind like a whisper into eternity. "It has been a while since I last saw you. How have you been?"

"Same old, same old," he whispered.

He wasn't attempting to be flippant; that reply was all that came to his lips. Maybe it had something to do with the fact that Boku Veeza's voice in his head was taking up so much mental space. Maybe it had to do with the fact that he was so close to her that she seemed limitless.

The bulk of the worm goddess's body towered over Dustin to more than twice his height. And her worm body was at least four feet thick—the lowest segments rose to the height of Dustin's chest and altogether, her segments were piled up in three levels, down the sides of which her udders discharged endless streams of Nightmare fuel into the silver tray that surrounded her silver throne. The ceaseless dripping of the iridescent liquid made the goddess look like a solid rainbow.

Dustin didn't look, but he knew that a few steps away from him, a man was busy scooping up the *Nif* with a ladle and pouring it into large wooden casks that were stored near the exit of the room, for the use (and mind control) of the Real Dreams faithful.

His attention was focused up at the top of the pulsing, dripping brown bulk, at the goddess-worm's human face.

Once again, he felt that she looked Native American.

He stared at that giant face that was so beautiful and yet so evil, so perfect and yet so misplaced on its grotesque, segmented body.

Outside in the clubroom, he'd needed Nightmare Fuel to put him in tune with his goddess. In here, her presence was sufficient.

In here, oxygen was nonexistent. Dustin was breathing in Nightmare Fuel. It was in his lungs and in his blood. His goddess's evil essence was all he needed to survive.

Boku Veeza didn't seem to care how long he stared at her. She approved of him thinking horrible thoughts about her.

"I love human beings," Boku Veeza told Dustin. "You're so insignificant and yet so conceited. And you're so tasty also. Do you like human meat, Dustin?"

He shivered in horror and shook his head and followed her gaze downward to her feeding mound.

She seemed to withdraw from his mind a little now, and he felt more in control of himself, sufficiently so that he could look around.

Jimmy Fisher from the Ghost Research Outfit Worldwide lay on the feeding mound. Jimmy was still all in one piece, except for that hole in his chest. He'd been stripped naked, and lay on his belly, with his head turned sideways.

With a squishy, sucking sound like the churning of diarrhetic bowels, Boku Veeza slithered down her mound and engulfed Jimmy's legs and hips in her mouth. She bit down, and then lifted her head again, leaving the upper half of Jimmy's body behind on the feeding mound.

She chewed slowly on the dead man's flesh.

Has she summoned me here so she can eat me too? Dustin wondered. *Of course, if she feeds on me, I'll live forever as a part of her, a cell in her revolting eternal body. All glory to Boku Veeza.*

Boku Veeza swallowed and licked blood from her lips.

"Why have you brought me here?" Dustin asked her.

"I'm not sure whether to eat you or not," she replied him. "You ran away from me."

"You told me to leave."

Her head came down till her chin touched the floor. Side by side like this, her head was taller than Dustin.

Each of her eyes was larger than his head, her nose was larger than his entire torso, and her mouth was the size of his bathtub at home.

"Don't argue," the goddess told him. "Once I change my mind about something, I'm automatically right where earlier I was wrong."

"O.K.," Dustin agreed, as first her head and then her entire body slithered around him. She felt both warm and cold and he didn't know what to think.

Finally, when he was wrapped in the coils of her and their slightest tightening might have crushed him to pulp, she peered down at him through the gap she'd left in the circle of herself and laughed.

"For the moment, I won't eat you. Don't you dare run away from me again. Do you understand?"

"Yeah, sure. I won't."

At the moment, he was completely deluged in Nightmare Fuel. As far as he could see, Boku Veeza had turned all of her udders inward and was squirting her rainbow juice all over him, maybe to teach him a lesson about herself, he couldn't tell.

Nif was in his mouth, in his nose, in his eyes and in his ears. His hair and his clothes were drenched with it, and his shoes were full of it.

And, the way she'd enwrapped him, she'd pinned his arms tightly to his sides. She felt like she was both an oven and a freezer.

He was getting so high on *Nif* that his very existence seemed rainbow colored.

"No more running away," the goddess repeated, twisting herself around him. "I'm serious about this. Do so and you die from me."

"Okay, okay. Listen, if you don't stop squirting your milk all over me, I'm gonna die from you anyway. I'll drown right here in the middle of you and you'll have me for tomorrow's breakfast."

She laughed. "I like your sense of humor, Dustin."

With an agreement reached between them, Boku Veeza first squirmed about around Dustin a little more as though she were making herself comfortable in some inexplicably divine way, and then she floated straight up into the air until she was hovering in a donut shape over Dustin, and then she floated sideways till she was positioned over her throne.

As she settled down over her silver throne again, Dustin looked around a little.

CHAPTER 51

Dustin was dripping from head to toe with Nightmare Fuel and was standing in a puddle of it. And yes, it really did seem to be the sole component of the air around him.

Wow! They say the human body is seventy-five percent water. Well, at the moment, I think mine is about ninety-five percent Nif!

Then his eyes fell on the man who'd replaced Buddy as the goddess's 'brewer.' The man was ladling away, filling casks with her mind-altering effusion.

Unlike Buddy, who'd been a giant just a few inches shy of seven feet tall, this man was shorter than Dustin, maybe five foot seven, or five eight in height. He was also skinny.

I guess size doesn't matter in this job, Dustin thought in some amusement.

"Meet Michael, my new husband," Boku Veeza told Dustin.

"Husband?" Dustin looked at her and then at the man again. "Husband?"

"Michael, don't be impolite. Say hello to Dustin."

Michael looked over at Dustin. "Hey, dude, how's it goin'?"

"Same old, same old," Dustin replied, but Michael possibly didn't even hear his reply. He had already turned away from Dustin, back to his task, but not before Dustin had clearly noted the same mental vacuity in his eyes that had characterized the late Buddy also.

So, this guy is six cans short of a six-pack too? Now how fucking weird is that?

He looked up at Boku Veeza, and gestured at Michael, who was just about to start rolling the trolley laden with casks of *Nif* along its track to the storage area by the entrance to the goddess's chamber.

"He's your husband? You're *married* to *him*? Were you married to Buddy too?"

The goddess laughed very loudly outside of Dustin' head. The rumble of her mirth made his brain vibrate. "He's my husband because I say he is. And, *yes*, I was married to Buddy before him." She frowned pointedly now. "Is that a problem, Dustin?"

"It's confusing, that's all."

"Of course, it's confusing," Boku Veeza readily agreed. "You're a mere mortal and I am a goddess; your goddess, whom you've agreed to worship for all of eternity."

"You're not gonna let me forget that, ever, are you?"

She smiled evilly down at him, but said nothing.

"Okay, so he's your husband, and Buddy was too. I get that part. But, can I ask you a question? First of all tho', you've got to promise me that you won't get angry."

"Ask. I won't get angry."

"Are you into half-wits or something? Do low IQs turn you on?"

"WHAT!?"

"Hey, you just promised you wouldn't get angry. All I wanna know is . . . listen, Buddy seemed mentally deficient and now this kid too? So do guys like that turn you on, or what's the deal here?"

"Dustin, I've a question for you too. Why are you whispering?"

He shrugged and went on whispering. "Because I don't wanna hurt his feelings if he overhears what I'm saying. You're speaking inside my head, so he can't hear you, but he can hear me."

Boku Veeza nodded to this. "No, I'm not sexually attracted to idiots. It's just the effect that I have on men. On humans in general, really."

"Which is?"

For the first time, the huge woman-worm looked uncomfortable. Before replying Dustin, her giant brown body squirmed back and forth and seemed to produce an excessive amount of *Nif*.

Yes, Dustin confirmed that this really was the case, *Nif* cascaded down over her pulsating segments and overflowed the trough built into her throne from which her new husband had been filling cask after cask with the stuff.

What the hell is the matter with her? Dustin wondered. *She seems almost embarrassed.*

CHAPTER 52

"The problem is myself," Boku Veeza told Dustin after a short while. "My personal atmosphere, that intoxicating state of being that you're experiencing now, it has a deteriorative effect on the human brain."

"You're saying that being around you for too long kills brain cells?" Dustin asked.

The goddess nodded, but looked very displeased. "Exactly. I haven't yet found a solution. Buddy used to be a university professor, and Michael here—" she squirmed her immense bulk till she was looking at her new husband "—has a wonderful mind too. But I already seem to be killing it off." She looked even more annoyed. "It's bad not being able to carry on an intelligent conversation with your spouse."

"You need to find someone who's immune to you."

Hearing this, Boku Veeza frowned. "Dustin, you're either very smart to suggest this solution to me, or very dumb to attempt to insult me with it." The goddess worm squirmed, and her head slid down the spiral of her body till she was face-to-body with him again.

Once more he was struck by how immense her head was; considered front-to-back and side-to-side, it was at least nine times the size of his body.

Dustin was suddenly glad that even though Boku Veeza's massive lips moved when she spoke to him, she was actually projecting her voice into his mind.

I'm certain I'd go deaf if she actually spoke to me this close up.

"Believe me," he replied the goddess, "I wish I understood why I'm finding it impossible to keep my mouth shut, and instead keep saying smartass crap to you. Trust me, lady, I'm shit-scared that I'm merely one wrong comment away from becoming one of your most favored meals." He frowned and then added, half to himself, "But if you asked me to guess the cause of my current verbal diarrhea, it has to be a function of the 'personal atmosphere' that you mentioned."

He raised a finger in the air, and just managed to stop himself from poking her in the nose with it. "But, concerning your man trouble,

121

that's the only logical solution: If you are tired of bad bedroom conversation, marry a guy who isn't overwhelmed by you."

Boku Veeza smiled her evil smile at Dustin. Her lips were like SUV bumpers; her pale teeth looked like large ceramic tiles.

Her dark eyes were so large, they resembled the stained-glass windows in the Christian houses of worship that she so despised. The blood vessels in her retinas were larger than those in his arms, while those that occasionally twitched in her forehead and her cheeks were easily the size of his arms.

"You're one of the strangest humans I have ever encountered," she told him. "I don't know if I like or dislike you. This is one reason why you're still alive, at least until I decide one way or another."

He nodded. "I'm flattered. But hanging around here seems to be killing my brain cells already. Is it alright that I leave and rejoin the party?"

She extended her tongue and licked him, up and down. He stood there and took it, and right as the tip of her tongue was covering him in goddess saliva for the umpteenth time, it struck him that she was tasting him to see what sort of a meal he might make for her.

What will happen if she thinks I taste good? Better not fucking dwell on that.

He was so relieved when she pulled her tongue back into her mouth again

"Yes, I guess that you can leave here now," she said with an air of disappointment, like he'd not tasted that good after all.

"Thanks."

"But remember, Dustin, if you ever dare . . . how do you humans put it? Yes, if you ever dare sleep with me . . . No, I mean, fuck with me again, I will consume you body and soul and mind and spirit, and you'll become a part of me, suffering forever in my glory . . . I will cocoon you in my hell, where they suffer forever and where their worm dieth not."

"Hey, isn't that part of the Christian Bible? I think I remember the bit about the worm in hell not dying from Sunday school. Goddess, back then that shit scared me shitless."

"It doesn't matter. Nothing matters except that you do not anger me ever again. Now, return to the—"

And then her facial expression contorted up into a look that Dustin found impossible to place.

CHAPTER 53

Quick as a recoiling spring, Boku Veeza's head shot back up her body. And once she was properly arranged on her spiral throne again, she yelled down at her husband: "Michael, an egg is coming!"

(No telepathy this time. This was a full-blown goddess scream, one that made the chamber floor vibrate and that made Dustin quickly cover his ears with his hands.)

Michael, who'd spent the entirely of Dustin and the goddess's conversation hard at work filling up casks and moving them across the room, now instantly hung the ladle on the side of the trough, and looked expectant and somewhat excited.

What the hell is happening now? Dustin wondered. *Yeah, I really should get away from here while the getting's good, but . . . This looks to become interesting.*

Something odd was already happening. Boku Veeza seemed to have forgotten he existed. The worm goddess was squirming like crazy, with an expression of pain on her lovely face, while the lowest segments of her repulsive body kept contracting and relaxing. And then, the portion of her body closest to Michael bulged outward.

In a few seconds, a hole had opened up in her side and something brown and oblong squirted out of her into Michael's waiting hands.

The oblong 'egg' was attached at one end to Boku Veeza, and the thing squirmed like it was alive, although other than for a hole at the end opposite its umbilicus, it was featureless.

And then Michael unzipped his pants. His penis came out hard and he stuck it into the hole in the goddess's worm-like egg . . . And began thrusting back and forth in the egg.

Dustin sighed at the perplexing copulation and then looked up at the worm goddess's face.

Boku Veeza didn't appear to be in any agony anymore. In fact, she seemed to be enjoying herself immensely.

Oops, the egg is connected to her, and she feels what it feels . . .

"Yes!" Boku Veeza gasped at him, this time not bothering to project her thoughts at him. "Once or twice a day I make eggs like this and then Michael fertilizes them for me, and then returns them into my body, where they grow until they die." She moaned like a human woman and her entire body contracted to almost half of its regular thickness and then swelled out again. "I'm unfortunately sterile," she went on, "but fertilizing my eggs keeps my milk production flowing and that is desirable to me and my worshippers. Where would you all be without my rainbow nectar?"

Dustin glanced over at her human 'husband,' who was fucking the egg for all he was worth, his pale and hairy buttocks clenching and unclenching like mad as he slid his erection back and forth inside of the wormy thing, the pale umbilicus of which was contracting along with the goddess.

The job of ladling *Nif* had clearly been forgotten for the moment.

"Now leave us, Dustin!" The worm goddess thundered in his mind. "I can feel our sweetest time fast approaching, and if you dare be so disrespectful as to witness us like that, I will eat you afterwards for sure. This I promise you."

Oops, she means she's gonna come soon and she doesn't want an audience watching her lose control of herself then.

Dustin got the hell out of there. He'd seen more than he wanted to.

Shit, there are marriages and then there are marriages. And then there's marriages from hell, he thought in amusement as he stepped along the corridor, dripping *Nif* and goddess saliva each step of the way.

"Make love off, Dustin, you deity-cursed back passage!" the goddess grunted throatily in his mind and then began gasping in delight. "Oooh! Oooh! OOOHHH!"

Laughing, Dustin headed back up the corridor, towards the main clubroom.

Since he'd decided not to look at his cellphone for the duration of his stay here, he had no way of telling how long he'd been with Boku Veeza.

But from the sound of things back in the clubroom, the party was well under way.

CHAPTER 54

By the time Dustin arrived back in the clubroom, the 'Nugget Auction' was almost over.

"Ladies and gents, now was that fun, or what?" Malarkey the clown was asking the audience. "I for one ain't had this much fun since I . . ."

The clown was dressed in, of all things, a long black coat with long tails and a massive top hat over his clown costume. He looked utterly ridiculous.

People were cheering loudly. It took Dustin a while to understand what they were so excited about.

On Malarkey's right, an operating table was set up in the middle of the stage. A man lay on the table, and another man wearing a red demon-mask was busy sawing his right arm off at the shoulder.

Dustin couldn't make head or tail of what was going on.

This could be the punishment of yet another infidel, but the guy whose arm is being amputated is grinning instead of screaming.

Dustin frowned. The victim/patient had already lost all of his other limbs, and recently too. The severed limbs sat in a pile on the floor . . . beside two other sets of severed limbs, eight in all, the male and female owners of which lay, looking like shapeless naked blobs, on the stage, while medical personnel tended to them.

As might naturally be expected to result from all of those 'surgical procedures,' the top of the stage was liberally splattered with blood, through which Malarkey happily trampled in his giant blue floppy clown shoes.

"What's been going on in here?" Dustin asked Grace Mills as he resumed his seat beside her. Her younger sister seemed to have vanished for the moment.

Grace was laughing, and tears were streaming down her cheeks, making a mess of her blue and red face paint.

"You missed a whole damn lot of fun!" she squealed in delight at Dustin. "I've never seen anything so creepy before in my life." Then she wrinkled her nose. "Something smells awful in here. Can you smell it?"

"That's probably me," he admitted.

Grace paid proper attention to him and realized that he was drenched in fluid. "Okay, I can distinguish the *Nif* part of your new fragrance, but what's the rest of it?"

"Worm-goddess cologne."

Grace wrinkled her nose again. "Ugh. Did she . . . ?"

He sighed. "Forget it, like I'm trying to. Where's Faith?"

Grace waved her fingers airily. "Off sucking dick somewhere, I suppose."

Dustin wondered if she'd said this specifically to anger him. "It's the night for it," he replied calmly. "Club rules are she can bang whoever tonight. You and I can too."

On hearing this, Grace gave a loud, clearly mocking laugh. "Yep, tonight anyone can have faith, even total assholes and infidels."

Then she sighed like she was disappointed that she'd not stirred him up to jealousy.

"You know," she told him, "I was gonna suck you off and maybe fuck you before she came back, but with the way you smell now, I'm gonna pass. Trust me, you need to find yourself a bathtub or a shower fast."

Dustin noted that a few people at the next table were also wincing and making disgusted faces. Taking a shower seemed the right idea.

"I'll need some clothes too," he said, pulling at one soaked sleeve of his jacket to make his point. "These ones have had it."

"Oh, there's lots of unneeded clothes somewhere here. We keep all of the dead infidels' clothes . . . just in case."

"So, what is this Nugget Auction all about?" Dustin asked.

Up on the stage the giggling patient's arm had now been completely removed and the wound was being cauterized with a blowtorch, despite which he was laughing as if becoming a circus freak was the most wonderful thing in the world.

Grace Mills leaned forward over the table. "I'll tell you if you promise to go take a bath once I'm done, and that we'll hook up afterwards if Faith isn't back yet."

"Aren't you worried about hurting your sister?"

Grace indicated her jazzed-up face. "Why the hell should I be? She's the whole reason I can't go out in public without tons of makeup anymore. I *want* to hurt her, and keep hurting her." She frowned. "I just don't want to hurt her so badly that I kill her or disable her, because then we'll be even and I won't be able to hurt her any longer without feeling shitty about it."

"Your concern for her wellbeing is heartwarming."

She smiled coldly. "Well, now you know, skunk man. Deal or no deal?"

He nodded. "Deal. Now what is this all about? I can see Malarkey up there dressed like . . . he's got to be the first damn clown in history to also dress up like P.T Barnum."

CHAPTER 55

"It's simple," Grace explained. "Apparently, a Russian crime cartel that does nugget porn is looking for American porn stars. So—"

Dustin raised a finger to halt her. "Hold on a sec. What is 'nugget porn?'"

"Porn starring the disabled—you know, amputees with no arms or legs and shit. They're called 'nuggets.'"

Even submerged under the spell of *Nif*, Dustin felt dizzy from deranged and derogatory concept-overload. "Okay, I think I get it already."

Grace laughed. "You don't want to hear the rest?"

He shook his head. "Nugget *Auction?* The wannabe freak-porn actors auctioned off their soon-to-removed limbs to the highest bidder?"

She laughed even louder. "You should've been here! It was so crazy. I tried to buy that skinny guy's left arm, but I didn't bid enough! Ha ha ha!"

"Grace, what did you want a severed arm for?"

She looked at him oddly. He had the sense that she felt that rather than she having made a dumb comment, he was asking a foolish question.

"What does anyone do with a severed arm? Masturbate with it, of course. They're all first gonna be chemically treated so that they don't rot. And, of course, they feel much more realistic than plastic sex toys."

"Of course," Dustin agreed and quickly finished up his glass of *Nif*. While not exactly disgusted (this was after all a witch's den of sexual perverts), he did feel an intense need to be alone for a while.

"Time to go take that shower," he told Grace, rising to his feet.

"Come back quickly," she told him. "Remember our deal."

"Yeah, yeah. And where do I find those spare clothes?"

"Go through the door over there, the one beside Chang. He's the Asian guy Tanana is sucking off, and then, you turn left and . . ."

CHAPTER 56

Dustin headed off to find a bathroom and those spare clothes. With the Nugget Auction over, people had dispersed towards the beds near the walls to have sex.

Some of the sex was quite gross. Take for instance, the slim thirtyish woman, a pretty lady with long black hair, extremely long red fingernails and toenails, and giant breasts. (Her breasts were even larger than the high priestess' own humongous pair, meaning she had to be a porno actress, and that she was very likely 'Penny,' whom Queen Bee had been joking with earlier from the stage.)

Each of this woman's labia majora was pierced by two gleaming and very large chromium rings.

This stalwart lady was being penetrated by someone's foot while she massaged her clitoris with a pink wand vibrator.

To her seductive credit, she had attracted quite a crowd of masturbating spectators.

Dustin was still dripping liquid and leaving little puddles everywhere he stepped, and folks kept wrinkling their noses as he walked past. One woman actually threw up when she smelled him.

While sighing because of this, Dustin walked by Tanana Reeves, who was now riding the Chinese guy.

The guy was saying, "Wow, Banana, your ass is so hot."

"It's *Tanana*, Chang, not *Banana*. Call me 'Banana' one more time and I'll grow myself a banana and fuck your ass with it."

The guy laughed and thrust himself deep in her ass. "Sorry, honey, I got you now. Oh, shit—your ass is hot as hell."

"Oh thanks, baby, I'm so glad you like it."

"No, I mean it literally. I don't know what you've been eating of late, but your asshole feels hot inside. My dick feels like it's in an oven."

"Shut up and bang, Chang."

Dustin began laughing.

While grinding her ass on her Asian lover, Tanana showed Dustin a stiff middle finger.

"Is that the toilet I smell walking past me?" she asked between sexual gasps. "Oh no, it ain't the shitter—" she aimed a fingernail at him "—it's you, Dustin. Motherfucker, go take a shower. You smell like goddess spit!"

She burst out laughing too.

Shaking his head, Dustin pushed open the door that Grace had pointed out to him and stepped out of the clubroom.

And just like that, with no fanfare of any kind, no 'crash, boom, bang!' or flashing lights, or even any sense of accompanying strangeness, he discovered that he'd stepped out of his neighbor's front door again.

Yes, he'd just exited the Mills' house and was staring at his own house across the road.

Craziest of all, it wasn't nighttime anymore.

The sun was up in the sky. The time now seemed to be mid-morning of the next day.

CHAPTER 57

I just hate these time-shifts. They're using up precious hours of my life.

Dustin sighed on realizing what had just happened. The fact that he was still soaked through with *Nif* and goddess saliva, however, was sufficient proof that he'd not just hallucinated last night.

That he'd simply imagined everything would have been very easy to believe, because Faith's Honda Civic, which she'd certainly driven over to her sister's house yesterday, was now parked in her garage again. Dustin stared at the shiny red car.

Faith's car being here means that she's back home now and sleeping off last night's debauch.

He'd already shut Faith's front door behind him. He considered reopening it, entering the house, and checking on her.

Then he glanced down at a small brown carton on Faith Mills' front porch. He'd noticed it earlier, but not what was written on it.

The brown box was labelled: 'Bury me, Dustin.'

Not knowing what to expect, Dustin crouched down and opened the box.

Inside it lay a dead kitten. From its brown color and tormented death grimace, Dustin realized that this was the same kitten that yesterday had been used to open up the portal into the Real Dreams club.

He sighed and felt intense pity for the cat, wondering why it had to get caught up in human bullshit like that.

"Alright, li'l fella, I'll bury ya," he told the stiff little feline body. "Better I do so than Boku Veeza having you for breakfast or lunch, not like she'd even notice she'd eaten ya."

There was a piece of paper in the cardboard box also. Dustin pulled it out.

The paper was a note that read:

'No sex for you tonight, Dustin. No night either. Make love off. Your loving Goddess.'

Dustin frowned at Boku Veeza's pettiness.

"Women," he said finally.

Carrying the box with the kitten, he crossed the road to his own house and let himself in.

CHAPTER 58

After confirming that today was the day it was supposed to be, that is, the day he thought it was and not two months in the future, Dustin relaxed a bit.

Problem was, today was Monday.

I'm due at work, but it's almost midday now. Once I'm cleaned up, I'd better call in and let Uncle Rich know I won't be in till much later.

Dustin then stripped off his soaked and smelly clothes, took a long hot shower, and did his best to clean all the mess off of himself.

When he felt clean again, he made the call to his uncle, explaining that he couldn't make it to the office until afternoon.

Then he went outside to his pickup truck to fetch the spade he kept in it.

Then he went round back to bury the dead kitten.

I really should bury this animal near the other cat over at Faith's house, he thought while digging up a patch of sod near the roots of a tree halfway down his backyard. *Then both little kittys will have company in cat heaven.*

The soil was nice and soft and the grass a bright summery green.

After a while he looked up. This Monday morning, the sky was nice and blue, and the weather nice and warm. He noted a few possible thunderheads on the horizon, so maybe it might rain later; he'd not listened to the weathermen today.

Humming a pop tune, Dustin resumed making the cat's grave.

Then, Dustin frowned as a memory came to mind, triggering thoughts of something he'd not previously really considered:

On the night that I rescued Bianca, she'd been strung up with a cat, but it didn't seem like any attempt had been made to 'open her up' as a door. I wonder what that was all about. Bianca said she'd explain it all to me, but because her throat still hurt so much, I didn't ask her the next day, and she fled and got recaptured before she had the chance to volunteer the info herself.

He sighed. Maybe in that case killing the cat had been merely symbolic. Or maybe it was just further evidence of the two demons' sadism and perversion.

Maybe it's even a calling card of sorts for them; like, 'Tanana and Malarkey were here—here's a dead cat as proof.'

When Dustin judged the grave to be deep enough, he placed the kitten's box solemnly into the hole.

He considered this cat's burial serious business. It was why, since his return from the Real Dreams clubhouse, he'd avoided drinking any *Nif* today.

"Okay, little guy, have fun in cat heaven. And if there's any truth in the rumors about reincarnation, pray you come back as a human being yourself next time, so you ain't gonna be on the receiving end of us humans' shit."

He crossed himself and then filled in the hole. Then he made a little cross out of a couple of twigs and two rubber bands and stuck it on the little burial mound.

He straightened up and wiped sweat from his brow.

Okay, that's taken care of. Now what else have I got planned for today? I'd better go see Faith. She's got to be wondering what happened to me last night.

Then he froze, staring at the back door of his house and frowning intently.

Hey, hey, hey! Hold on a sec! Am I figuring this out right? What if, rather than shove me forward through time, what Boku Veeza did instead was to freeze me—freeze my body and my mind—so that time went on without me being conscious of its passing. I could have been standing frozen by that clubroom doorway for eight or nine hours—maybe invisible even—with everyone coming and going past me, without me noticing, until she decided to unfreeze me, and then it would be just like no time had passed in the interim. She's a goddess, she can play dirty like that if she wants to. I don't know why she thinks I'm so impor—

Dustin realized that for the past minute or so, he'd been hearing a rustling noise coming from the nearby trees.

His first thought was that some woodland creatures had watched him bury the kitten and were waiting for him to depart so they could dig it up for their breakfast.

He stared into the woods, trying to locate the animals so he could drive them off.

But then Woody Taylor hurried out of the woods towards him. In one hand Woody held his gun; in the other he gripped his laptop.

"Where've you been, man?" Woody asked Dustin in a scared voice. "This is the third time I've been here looking for you."

Woody looked like he'd not slept all night. He stank of sweat and dirt and had a harried look in his eyes like he'd been evading capture by law enforcement for the past twenty hours.

"Come on, let's get inside the house where it's safe," Dustin told Woody.

Together they hurried back inside.

CHAPTER 59

"I knew it!" Woody said, pacing Dustin's living room while also slamming his clenched right fist into the palm of his left hand. "I knew it! I just knew it!"

Woody was so agitated that Dustin found it easy to hide the worm-shaped decanter of *Nif* from him. Woody had no idea what it was anyway.

"Dude, let's have some breakfast," he told Woody afterwards. "And some coffee. I didn't get any sleep last night. I'll need caffeine if I'm gonna hear you out."

"No, not coffee," Woody quickly countered. "Beer, if you've got it, or whiskey. I'm all hyped up now and I need to calm down. No breakfast for me yet either."

Dustin nodded. "Sure, there's beer in the fridge. Help yourself."

They walked into the kitchen together. While Woody got himself a couple of beers from the fridge, Dustin pondered this new development.

The Real Dreams club are looking for this guy, and he's here with me. I really don't know what to do. Sure, Woody's an infidel, but he's also a friend of mine and I won't hand him over to be killed by Tanana and Malarkey. Damn my sentimentality, but I'm not gonna do that to the guy!

"Dammit, Dustin, I don't know what to do," Woody said, leaning against the kitchen counter with an opened beer in hand while Dustin scrambled himself some eggs. "You saw what happened, man!" Woody was trembling with emotion and looked like he might've spent part of the night crying. "Man, you saw how those two freaks killed Jimmy. And now they've got Jen too." He began thumping his fist on the countertop. "Damn, Damn, Damn!"

Dustin concentrated on not burning his breakfast.

"Woody, what the hell was that clown that killed Jimmy?" he asked while pouring out his coffee. "I hate saying this, but watching Jimmy die like that was like watching a horror flick with top-notch CGI."

Woody stopped thumping the countertop, took a long swallow of beer, and replied: "Same shit as was in the photos, Dustin. You saw those, right?"

"Yeah, but how did the clown's hand . . . ?"

Woody stared woodenly at him. "Fuck me if I know, right? Those two—the damn clown and the hot black chick with him—they're both demons. Demons do shit like that, bro."

Dustin picked up his tray of food and nodded to Woody that they return to his living room. "Demons? C'mon, man, you know I don't believe in that stuff."

Woody followed behind him, saying, "Believe it or not, your own eyes watched Jimmy get killed by those two." He laughed. "Dustin, you must've also seen how I shot the damn clown twice and the bullets just went through his head like he was made of rubber; no effect whatsoever. And then . . . then they took Jen to only God knows where the hell they took her to. And they did so without leaving the apartment by either of its doors. Just like they somehow arrived out of thin air into an apartment which was completely empty when we got there."

In the living room they sat in opposite chairs, Dustin with his breakfast tray on his lap, Woody holding his beer bottles.

"Okay, I admit that I did see you shoot the clow—" he began saying before Woody cut him off.

"Permit me to interrupt you," Woody said. "What you're forgetting is that those two also sent us—by 'us' I mean GROW, of course—they emailed us those pics of my bro Seth and Amy Weinstein being killed. I think what happened yesterday morning at my place confirms that both Seth and Amy are dead. Shit, shit, shit!"

Woody finished that bottle of beer, dropped it on the rug, and opened the second one. Tears began spilling from his eyes. "My bro's dead, man, because of those two!"

Woody drank his beer and wept, while Dustin drank his coffee and ate his breakfast. Dustin also missed Seth Taylor, and now that he wasn't tripping on *Nif*, it upset him that he couldn't tell Woody what he knew about Seth's killers. He felt like crying too, and also didn't like pretending he knew nothing about what was going on.

Woody's tears dried. He finished that second beer, and then held the empty bottle out to Dustin. "Can I have some more? It's making me feel better."

Dustin nodded. "As many as you like. There's four six-packs in the fridge. Just don't make yourself sick."

"Thanks, and I won't. I still got stuff to discuss with you." Woody headed off to the kitchen and Dustin finished eating.

"So, what do you plan on doing now?" Dustin asked Woody when he was back with two more beers. "I'm figuring you've not informed the cops about Jimmy's death."

Woody nodded. "You know I can't do that. For one thing, there's no body. And second, who the fuck am I gonna say killed him!? Cops are gonna think I did it!"

"Calm down, man. Hey, didn't the gunshot noise bring the cops to Jimmy's place?"

Woody shook his head. "I dunno how Malarkey and Tanana did it, but I think they blanked out the sound from Jen and Jimmy's apartment. That way no one could possibly hear us screaming when they killed us, right?" He frowned. "That seemed to be their plan anyway."

"Man, we really need to figure this stuff out," Dustin told him.

"You are so freakin' right." Woody settled down and drank some more beer.

Dustin leaned back on the couch. "Dude, you're in serious shit here," he told Woody. "And . . . I honestly don't know what the hell we can do. 'Cos I'm sure the killers must be searching high and low for you too."

"Yeah, yeah, but they won't find me."

"Okay, now let's retrack a little bit. Tell me what else you guys discovered about them, maybe we can find a clue as to where Jen is now."

Woody nodded and then looked coldly at his handgun, which lay on the coffee table. "Yeah, if we can figure that out, maybe we've still got a shot at rescuing Jen."

CHAPTER 60

Woody told Dustin a lot of stuff he already knew and a lot of things that he didn't know:

"Shit, dude, those Real Dreams freaks are psychos. So, they have this messed-up ritual using cats as sacrifices. A human—usually a woman—is called the 'door' and the cat is called the 'key.' And the cat 'key' is used to unlock the human 'door,' to wherever it is they go to. Of course, both 'door' and 'key' die in the process.

Dustin scowled; he still found it hard to come to terms with the cat-killing. "Sounds completely effed-up. I thought cats were supposed to be friends of witches."

Woody slurred a loud laugh. "If cats have guardian spirits, this stuff is certain to have pissed them off big time—I think they even have cat fry-ups for their worm goddess."

Despite promising Dustin that he'd stay sober, Woody Taylor had gotten progressively more drunk. The evidence bottles stood on the coffee table. A six-pack-and-a-half was Dustin's latest estimation of Woody's alcohol intake. This helped in the sense that the guy hadn't remained miserable, but it sucked in conversational terms, as it meant their discussion rambled from point to point that revolved entirely around whatever details Woody's alcohol-addled mind dredged up next.

To calm himself in the interim, Dustin had sneaked into the kitchen and drank a little *Nif*.

The *Nif* helped him see his supposed friend for what he really was: a pathetic human creature who dared go up against a mighty worm goddess.

"There's more and worse," Woody went on after opening up yet another beer. "You might remember a few years ago, when a preacher's entire family went missing one night, over near Halifax?" He waited till Dustin nodded before continuing. "Well, that was them too. That was those fucking Real Dreams assholes. Hold on a sec, while I find you some pix."

Woody's laptop was open beside him and he fiddled with it for a while as if the alcohol was making the images dance on the screen before his eyes. But finally, he got up, staggered across the living room, and shoved the laptop in Dustin's face.

"The victims," he said, looking exceptionally sad. "Little kids too, abducted by a sex club. How sick is that?"

Dustin stared at the faces of the missing in an online newspaper. The reverend Paul Smith, his old sister-in-law Madison Smith, and their children. Three of the kids were under the age of ten, and Madison's son, whom according to Queen Bee, had escaped with her that night, was in his mid-twenties.

Looking at Frederick Smith's face, Dustin frowned as recognition dawned:

Bianca's boyfriend Freddy Reid, whom I watched get pulled apart last night is this same young man who survived the family abduction three years ago! Now his motivation makes sense to me. The guy risked the dangers to expose the club because he wanted justice . . . or revenge, for what they did to his family!

"This is really messed up," Dustin told Woody, who nodded drunkenly and then retrieved the laptop from him. Woody tramped back across to his armchair, dropped the old beer bottle, twisted open a new one, and then began laughing. Woody laughed and laughed and laughed.

Just when Dustin had concluded that the guy was having a nervous breakdown, Woody calmed down again.

"I dunno whatever possessed me to go into paranormal investigations," he slurred at Dustin. "Maybe I was jealous of the fame my older bro Seth was getting. And the chicks too. Lots of geeky chicks dug Seth—say, you ever see Kelly Ann Duffy's show Paranormal Wives? Total jerk-off material, if you ask me. Any young boys watching that show are gonna grow up with an unfixable boob fixation."

"We're still no closer to locating Jen," Dustin pointed out. He felt ready to slip back into the kitchen for another drink of *Nif*.

"Locations?" Woody burped. "Man, I'll tell you somethin' about locations." He leaned forward in his chair and burped. "Dustin, take it from me that your Uncle Richmond is a sleazeball. You know the greedy motherfucker paid GROW to say your neighbor's house ain't haunted?"

Dustin feigned surprise. "Are you saying *it is* haunted?"

Woody waved his beer at Dustin. "Fuckin' A it is. Most haunted place I've ever been inside, in fact. Hey, how'd we even get to talkin' bout this shit in the first place? Yeah, yeah—I was tellin' you I must've been crazy to start hunting spooks and Bigfoot with Seth and Amy and Jimmy and Jen."

Woody got up and stumbled over to the living room window and then added: "And that house over there is one prime reason why I think so. You know, Dustin, a lot of weird shit has gone on in that house. Stuff that I'm scared to even theorize about."

Woody was speaking over his shoulder, his eyes staring outside of the house. Dustin could see that he was shaking, and knew it wasn't just because he was discombobulated by beer.

"Damn, bro," Woody went on. "You need to've been in there and felt it like we did when Seth and Amy had all of their gizmos set up. We got this sense of extremely vexed spirits. I mean, really upset ones. Amy told us one of the ghosts was a pregnant woman who was looking for her unborn child."

Now Woody did turn around, and there was a chilling look on his face.

"Do you understand me, man? How can a pregnant woman be looking for her *unborn* child? As far as you and I know, they generally go around together. What the hell could've happened to that baby?"

He walked back round to his chair, sat on it and then got back up to his feet again.

"I gotta go piss, man, and then I'm gonna sleep in your guestroom. Maybe when I wake up, the world will be a nice place to live in. Cuz right at the moment, it's a damn shitty place to be."

Dustin watched Woody stagger off in approximately the right direction. Then, just before he stepped into the hallway, Woody turned around and cracked a cold smile.

"You know what I feel like doing now?" Woody said. "I feel like saying 'fuck it' to the world and hiring myself some strippers or hookers for a party. Call it a funeral party for my deceased bro and friends, if you like. Call it my own funeral bash if you will."

Then he walked off down the hallway.

Dustin immediately visited the kitchen for a fresh drink of *Nif.* This time he filled the glass to the brim and drank deeply.

A lot of what Woody had said had really troubled him, and if there was one thing Nightmare Fuel was good for, it was soothing troubled minds.

Dustin drank and tried to figure out what to do about Woody Taylor.

Nif-influenced or not, he was resolute in his decision not to turn his friend over to Boku Veeza's demon assassins.

But how to keep him safe from them; well, that's the problem.

CHAPTER 61

With Woody out of the way for the foreseeable time being, Dustin felt no worries about seating himself opposite the TV with his tall glass of *Nif*.

He drank and his worries about Woody all seeped away through the wall. This was a good day.

I'll just drink a little more Nif and then go see if Faith's woken up yet. Then, maybe around 1 p.m., I'll head out to work.

And then, while lounging comfortably on his living room couch, Dustin watched Bianca Sanchez materialize before his eyes.

Bianca was dangling from his living room fan with the cat stuck to her neck like a hairy conjoined fetus.

The crazy thing was, Dustin knew he wasn't dreaming. Bianca really was in here with him, though of course, she couldn't be.

And how can the cat be here too, when I just buried it out back? But hey, Nif does crazy stuff like that to you.

He stared down at the liquid rainbow in his hand with renewed respect for its paranormal abilities.

"Ha ha, you're already in love with Faith." Bianca wheezed at him, managing to spit the words through the noose's constriction.

"Hey, don't jump to conclusions like that," Dustin said. "I don't know that I'm in love with her. It's just that . . ." He frowned. "Well, it did happen once upon a time. I once fell in love with a woman on first meeting—met her that night and was instantly head-over-heels."

"You're talking about Jordan Hayes, aren't you?"

He sighed and nodded. "Yeah, that was a crazy experience. And regrettably, one with a very sad ending too."

Bianca wagged a finger at him. "But, are you sure of what you're feeling for Faith Mills? I mean, I lived with you for two days and you didn't once hit on me."

He looked at her in surprise.

"Surprised?" she asked him. "Don't lie that you didn't consider screwing me when I was hiding here. I offered you a blowjob once, remember?"

"But that was under difference circumstances," Dustin protested. "At the time when you offered me that blowjob, we were both under the influence of *Nif*, and you know how Nightmare Fuel waters down one's sexual inhibitions. So, I never imagined you had any real feelings for me."

"Okay, that's fair enough," she replied, with her dangling body swaying slightly beneath the fan. "But even assuming *I* didn't, why didn't *you* hit on me while I was at your place?"

"Bianca, you were my guest. You also had a boyfriend at the time. You were also a fugitive. If I'd suggested we sleep together, you might have said 'yes' simply so I didn't throw you to the wolves. In such a situation, it would be unfair of me to take advantage of you like that." He gestured window-ward. "Faith, on the other hand, isn't running away from anyone or anything that I know of. If she likes me in return, it has to be because she really likes me, not because—"

"Oh, just admit it. You've fallen for her."

"But I don't think I have. You're still jumping to conclusions."

"No, I'm not," the hung woman said with some irritation, though the anger Dustin perceived may just have been the result of forcing the words through the tightness of the noose. "I can see it in your eyes and hear it in your voice. You're in love with Faith Mills. I'm worried for you though. What if she doesn't love you in return? What're you gonna do then?"

He waved his glass at her. "Please, stop jumping the gun. I don't feel like I love her. I do feel very attracted to her, but that's only natural because she's so damn beautiful. Do I desire to continue sleeping with her? Yes, for the same reason. I suspect every man she meets wants her pussy."

"Just listen to yourself. You sound incurably smitten."

"And those lovely blue eyes she's got. Looking into Faith's eyes feels like standing on the deck of a yacht, with the sea stretching endlessly on all sides of me. For me, being with Faith Mills is almost a crisis of faith."

Bianca rolled her own eyes. "Oh, just forget it. But, know this: she's gonna get you into big trouble. You were very good to me, Dustin. So don't say I didn't warn ya."

And then Bianca faded to nothing and Dustin was left with his glass of *Nif*.

What the hell was that all about? he asked himself and took another sip of sweet rainbow logic.

CHAPTER 62

Maybe five or six minutes after Bianca had vanished, Dustin's front doorbell rang.

Oh great, Faith's come to visit me!

Feeling delight, he got up to let her in.

But it wasn't Faith on his doorstep. It was Tanana Reeves.

Dustin stared at the black demoness in surprise, and then automatically stepped aside to let her in.

This time she wasn't dressed like a congresswoman, but instead like a hooker, in a skintight red minidress that revealed half of her boobs and only covered half of her massive ass, and red six-inch high heels. As a fashion accessory, she carried an alligator skin purse.

Dustin doubted that she was wearing panties. She had a Basic Instinct vibe to her; the 'shadow' between her thick thighs seemed to be her pubic hair.

"What brings you here?" he asked Tanana while accompanying her into his living room.

"Oh, I'm Woody's blowjob," she replied airily, waving aside his indication that she have a seat. "Orders of Queen Bee, of course."

Dustin frowned. "Of course. He's in the guestroom."

Tanana pointed towards the hallway. "That way?"

"Yep, thatta way." Dustin saw no point in pleading Woody's case. Tanana's presence in his home meant the Real Dreams organization had been watching him closely.

"But, Tanana," he said. "Don't you think the high priestess should've sent someone Woody doesn't know? The moment Woody sees you he's gonna recognize you from yesterday and then he'll try to get away."

Tanana smiled. "Oh, he ain't gonna recognize me. Bet your bottom dollar on that."

While speaking, her body was changing. From a tall black diva with long yellow braids hanging down her back, Tanana Reeves was suddenly a petite white lady, a freckle-faced blonde with large breasts, a wasp waist, and lots of heavy metal tattoos. The boob-low/ass-high dress, high heels, and gator-skin purse remained the same.

"What do you think?" she asked, pulling a compact and tube of pink lipstick from her purse and making up her lips.

"You look like someone's high school sweetheart run wild into a hot mess." Dustin was impressed. Even her voice was flawless white honey.

She grinned and put the compact and makeup away. "Perfect then. He's gonna want me for lunch."

"One more thing," Dustin said.

"Yeah, what?"

"Your ass is too big for a white girl. That's a red flag if I ever saw one. You need to be less Nicki Minaj, more Miley Cyrus."

"Oh." Frowning, Tanana looked back at the sole physical asset she'd not adjusted. "I guess you're right."

A few seconds later, her buttocks were smaller and tighter.

"Yeah, that's fine," Dustin acknowledged. "Remember, don't talk ghetto. That's a giveaway too."

She scowled at him. "Man, quit with the lecturing already. Quit sounding like my mama."

Dustin laughed. "Honey, demonesses don't have mamas. You were born from a fiery pit, not a pussy."

"Fuck you, wigga."

Tanana walked (or stalked) off.

Dustin relaxed. A few seconds later he heard her knocking on the door to the guest bedroom. Then, after a short pause, he heard the bedroom door open.

"Hey, who're you?" Woody asked in a drunken voice.

"Hi honey, I'm Cindy, the escort Dustin hired to come cure your blues."

"Really?" Dustin could hear the interest breaking through Woody's alcoholic haze. He nodded; Woody had likely just gotten an eyeful of Cindy's breasts. Big tits had a way of waking up a guy's dick.

"Well, I agree I could really use some sexual healing right now," Woody said.

"Well then, invite me in, baby. What're are you waiting for? We don't want Dustin's hard-earned money to go to waste now, do we, hon?"

147

The door creaked as it opened wider. And Woody must've been in a real hurry to get started, because Dustin didn't hear the bedroom door close again.

Sounds of unrestrained carnality began ensuing from the guest bedroom.

I guess the dude's gotta enjoy his last fuck, Dustin thought soberly and watched TV.

He drank his *Nif* like a good worshipper of Boku Veeza and tried not to visualize what was going to happen to Woody Taylor. Still, it was hard knowing that a friend of yours was only minutes short of dying and that there was nothing you could do to prevent it.

Dustin had somehow gotten the TV tuned to Paranormal Wives again. He watched the busty wives chase down a poltergeist and got quite into it, almost forgetting the sexual activity going on a few yards away.

But then he heard a short yelp, and Tanana's voice—her 'black' voice not her 'white' voice—saying, "Hey, you promised to close your eyes!"

And then there was the sound of a loud struggle in the bedroom.

Knowing that the nonsexual climax of Woody's existence was now at hand, Dustin got out of his chair and walked towards the bedroom to see what was going on.

Dustin didn't hurry. He walked leisurely, sipping his *Nif* as he went.

What is happening to Woody now, is his fate as decreed by Boku Veeza. It is perfect.

CHAPTER 63

Dustin reached the bedroom and leaned against the door jamb, watching Woody's passing unfold.

Woody was on top of Tanana. But as Dustin had expected, this wasn't the regular 'human Tanana,' but the demoness' 'bug version.'

It looked like Woody was having sex with a giant black insect, something like a giant charcoal cockroach with female breasts and at least sixteen legs. The legs were stupendously long and thin and were wrapped all around Woody, almost like a perforated cocoon, and their claws were digging deep into his skin, drawing blood. Several of Tanana's claws had already sliced Woody's skin open and were tearing his muscles off of his bones.

Disgustingly, while this was going on, the black insect demon was still thrusting her hips up at her victim as if they were still having intercourse.

In a case like this, one would naturally expect the victim to be screaming in pain and calling for help. This wasn't the case here because Tanana's head was once more inflated like a featureless black beachball, and Woody's lips were stuck *inside* her head.

Dustin saw this clearly. For a few seconds Tanana's head became almost transparent and he could see Woody's lips and the tip of his tongue *inside* the massive black sphere, while the rest of his face was outside of it.

Poor guy must've been kissing her when she glued herself to his face like that!

Woody's eyes showed his terror and pain. He was trying to fight Tanana, trying to escape from her, but with his lips trapped like that, he wasn't going anywhere except if he could rip or slice them off his head.

And that was how Tanana's many legs slowly stripped him of skin and flesh and tore him to pieces. Dustin watched the Tanana creature pull Woody apart like she was cutting up a steak. He came apart with the ease of cotton candy, in sheets of skin, strips of flesh, splashes of blood, and slivers and splinters of bone.

While doing this, Tanana was emitting a chirping noise like a cricket, a sound that Dustin felt certain would have unnerved him except for the *Nif* he was drinking.

But for the fact that Tanana's multiple limbs were visible inside Woody Taylor as the engines of his destruction, one might have believed that Woody was exploding.

It *was* that crazy. Parts of Woody flew through the air and hit the walls and ceiling, the drapes and windows, and the dresser, the closet, the wall clock, and the calendar hung up beside it. Just about everything in that guest bedroom was soon covered in bloody fragments of Woody Taylor.

Dustin had to cover his drink with a hand to prevent Woody's blood ending up inside it also.

Dustin stared at the blood everywhere. Then he stared down at the Tanana monster. She lay alone in the bed and Woody lay scattered everywhere else in the bedroom.

The monster's black globular head was as featureless as a bowling ball. Woody's head lay in five or six parts in different corners of the room.

The monster was moaning in pleasure. Dustin looked at the lower part of the creature's body.

Fuck!

Yes, he'd seen right. Woody's cock was still stuck in Tanana's body, a bloody chunk of flesh around which strange vaginal muscles continued clenching as if the monster was still bent on having her orgasm even with her lover demised.

"Hey, Tanana!" Dustin said.

The demoness insect twitched in irritation. "Go away, Dustin. I'm about to come."

"I'm going. Just clean up the mess before you go, alright? I don't know why you couldn't just behead him."

The demoness kept clenching her crotch muscles around Woody's severed penis, but managed to vocalize a reply:

"I did it like this cuz Queenie wants an example made of the infidel. I'm recording everything. Now fucking leave me alone."

The horrible creature began moaning in ecstasy again and Dustin left the room, not bothering to search for the recording camera, though he did wonder how it could possibly have escaped being splattered with all of that bloody mess that had once been Woody Taylor.

CHAPTER 64

With his peace of mind no longer what it might have been, Dustin left his house to go see Faith.

However, once outside, he saw that Faith was reversing her car down her driveway.

He walked quickly to the road. She backed the car into the street, straightened it out, and parked.

She was not alone in the car. Her sister Grace sat in the front passenger seat. This afternoon, Grace wasn't sporting last night's zig-zag face paint, but was instead wearing a face mask, like the pandemic was still happening. Her face mask was flesh-toned in color, with a giant replacement female mouth and chin painted on it.

Her brunette hair still obscured her eyes though.

"Hi, honey," Faith said when Dustin leaned on her window. They kissed and then Dustin greeted Grace, who didn't reply.

"She's pissed at you for standing her up yesterday," Grace explained. "She says you promised to come back and then . . . what happened anyway? Queen Bee called me over and by the time I got back to our table, you'd left."

Dustin quickly filled her in on what had happened when he stepped through the clubroom door, how he'd suddenly exited her own front door at around 10:30 a.m. this morning.

Both sisters now stared at him. "Wow, the goddess did that?" Faith asked.

"You must've *really* pissed her off," Grace now said.

Faith turned to her sister. "See? I told you he didn't stand you up on purpose. He wasn't avoiding sleeping with you." She frowned at Dustin. "Were you, baby?"

He shook his head. "Not at all. But where are you two going?"

Faith gestured with her head at her sister. "I'm running 'grouchy' here home; she spent the night here, and all she did was bitch about how nasty you were to her." She grinned. "Hey, I'll be back in a short while. You wanna come over and have fun later?"

Dustin shook his head. "Not later. Lemme have your keys, please. I'll wait in your place."

Both sisters stared at him again. Two sets of similarly inquiring similar blue eyes.

"Tanana has just made a huge mess in my guest bedroom," Dustin explained. "The huge mess used to be a good friend of mine. I need to be somewhere else until Tanana leaves."

Faith fished in her purse for her keys. "Here you go. So, I'll see you in a bit."

They kissed again.

"Bye, Grace," Dustin told the masked woman.

"I expect you to make amends to me at the next Real Dreams meeting," she replied him coldly.

He stood scratching his head as he watched their car drive off.

Damn, where those two are concerned, a massive storm is brewing, and if I'm not careful, I'm gonna be caught right in the middle of it.

CHAPTER 65

Once Dustin stepped inside Faith's house, he felt strange again.

Okay, so he'd long since gotten accustomed to feeling odd in this building, but today, maybe because of what he'd just witnessed transpire between Tanana and Woody, he felt especially odd.

This recurrent feeling in here was clearly something *Nif* could do little about.

Maybe it's the house, he told himself. In the course of his work as a realtor, Dustin had come across a few 'weird as I heard' places that more than lived up to their creepy reputation.

Most times, however, even such houses merely had strange acoustic properties that made them appear haunted to persons of a credulous disposition. Usually, on careful investigation, Dustin had discovered that the problem was simply a matter of wall angles. Just a few degrees off and sounds produced in the basement could sound like they were coming from the roof. And if someone opened a living room window, you'd think ghosts were descending the stairs.

Not in this case however.

Alright, I've been told twice now—both times by people who are likely now ghosts themselves—that this building is haunted. It seems quite dumb that I'm coming in here all alone, but Faith and her sister slept here last night, so the haunting can't be all that bad, right? Oh, I mustn't forget that one of the house's previous occupants was himself a ghost!

In this spooked frame of mind, Dustin poured himself a glass of *Nif* in Faith's kitchen and then sat in her living room to await her return. After a while, however, he began feeling uncomfortable.

Why the hell do I feel now like there's eyes watching me?

He soon decided that the creepy feeling stemmed from the fact that he was sitting with his back to the painting on the wall, the painting that depicted the worm goddess's Human Grove.

Of course, the background of that painting showed a multitude of watching eyes.

Absurd as the idea was, Dustin felt the eyes in the painting were watching him. He tried to ignore the ridiculous worry that this idea created in his mind, but it persisted, so he changed seats so that he was looking towards the painting instead of away from it.

Oddly enough, this didn't help. Now that he could see the painting of the tree-headed human sufferers and their three orange reptilian guardians, he felt even more bothered.

Why do I feel like that painting is alive?

He almost left the living room then to go sit outside on the front stoop.

But instead, as if compelled by a force outside of himself and beyond his control, Dustin got to his feet and walked over to the wall to stand beside the painting.

He stood there staring at it for he didn't know how long. He'd entered some kind of trance, over which once again he had no control at all.

"The guardians are Boku Veeza's most cherished worshippers," a voice whispered in his head.

"I know that," he replied aloud. "She finds them delicious."

And then, he couldn't explain what happened next. It felt as if he'd been sucked into the picture and was staring out into the past through those multitude of eyes.

CHAPTER 66

Dustin saw and knew things. He understood that he wasn't either seeing or knowing everything there was to know about what he was seeing, but what he did see and know, he saw and knew with crystal clarity.

Nothing was hidden, except what wasn't revealed.

Did he see with just one set of eyes, or with a thousand? He couldn't tell.

CHAPTER 67

He was in this same house, but at some point in the past. Not too soon after it had been built actually. The color of paint on the walls was different. There were also lots of hung satanic decorations.

Okay, this is back when Jeff lived here.

Jeff had been a Satanist.

The view moved forward in time. Suddenly it was night, and all the living room curtains were drawn. The house interior was lit only by candlelight from black and red candles.

Dustin was suddenly staring at a gruesome surgical operation.

The 'patient' was a pregnant blonde woman. The woman's pregnancy was very advanced—Dustin 'knew' that her baby was due in a month's time.

The woman was gagged and was tied down on a round wooden altar carved with a pentagram. Three satanic 'doctors' were in attendance, all of them dressed in hooded black robes.

Dustin looked from face to face.

Jeff the Satanist was one of the three.

The second 'doctor' made Dustin gasp. It was Beatriz Greme, aka Queen Bee, high priestess of the Real Dreams cult.

The third person was a man that Dustin thought he'd seen at Real Dreams, but he wasn't certain of this.

What were the three doing?

They were giving their pregnant 'patient' a caesarian section. Without anesthetic. The woman's eyes bulged in agony as Jeff carefully sliced her baby bulge open from left to right and then pulled out her premature child, a boy.

Without ado, Jeff next slit the little boy's throat and sucked out some of his blood. Then he passed the baby to Queen Bee who did likewise and who then passed the child on to the second man.

After they'd all drank their fill of fetal blood, Jeff cut off the fetus's umbilicus close to his navel and threw his premature corpse somewhere out of sight.

"The door to welcome Boku Veeza is prepared," he announced in stentorian tones.

Queen Bee wiped blood off of her lips. "Hand me the key," she told the third man.

"Now, why aren't I surprised?" Dustin wondered aloud when the man handed a fluffy white kitten to Queen Bee. The kitten seemed so damn cute and so full of life and so nice and so trusting. Dustin felt so damn annoyed.

"Now we unlock the door with the key," Queen Bee proclaimed and then she proceeded to stuff the little cat into the pregnant woman's emptied womb.

Amazingly, the not-to-be-mother was still alive, kept so by magical means. She groaned in pain and twisted and turned and her weeping eyes registered her disbelief at the horrors being inflicted on her, but the one thing she didn't do was die on her tormentors.

The kitten protested a little at being stuffed into her womb, but finally, after it was wrapped up in the severed umbilical cord, it was forced properly in there.

The third man said, "And now we turn the key in the lock."

Stepping forward with needle and thread (not surgical suture), he began sewing up the woman's womb with the little cat inside of her.

Halfway through doing so, the kitten stuck a bloody paw out through the womb slit. The man patiently pushed the paw back inside the slit and continued stitching up the woman's flesh over it.

Dustin realized two things now: First, that the reason a woman this pregnant had been used was because they needed sufficient womb-space to house the kitten, and secondly, that the kitten was still alive inside the woman's body, surviving on the traces of air leaking in between the stitches.

"And now we unlock the door," Queen Bee said with a broad smile.

And now the pregnant woman was unbound from the wooden altar and the two men lifted her up into the air while Queen Bee slipped a noose that dangled from the ceiling fan around her neck.

Her body was released. She hung there choking to death, while the three witches chanted incantations.

And both the woman and the cat died at exactly the same time, at the stroke of midnight.

Dustin saw the dead kitten turn through space-time like a key. He saw the dead woman's body open up like a door. He saw a black tunnel extend from her to hell, from *here* to hell.

And at the end of the tunnel, he glimpsed massive brown squirming coils, and he understood that Boku Veeza had just been welcomed into the human world.

CHAPTER 68

Dustin watched the past from within the picture and the scene changed.

This was still in the past, but now further in the future.

Dustin saw Boku Veeza, massive, segmented, and repulsive as ever, lying in a pool of her rainbow juices. Beside the worm goddess lay a bleeding human corpse.

Queen Bee was just unbending from slitting the corpse's throat. The high priestess had blood on her hands and a wide smile on her face.

"He looks delicious," Boku Veza said of the corpse with deep approval while licking her lips. "Where did you find him?"

Queen Bee gestured dismissively at the dead man.

"He's Paul Smith, the Christian preacher I told you about, the one who kept trying to expose us," she replied in an amused voice. "Unfortunately, his sister-in-law and her son escaped."

Queen Bee was barefoot and Reverend Smith's blood had now surrounded her feet, leaving her standing in a crimson pool. The blood spread further to mingle with Boku Veeza's *Nif* drippings.

Dustin could see that the high priestess was delighted. Her pet goddess was everything she'd ever hoped for.

"Remember, priestess," Boku Veeza said, "always remember that here there is no salvation for anyone."

"Only sex, sadism, and suffering," Boku Veeza said.

"Yes," the goddess agreed. "Here there is no mercy, only pleasure and pain. All who worship me will have delight and *Nif*. Those who offend me will suffer my wrath and become my meals."

Then she dipped her giant head and began to eat the dead man on the floor. Soon, the top half of the man was all gone; just his buttocks and legs remained.

After a while, Boku Veeza smiled at Queen Bee.

"You were right, priestess," she said in a delighted voice. "Infidels do taste delicious. Feed me more of them. Many more, for God so loved the world that he gave his only begotten son, so that whosoever believeth in him should not perish—"

Boku Veeza stopped speaking and then looked shocked at what she'd just said. "What nonsense am I saying?" she worriedly asked Queen Bee.

Queen Bee looked apologetic and gestured down at the half-eaten corpse. "It has to be a side-effect of this preacher you're eating. Their heads are usually full of such horrible ideas. It should wear off once you poop him out."

Boku Veeza nodded. "I definitely hope so that whosoever believeth in him should not perish but have everlasting life!"

Boku Veeza stopped again and looked miserable. "I had intended to keep him in my anus forever, but except ye be born again, ye shall not see the kingdom of God."

Boku Veeza stopped speaking again. Now she had rainbow-colored tears in her eyes. Her giant bulk squirmed uncomfortably, as if she was doing her best to hasten the preacher's passage to her rear end.

But the goddess's tongue now seemed to have a mind of its own:

"Oh yes, ladies and gents, my Christian brothers and sisters," she went on saying, while weeping rainbow tears of rage, "these are the words of our Lord and Savior, Jesus Christ the holy son of God. For didn't our dear Lord himself say, "I am the way, the truth and the life; no one comes unto the father except by me? So then, let me tell you, folks . . ."

Dustin knew that Queen Bee was doing her best not to laugh at the mortified worm goddess.

Oh, so that's why she hardly ever eats the heads of infidels: they give her spiritual diarrhea, Dustin realized and burst out laughing himself.

CHAPTER 69

Again, time shifted. Once more Dustin viewed this same house, but further still in the future.

Both the color of the walls and the furniture were now familiar to Dustin, as were the decorations on the wall. Now the house was as Dustin remembered it when Candice Raveling lived here.

In fact, this was the night that Candice Raveling died.

Once more there were three people in the living room.

Candice Raveling was one of them. By the time Dustin began watching, Candice was already bound up and standing beside the fatal noose.

Once more, Dustin was surprised by the identity of two of Candice's murderers.

He had no difficulty recognizing Faith Mills. And her assistant, who was stroking Candice's cat Pookie, was her elder sister Grace Mills.

"It's great that witches keep cats as familiars," Grace was saying. "It means we don't need to buy or steal one."

Dustin sighed at her statement.

Woody was right. If there is a cat-God, that deity must be even more pissed off now than Jehovah used to get at the Old Testament Jews.

The fourth person in the room, wasn't exactly a person. There was a shadow on the wall. A female-ish shadow with a massive ball for a head and long praying-mantis limbs, and which kept moving about like a dog guarding the house against intruders.

Dustin returned his attention to the main parties in this drama of the conclusion of Candice Raveling's earthly life.

"Listen, girlfriend, we hate to have to do this to you of all people," Faith told Candice, "but you shouldn't have publicly gone up against Queen Bee like that. Now you're simply a nuisance and a threat to her and so we've gotta eliminate you."

"Yeah, this really blows," Grace agreed. "Yeah, I know that we're friends and all, but we're the Security Council. Our first loyalty is to Boku Veeza and then to the high priestess. And you pissed Boku

Veeza off too, so—" she sighed, "—up, up, up and away you go to down below."

Candice protested through her gag to zero avail.

"Okay, we're all set," Faith said. "Let's get this over with." Then she looked over at the shadow on the wall, which was now near the TV. "Hey, Tanana, stop looking for spooks and help us get her head up in the noose!"

Tanana seemed to slip out of the wall. The ball-headed long-limbed shadow became a ball-headed woman, then regular Tanana Reeves.

"Do you *really* have to do that creepy transformation thing all of the time?" Grace asked Tanana.

Tanana looked surprised by the question. "Creepy? But that's what I really look like." She gestured dismissively down at her hot Afro-American body. "This is just my human avatar."

"Whatever, biatch," Grace smirked back at her. "Hoist Candice up, she's long past her expiry date."

"Hey, be nicer to her," Faith objected. "She's a friend of ours."

"Not any more she ain't," Grace retorted. Then she nodded to Tanana. "What're you waiting for? Let's do this."

Tanana shook her head. "I don't get you humans. Us demons are supposed to be nasty and evil. But . . . You two, for instance, are almost as bad as we are. Grace, when you fucking die, I'll put in a demon-recruitment request for you. You've clearly got what it takes."

"All hail Boku Veeza!" Grace replied.

Tanana and Grace laughed at this. Faith and Candice didn't.

The killing went ahead.

Tanana lifted Candice Raveling up as easily as if she was a roll of tissue paper.

With sad eyes, Faith slipped the noose around Candice's neck.

With a broad grin, because she'd never really liked Candice to start with, Grace slipped Pookie the cat in between the noose and Candice's neck.

Tanana let Candice down slowly.

The noose began choking Candice and her cat.

Pookie started trying to get free. His front claws dug into the duct-tape over Candice's mouth and ripped it away.

Though the noose was strangling her, Candice still had a little breath and strength in her.

Her last words were, "I curse you, Grace Mills. I curse you with intense misery for life!"

She managed to grunt out a follow-up incantation and then she ran out of air and began gasping for breath.

"Fuck, the bitch cursed me!" Grace growled, staring at Candice like she'd kill her if she wasn't already dying. "She cursed me."

Faith shrugged like her older sister deserved it.

"Don't worry about it," Tanana told Grace. "Candice is just mad that you gon' still be here when she's gone. Dying like this? She's going to the morgue. Bitch knows that by killing her this way, Queen Bee has totally screwed her over: she don't even get to live forever in Boku Veeza's asshole like infidels do."

Grace laughed. She, her sister, and the demoness watched Candice dangle there, kicking and jerking. Poor Pookie was already long dead.

Then Faith remembered they were supposed to recite a spell to open the door.

The door opened in Candice, or Candice became the door.

"Let's get out of here," Grace told the others.

After a final sad look up at Candice by Faith, the three of them walked through the Candice-door and left.

CHAPTER 70

Time and location shifted.

This was the same night of Candice Raveling's murder, but later. The door that the trio of assassins had opened through Candice Raveling must have returned them to the Real Dreams club, because now the Mills sisters were emerging from the building at the rear of the dead preacher's house on Route 106.

They were walking towards Faith's Honda Civic.

"Really, I don't feel good killing Candice that way," Faith said.

"Damn, I can't believe the fucking bitch cursed me," Grace said. "Everyone knows a dying person's curse isn't a joke."

"Don't worry about it," Faith replied. "Nothing's gonna happen tonight. Let's just go get some sleep and we'll work out how to counteract Candice's curse tomorrow."

Dustin wondered why Grace was so concerned about Candice's curse.

But then he understood; it wasn't so much that a dying woman had cursed her, but that this particular dying woman had.

At Real Dreams, Candice was second only to Beatriz Greme in the spellcasting department. Everyone feared her and everyone respected her and everyone thus expected her to usurp Queen Bee's authority at the earliest opportunity.

But the wily Beatriz had struck first.

Their goddess Boku Veeza didn't care who her high priestess was. So long as she was worshipped and fed the flesh of infidels on a regular basis, any hen could rule the roost.

Dustin was momentarily unsure which Boku Veeza was: the cult's all-powerful goddess or simply a pampered paranormal pet that Beatriz Greme had summoned from hell to advance her own wicked schemes.

Maybe both, he decided. *The pet may have become mistress of its mistress.*

Meanwhile, back in the past, the Mills sisters were now in their car.

"Sis, fasten your seatbelt," Faith told Grace. "How many times do I need to remind you of that?"

Grace nodded and bucked the seatbelt. "Yeah, especially tonight," she agreed. "Tonight, I feel like a disaster preparing to happen to myself."

Faith glanced sharply at Grace and then put the car in motion.

At first everything went fine. Grace lived in nearby Bridgewater, and they'd be there in mere minutes.

(To Dustin, it seemed like he was sitting in the center of the backseat and looking between the sisters, staring out along the red hood of Faith's car, seeing the green and white of a street name sign approach them and then flash past . . .)

But then . . . a short distance into Bridgewater . . .

Without warning, the Honda flipped over onto its left side, and went careening down the street like that.

Total Mission Impossible shit, with both sisters screaming in the front seats, while Faith tried to steady a vehicle that was well out of her control.

The only possible cause for the car's tilting sideways that night on a dry and level road and with Faith driving well inside the speed limit, was Candice Raveling's curse.

Faith had told Dustin the truth about one detail of their accident: Yes, a steel girder from the back of a truck *had* rammed into their car.

But the specifics for the accident were quite different from what he'd been told.

Contrary to Faith's version of events, the truck carrying the girder hadn't been in motion, but had been parked.

They had rammed into it, not it into them.

The impact of the collision then dislodged one of the girders from the truck bed and this girder then slipped backwards through the front windshield of their Honda Civic, through the inflated airbag on the passenger side, and into Grace's face.

Ironically, had Grace not been wearing her seat belt like Faith had insisted, she would have completely escaped injury, as she would have fallen down onto Faith when the car went from horizontal to vertical.

Faith was down on the window of the sideways car (and was knocked unconscious in the collision) and was thus well below the 'danger height' of the killer girder, though she was soon coated in her sister's blood.

Oh, that's why she blames Faith for what happened to her, Dustin understood. *If she'd not reminded her to belt up . . . Crazy shit definitely happened that night. Never joke with a witch's curse.*

Fast forward to an operating theater, with Grace Mills anesthetized on a surgeon's operating table, with half of her face looking like an eggplant omelet.

The plastic surgeons began their reconstructive work and the replay blinked out

CHAPTER 71

The scene transitioned in a splash-screen of images.

In this collage of visual flashes, each lasting the merest of split-seconds, it was revealed to Dustin that the true reason why Candice's house had remained untenanted for over a year—why Beatriz Greme and Real Dreams hadn't attempted to purchase it in all that while—was because at first the building had showed no signs of possessing any psychic charge.

In layman's terms, the building hadn't appeared to be haunted.

This was why Doris and Reginald Mills had first insisted on renting it to discover if it was indeed haunted, though of course Dustin's uncle Richmond Mitchell had no idea of this.

CHAPTER 72

Back in the here-and-now, Dustin realized he wasn't exactly back in the here-and-now yet.

He'd just realized out of whose eyes he'd been staring at the past.

Wow! I'm inside of . . . I'm actually one of the guardians of Boku Veeza's human grove. I'm the male guardian!

It was a crazy perspective. He was in the painting, in a kind of vivid virtual reality.

He looked down at himself. His body was bright orange and scaly. His arms and chest were very muscular and leopard-spotted. He licked his lips and his tongue shot out to almost a foot in front of his face; its tip was forked like that of a snake.

His hands and feet ended in razor-sharp metal claws. He clawed the air, feeling a rush of power in the understanding of what these claws would do to anyone rash enough to disturb Boku Veeza's grove.

He felt exalted; greater than all who had come before him. He looked sideways at his wives and their perfect bodies filled him with lust. They smiled back at him and the reptilian beauty of their faces, those snakelike eyes, filled him with delight. Both of his wives were as perfect as he was, and he would mate with them forever and ever, as guardians did. Boku Veeza approved of this.

"The guardians are the most cherished of all of Boku Veeza's worshippers," he grunted in a voice an octave lower than his regular human one.

He felt strong, stronger than any human, and he laughed and laughed and laughed and awaited the infidels who were foolish enough to defy his mistress's will.

And then, Dustin was out of the painting and back in himself and still confused as to how what had just happened had just happened.

Now he knew more than he wanted to. The roots of the tree that was Real Dreams were planted in Murder and Gore and more Murder and Gore.

He frowned at the painting, which was now once again flat and dead.

I left my house to get away from murder and gore. But here I found more, oh so much more.

He did what any sensible Real Dreams member would under the circumstances: he drank deeply from his glass of *Nif.*

Then he relaxed and let the rainbow drink fill his head with its perfect delusions that all was alright.

Nothing's alright, Dustin knew, *but that's alright too.*

I really liked being the guardian creature though. It felt like being a video game warrior . . . or monster. Too bad that opportunity was lost for good.

CHAPTER 73

"My older sister wants me dead," Faith told Dustin once she was back home. "I'm so, so tired of her anger trip. I'm worried that one of these days she might try to murder me."

"I believe you," he replied. "I really do. But what can we do about it?"

"For a start, you can make love to me," she said, snuggling closer on the couch. "I really missed you last night. I had a few good fucks, but I felt no emotional connection to any of them."

Dustin smiled and thought: *Or maybe, honey, what really happened was that you and some other members of the Security Council went on a short assassination trip and killed a few infidels.*

Faith paused in unzipping his fly. "Are you alright? You seem distracted."

He laughed and drank *Nif* and kissed her. "Nothing serious. Nothing that matters. All hail Boku Veeza."

Dustin never made it to work that Monday.

CHAPTER 74

"Faith, darling," Dustin said during the pleasant afterglow of their lovemaking.

"Yes, baby?"

She relaxed her body luxuriously against his, which prompted a return of his erection, and almost converted their verbal conversation into a physical one again. But Dustin managed to restrain himself from once more making love to her.

"Something continues to puzzle me about that infidel bitch Bianca Sanchez," he told Faith.

Hearing that name, Faith gave him a jealous look. "What? You weren't in love with her, were you?"

"Don't go on a jealous trip, honey. This is merely a puzzle I'd like to have resolved."

She snuggled closer to him. "Oh, alright then, I'm listening."

Dustin said. "Well, of course, this wasn't any issue when I didn't know that you were also a member of Real Dreams. But now that I do . . ."

"Oh, honey, stop keeping me in such suspense. I already want you to make love to me again."

Dustin nodded. "Alright, here's the problem: Why didn't Bianca, who worked at Real Dreams, recognize you for who you were when you moved in here?"

Faith thought on this. "I dunno. Did she get a good look at me?"

Dustin shook his head. "No, she didn't. But your name should've been a giveaway . . . at least it should have rung a bell in her memory . . . And, yes, Bianca *did* ask me what you looked like." Dustin now looked confused. "But when I described you to her, she shook her head and said you didn't sound in any way familiar."

"Grace and I don't always attend club meetings," Faith told Dustin. "And—we'll need to confirm this tho'—but I don't think Bianca had been working at Real Dreams for very long before she went astray, maybe two or three months at most. So, I guess, we simply never saw one another."

Dustin nodded. "Yeah, I seem to remember her mentioning that too; about not having been working there for very long."

"But anyway, we never met," Faith said. "Why? Is something the matter?"

Dustin shook his head, and reached for his glass of Nightmare Fuel. He smiled at the liquid, which shifted like a liquid chameleon in its glass.

Faith grabbed his penis and jerked it, so that he moaned. "Come inside me again now?" she asked him softly.

He nodded. "One more question first."

She continued stroking him while nodding. "Fire away."

"What's your actual surname? I mean, now that I know you aren't really Reggie's niece?"

Faith laughed. "Oh, it actually is 'Mills.' Just from another Mills family."

After saying this, she pulled Dustin on top of her, and then inserted his hard manhood into her soft womanhood.

"Now, prove to me that you never had any feelings for Bianca Sanchez," she whispered in Dustin's ear. "You know the sort of proof I want."

Dustin did his best to prove to Faith that he loved her only. And from Faith's loud moaning, it seemed that he succeeded in convincing her of this.

CHAPTER 75

On returning home the next morning, Dustin was happy to discover that Tanana had cleaned up the guest bedroom like he'd asked her to.

But . . . how . . . ?

He was surprised that the guestroom showed no sign whatsoever that the demoness had torn Woody to pieces in it. She'd even removed Woody's clothing.

All that remained to mark Woody Taylor's exit from life were his pistol and his laptop; both of which still lay where he'd left them.

If anything, the bedroom was cleaner than Dustin last remembered seeing it.

She even sprayed it with Febreze, he thought and shut the door again.

CHAPTER 76

This week of Dustin's life was a kind of replay of yestertime.

In the morning I go to work and in the evening I go to fuck, he mused on Wednesday morning. *Seems like I've lived exactly this life before.*

Dustin's workload was light this week, Uncle Rich having decided not to attend their distant relative's funeral after all. (This was a relief to Dustin, as, with all of the drama currently happening in his life, he had forgotten all about the proposed trip himself.) He showed a few houses to folks, supervised some renovations on a new property, and drank a few beers with the guys from work.

Then he'd return home to Faith Mills, who always seemed to be sexually aroused. She'd cook them dinner and afterwards they'd watch TV or have sex, usually the latter.

Grace Mills visited thrice, each time wearing a face mask that she wouldn't take off. As far as Dustin could tell, Grace had lots of those masks, ranging from cute and funny, to freaky, to scary.

Each time Dustin saw Grace drive up in her white Volkswagen, his heart seemed to skip beats. He couldn't help wondering how long it would be before Grace sliced through the thin veneer of civility that still constrained her, and then sliced off Faith's face, so they could share a uniform deformity.

Although, I'm not sure that her 'deformity' isn't just in her mind. From the little I've seen of her, she still looks good. She has no visible scars.

But mental scars were clearly just as grotesque.

Whenever Grace visited, Dustin would excuse himself and go home. Grace never stayed long; it seemed her sole purpose in visiting Faith was to remind her of her guilt; to let her know that she had no business being happy when her 'victim' wasn't.

Usually, twenty or thirty minutes after Dustin left Faith's house, he'd hear Grace driving off again. Then he'd go back over to Faith's place and find her mood altered.

If she'd been happy before her sister's visit, she'd be sad afterwards. If she'd been low before Grace came, she'd be high afterwards. In this latter case, her good mood seemed to stem from the satisfaction that she'd given 'the bitch' what she deserved.

Whatever her mood though, she'd be in the mood for sex.

Dustin began suspecting that maybe Faith (who seemed normal on the surface), was as emotionally scarred as her sister was, although if this was the case, he had no idea what the cause of her own neurosis might be.

CHAPTER 77

When Dustin arrived home from work on Wednesday, Queen Bee was in his house.

"I dropped by to see my ass doctor and thought I'd best make him some dinner," she told him, greeting him at the front door in nothing but a thong and slippers.

He could smell cooking, a rich roast and other things he'd not eaten in ages.

Staring at the high priestess's naked body, he silently applauded the benefits of living on a sparsely populated street.

I won't even bother asking her how she can get into my house without the keys.

"What's on the menu?" he asked the old girl instead, wondering how for the life of him he couldn't get her breathtaking bosom out of his brain.

No, that's not true. I don't go around having granny sex fantasies . . . but once I catch sight of these huge tits of hers . . . !

"Lots of ass grapes, that's for sure," Queen Bee answered and let him in through his own front door.

"You really need to let me know when you'll be stopping by," Dustin said. "Then I can stop at a restaurant on my way home from work and buy something for us to eat. No need for you to go to the trouble of cooking for me."

"Oh no, it's no trouble," she told him. "I felt like cooking us both something. And I brought you some *Nif.* I'd have given it to you at our last meeting if the goddess didn't send you home early like that."

He smiled at the 'send you home early.'

They ate the delicious dinner she'd prepared and afterward retired to his bedroom, where he sucked on her swollen hemorrhoids until she couldn't stand it any longer.

Once he'd come too, they lay side by side and talked:

"Honey, you're so good at sucking ass that I wish I had a cock you could suck for me too," she said.

After they'd laughed over this for a while, the old lady told him, "On a more serious note tho', I need to give you some advice."

"About what?"

"Listen to me, Dustin. Those two Mills girls are nothing but trouble."

He frowned. "How do you mean?"

"Oh, don't play dumb, honey. Don't pretend you've not noticed the enmity between Faith and Grace."

"Yes, I have. But that's normal enough between siblings. They've likely been like that all of their lives."

Queen bee shook her head pointedly at him. "Not in this case. Grace flat-out blames Faith for causing the accident that ruined her looks. You've seen how she wears a mask everywhere now. How do you ever expect her to forgive that?"

Recalling his vision of the accident that had scarred Grace for life, Dustin nodded. "Yeah, I guess that's true."

"Grace wants Faith out of the way. Along with Malarkey and Tanana, Grace is a member of our club's Security Council. She claims her sister is a security risk to the Real Dreams organization."

"But that's preposterous!" Dustin instantly protested. "Faith is also a member of the Security Council!"

"And how do *you* know that?" Queen Bee asked Dustin, raising inquiring eyebrows.

Dustin felt comfortable whenever he was Queen Bee, but not enough to tell her the vision he'd had in the Mills' house, particularly as it concerned both how she'd come to power originally and also how she'd maintained her grip on authority by murdering Candice Raveling.

"I don't remember, I guess Faith told me," he replied instead.

"See what I mean?" Queen Bee retorted right away. "Grace claims her younger sister can't keep her mouth shut. You've just proved that's true. I wonder what else she told you."

Dustin knew he had to defend Faith. "Mostly that her older sister hates her guts because of the accident and would kill her if she had the chance."

Queen Bee rolled her eyes skyward. "According to Grace, her younger sis thinks with her vagina instead of her head. Our secrets are safe until she gets fucked properly." She pierced Dustin with her steely gaze. "Have you been fucking her properly?"

"Aren't you being rather harsh? Has Faith caused any security breaches yet?"

Queen Bee shook her head. "None that we can prove, and that's what's still leveraging in her favor. But Grace insists that her sister is halfway to becoming an infidel now and that she'll get us proof if it's the last thing she does."

Dustin sighed. "Oh, come on, mama. Surely you can't just let one woman's bitterness destroy another."

She grinned at him. "Hmmm. I love the way you just called me 'mama.' Say it again like you just did."

"Mama. *Mama.*"

She momentarily grabbed his penis and jerked on it. "Ooh yeah, sweetie, that's real nice." Then she frowned again. "Listen, kid, it's not like I like Grace's attitude to her sister. I'd stop her if I could, but you're forgetting that lots of times the goddess hears what I hear."

Hearing this quite surprised Dustin. "Really? Does Boku Veeza eavesdrop on her worshippers?"

Queen Bee made a face. "I've never really figured that out. I've asked her, but she's coy about it. But the way I've got it worked out, she can either hear us talking when she's awake, or when she's asleep—maybe then she hears us in her dreams, in her unconscious mind. She's not omniscient tho'—I'm certain of that. There's a limit in distance to which she can hear people speaking." Queen Bee shrugged. "And then of course, she can read minds to a degree."

Dustin nodded to this. "Yeah, I got that last part. Okay, so I get what you mean about Boku Veeza knowing what's being said about Faith. You're suggesting the goddess might order you to feed Faith to her?"

"Or sacrifice her, even," the high priestess agreed. "Sometimes it's really hard to tell what she wants from us. Sometimes, I'm not sure she herself knows what she wants. She just knows *that* she wants."

"Really?"

Queen Bee nodded back at him. "Definitely looks that way to me. Our goddess simply possesses *desire*, and she channels this *desire* into whatever physical, mental, or emotional urge is closest to the surface of her mind at the time. And once that urge or lust is satisfied, she is herself satisfied, fully content until her *desire* overflows again."

"And if she hears what we're saying about her now?"

Queen Bee smiled coldly. "No problem. The goddess doesn't really mind being insulted. She knows we're too puny to act against her, and we need her anyway, so . . ." She waved the rest of her statement away, and crossed her hands over her immense breasts. "My point is . . . Grace is in Boku Veeza's good books; Faith isn't. While you . . . our goddess apparently can't make up her mind if she likes you or detests you."

"She told me as much herself," Dustin said.

"Say, you haven't been going to church, have you?"

"I went twice," Dustin admitted. "I haven't been back there since. I dunno, but I felt like something was lacking."

"What was lacking was the immediacy of the deity's response," Queen Bee said with a fervent look in her eyes. "But we'll discuss that later. Just stay away from holy rollers. Boku Veeza detests them; she feels threatened by any deity other than herself. If you go to church again it'll start to 'smell' on you and then she'll eat you for sure."

"And what are you gonna do to protect Faith Mills? This situation with her sister needs to be resolved."

"Because you've developing feelings for her? Because you've fallen in love with her?"

"Maybe. But even leaving me out of the picture, you owe it to your congregation to watch out for them, don't you?"

Queen Bee laughed. Oh, I do my best. Listen, there's little I can do for your little Faith. It's really out of my hands. Malarkey and Tanana like Grace; those demons think Faith is too soft for the disciplinary committee, and they'd love to replace her with someone else. If Grace finds 'evidence,' they're gonna attempt to throw her li'l sis to the wolves. And you too, Dustin. If you're still balls-deep in her pussy when the wolves come for Faith, there's a good chance they'll take you too. Remember, Boku Veeza loves the flesh of infidels best of all."

Dustin sighed. "O.K., O.K., so I've gotta keep Faith out of trouble."

Queen Bee shook her head at him. "No, no, no. Faith Mills *is* trouble. You need to keep your dick out of *her*, so you're not judged guilty by association."

While Dustin was still thinking on this, Queen Bee spread her legs wide so he could see her asshole.

"All this talk is making me itchy," she told him. "Suck me one more time, honey. For the road . . . or maybe, just in case you do piss Boku Veeza off enough that she eats you and I don't have my ass doctor no more."

With a whole lot on his mind to think about, Dustin nevertheless got down on hands and knees and began sucking her 'ass grapes' again.

CHAPTER 78

After Queen Bee left him that night, Dustin did one of the hardest things he'd done in recent times:

He decided to go cold turkey on *Nif.*

Queen Bee left his house at 8:30 p.m., leaving him more than enough time to go visit Faith. (He still found it inconvenient sleeping at her house, since he'd have to wake up early to come get dressed for work in the morning.)

But first he sat down and did some hard thinking:

This problem between Faith and her angry sister is ripe as a peach. It's about to come to a head. That's exactly what Queen Bee just warned me about. Grace will shoot her shot in the next few days, and Faith had better not be holding the 'dead woman's hand' and be caught sitting with her back to the door. To protect Faith, I need to be clearheaded. And I don't mean Nif clearheaded, as Boku Veeza might agree with Grace's trumped-up evidence. I need to have my wits about me.

So, with deep feelings of waste, he poured the sweet rainbow liquor down the kitchen sink.

Then he went to the guestroom and got out Woody's pistol out of the nightstand.

CHAPTER 79

Staying off of *Nif* was as hard as Dustin had anticipated it would be.

Though Faith grudgingly accepted his excuse of "Babe, it's essential that I keep my head straight at work this week," the real abstinence problem lay in the sheer abundance of the drink nearby. Once or twice, he found himself halfway to Faith's kitchen to pour himself a drink of Nightmare Fuel, powered purely by his subconscious, and had to backtrack to the safety of sobriety.

Not that he really felt safe. With his abstinence came a torrent of those feelings that *Nif* had suppressed.

Foremost amongst these feelings were worries for his girlfriend's safety.

Okay, Faith is no saint. She's a murderess, or at best an assassin for the goddess's cause. But somehow, I'm now hopelessly in love with her. It feels to me like she's all I have, and I need to protect her with my life.

Dustin's other feelings alternated between disgust at his personal involvement with Real Dreams and terror that resulted from the visions he'd had in Faith's house.

He couldn't stop seeing the pregnant woman having her fetus replaced with a living cat, after Queen Bee and her associates had first drunk the fetus's blood.

We're all crazy here. I'm right in the middle of this; no way out. So, alright, my current task is just to keep Faith safe from her sister. But once that's finished, what do I do?

Right now, Dustin wished he could drink *Nif* and let it soothe his doubts and worries. He really did.

But Dustin didn't break down and drink Nightmare Fuel. Instead, he waited and watched for the storm that was surely about to break around he and Faith's heads.

That storm was coming soon. He was certain of it.

CHAPTER 80

By Friday, Dustin felt passably normal again. Except for when he was directly in the presence of the rainbow drink, his craving for *Nif* had subsided.

He felt mostly in control of himself.

The day went smoothly enough until 2 p.m., when he was driving back from a house showing.

Then a call came in from Faith.

Dustin parked to accept the call.

"Hey, baby, how's it—"

"Help me, baby!" Faith whispered urgently over the phone. "Grace has . . . !" Then there was the sound of a slap and Grace's angry voice yelling: "Give that cellphone, infidel bitch!" Then silence, then the sound of a scuffle, then Faith again, this time moaning: "Help, baby, she's snapped . . . she . . . and Queen Bee . . . they're gonna sacrifice me to—!"

Then Dustin heard a loud thud, like a fist hitting someone's jaw, and then a loud thumping sound like a body hitting the floor, and then triumphant laughter that could only have come from a psychotic Grace Mills.

"Faith? Faith?" Dustin queried the phone for a few seconds before realizing it was dead.

On an impulse, Dustin dialed back. Maybe, just maybe, he could persuade Grace not to do anything rash and murderous.

But Grace didn't pick up.

Dustin felt cold all over. For endless moments he sat gripping his steering wheel while a wind of mindless rage blew over him. He felt mad enough to kill someone, anyone who interfered with him at that moment.

He waited till the wave of rage had passed. Then, in a much calmer frame of mind, Dustin started up the F-150 again.

He'd been on his way back to the office. But now, he turned the car around and sped home.

Dustin knew he had to get over to the dead preacher's house as soon as possible.

But first, he needed to pick up Woody's gun.

CHAPTER 81

By the time Dustin arrived at the deserted mini-mansion on the outskirts of Halifax, he'd realized one critical flaw in his rescue plan:

I've no way to open up the portal to Real Dreams! Damn, what am I gonna do? Then he calmed down again. *Bianca was the last so-called 'door' that they opened. According to Queen Bee, the doors never close immediately; sometimes they remain open for weeks. I hope that's Bianca's case too.*

While hoping that this was one such case, Dustin skidded his pickup truck across the house's gravel driveway.

He looked around for Grace's car. Faith's own car had still been parked in her garage, which meant that her abductor(s) must have brought their own vehicle to her place.

Damn, Grace's damn Volkswagen isn't here. But that doesn't mean anything. Someone else could've brought them both here and then driven off!

Leaving his car keys in the ignition, Dustin leapt down and, gun in hand, began running for all he was worth around the side of the Smith house.

I already wasted enough time getting here!

He reached the small rear building, pushed its door open and ran through it till he reached the stairs to the basement.

CHAPTER 82

"Hey, it's Dustin," Tanana said as he reached the bottom of the stairs.

"Hey, man, what's with the gun?" Malarkey asked him. "You planning to shoot someone?"

Dustin sighed. The demons weren't alone either. Between them stood a gagged old woman. They'd apparently been about manhandling the old woman through the human-door when they'd heard the sound of Dustin's feet.

This has to happen today of all days. I have to meet these two demonic assholes here of all places. The pair of them are standing between me and the damn human door, and of course, bullets won't hurt a fucking demon.

He stared down at his gun. "Not really, but I'm in a hell of a hurry."

"A *hell* of a hurry?" the demon clown burst out laughing. "Ah, you always crack me up, man. I already told ya, you should be a clown too. What d'ya think, Tanana? This guy's good at comedy, ain't he?"

"He's real good," Tanana nodded with a sly sidewards glance at Dustin.

Dustin looked the demons' elderly female captive over. She looked both shocked and scared, but she was peripheral to his concerns, which all revolved around rescuing his abducted girlfriend.

"You're in time, bro," Malarkey said, "We just got through opening the door."

"What do you mean?" Dustin asked, but then a sideways glance revealed that Bianca's withered and shriveled corpse lay over by a bookcase.

Seeing the waitress's dead body made a lot of sense to him. Hadn't he already buried the cat she'd been hung up with?

"She didn't remain open for long," Tanana informed Dustin. "Thank hell we already had a replacement handy."

She stepped aside so that Dustin could see who they'd sacrificed this time.

He sighed deeply. It was Jen Carlson, the last member of the Ghost Research Outfit Worldwide.

"At this rate, I'm soon gonna be out of friends," Dustin quipped in disgust.

Both Tanana and Malarkey burst out laughing now.

"Honey, you're so damn funny," Tanana told him, almost bent double with laughter.

The demons' old female captive was staring at Dustin as if pleading with him to shoot them. But he didn't dare try, as in addition to not harming them, attacking the pair would most likely end his rescue attempt.

Instead, he stared for a while at Jen Carlson. She wasn't dead yet. Still wearing her spectacles, she hung there, with her mouth gasping for breath and her eyes out of focus, while meanwhile she was out of focus herself, being now the transparent centerpiece of a hellish portal. Of course, her 'key'—the black cat that had 'unlocked' her—dangled over her shoulder, just as transparent as she was, as it gasped out its last breaths.

Dustin glanced at the bound and gagged old woman that Malarkey was holding onto. The captive lady possessed an ambience of minor familiarity; he'd seen her before, and recently at that. But the possible implications of this knowledge ricocheted off of Dustin's troubled soul like tennis balls off of a military tank.

Then suddenly Dustin felt bolder, or maybe he felt crazier. Anyway, he asked the demons: "Guys, has either of you seen either of the Mills sisters?"

"Yeah, of course," Malarkey immediately replied. "They came through here a short while earlier."

"Grace was taking Faith to the temple to sacrifice her for betraying Boku Veeza," Tanana added with a sort of laugh. "Dumb bitch oughta know better."

Malarkey nodded. "If you hurry, you'll be just in time for the ritual. Should be lotsa fun."

"What the fuck!" Dustin yelped, and then he dashed between the pair of demons, ran through the door that hanging Jen Carlson had opened up, and raced down the corridor it opened into.

CHAPTER 83

Dustin sprinted towards the main clubroom. He'd already run past the connecting corridor before remembering that he needed to turn into it. He skid to a halt, backtracked, and then corrected his direction.

Half a minute later, he'd crossed the corridor that ran parallel to the one he'd originally been on, and was standing at the entrance to the temple.

The temple entrance was wide open. Inside the temple, ranks of black-robed cultists stood in concentric circles between the red temple walls and its central Human Grove, those six suffering humans with trees growing out of their heads.

The odor from the trees in the grove's heads was already tampering with Dustin's thinking. The experience was similar to that of being in Boku Veeza's presence. Dustin once more felt like he was immersed in Nightmare Fuel, as if *Nif* was the oxygen in there.

This felt even more intense than the last time. And he'd not yet stepped through the temple door.

Crap! Maybe I should have planned this better. If my arrival is expected, there'll be guards lying in wait for me. But then, Malarkey and Tanana didn't seem to care.

Anyway, he couldn't turn back now. His beloved Faith was somewhere here in the temple and he had to save her.

With his gun held ready to shoot, Dustin stepped cautiously inside the temple.

To his surprise, no one attempted to grab and disarm him. He heard the murmurs as the congregation noticed him and some of them even nodded at him when his gaze met theirs. But no one left their positions to try and stop him.

Puzzled and encouraged by this, Dustin walked quickly between them and through the nearest arch in the Human Grove, until he was standing on the sexagram in the middle of the temple and was face-to-face with Queen Bee.

Queen Bee stood alone in the sexagram. Dustin felt relieved. Faith hadn't yet been sacrificed then.

Today (or was it actually tonight? Dustin imagined he might have been shifted through the hours again on stepping through the human portal), the high priestess was dressed like her acolytes, and her black robe managed to diffuse the seductive effect of her generous mammary endowment.

Dustin didn't need the distraction that seeing her breasts would cause him. The odor in this place was distraction enough.

"Hello, Dustin," Queen Bee told him in a solemn voice. "We're just about to start a ritual to expunge a traitor from our midst. You're welcome to join in, but first you'll need to change your clothes."

Her comment provoked laughter in the temple. Dustin was not in the least bit amused by the amusement he'd generated. He was also worried because Queen Bee was showing not the slightest concern about the gun in his hand.

"Where is Faith?" he asked the old woman. "What have you done with her?"

Queen Bee's eyes narrowed. "Nothing yet," she replied in cold tones. "But, Faith is the traitor I just mentioned. We're about to sacrifice her to the glory of Boku Veeza. Put on a robe and join us."

Dustin shook his head. "No, you're not sacrificing Faith, you old hag. Where is she? Let her go at once!"

Now the high priestess looked angry. "Watch your tongue young man, before I have it cut out."

Dustin's response was to take three paces forward and grab Queen Bee. Then he spun her around, wrapped an arm around her neck and stuck the gun in her back.

His actions caused a loud mumbling in the temple, but no one stepped forward to stop him.

"Now listen to me, you old hag," Dustin whispered angrily to Queen Bee. "Enough of your satanic fun and games. Order Faith released right now. You can kill her crazy sister if you like. You know like I do that Boku Veeza doesn't give a shit who she eats; we're all just meat to her. But you aren't going to kill Faith."

Queen Bee began squirming. "Dustin, I'm warning you!"

Dustin jabbed the gun hard into her back. "And I . . . I'm telling you, Queenie, I'm gonna count to five and if by then you haven't released Faith, I'm gonna shoot you!"

Queen Bee laughed. "You pathetic fool! I have the power to turn you into a worm with a mere command!"

"I'm serious. One . . ."

"Never! Faith betrayed us. She belongs to Boku Veeza now!"

"Two . . ."

"Listen, you little shithead, once we're through sacrificing your silly little lover, we'll castrate you and feed what's left to the goddess too. ALL HAIL BOKU VEEZA!" she then screamed.

"ALL HAIL BOKU VEEZA!" the congregation dutifully intoned, and yet none of them moved to intervene in her plight. Their lack of action now struck Dustin as strange; it seemed like no one bothered to help their high priestess because they didn't believe she was in danger.

Or, do they think she's bulletproof. Or is . . .

He stared up at the far-off ceiling of the temple chamber, in case Boku Veeza lurked up there, waiting to make a meal of him.

But the goddess wasn't floating overheard and so he relaxed a little.

"Three . . ." Dustin said. "And no, you won't dare kill me, because if you do you'll have no one to suck on your filthy asshole!"

Queen Bee laughed nastily. "Oh, you can still suck my grapes without a penis. And I'll first have all of your teeth pulled out, so you can't bite them like you sometimes do."

This threat really worried Dustin.

"Because of this rebellion," Queen Bee went on, "I'm going to torture your little slut girlfriend myself. I'll rip her throat out and drink her blood. I'll let Tanana and Malarkey rape her!"

On hearing this, Dustin got really angry. He remembered how Queen Bee had drunk the blood of that fetus.

Oh no, that isn't gonna happen to Faith. I need to hurt this old cow in some way, so that she won't keep acting like this is all a big joke!

He put off calling out 'Four' and did some quick thinking.

I really don't know what I'm gonna do, if I get up to 'Five,' and this nasty old witch calls my bluff!

Sensing his indecision, Queen Bee laughed. "Sorry, Dustin, but this isn't gonna work. I'll have both you and Faith raped and then—"

"Shut up!" Dustin growled at her, then he quickly slid the gun down to her ass and jabbed her in the hemorrhoids with it. He didn't do this gently; he first pushed the loose rear folds of her robe in deep between her buttocks and then really jammed the gun barrel in there amidst her ass grapes.

So, you'll have us both raped, huh? Have a taste of what an ass-rape feels like!

Queen Bee screamed. She screamed so loud that Dustin let go of her.

Once she was free of Dustin's grasp, Queen Bee wheeled around and slapped him hard in the face. Then she shrieked at him: "You dirty sonofabitch! What the hell did you do that for?"

Dustin's face stung from the slap, but he retained his cool. "That's 'Four,' old lady. Now have Faith brought out here." He waved the gun in Queen Bee's face, then poked her in the left breast with it. "Do it, or I'll stab you in the ass with the gun again . . . this time *under* your robe."

Queen Bee looked like she was going to slap him again, but then she calmed herself.

"Okay," she said. "You can have her if you love her so much."

"I do love Faith," Dustin said. "Enough to die for her if I have to." When the old woman seemed to smile sadly at him, he added. "I don't care if the entire cult of Boku Veeza comes after me after this, I'm not letting you kill Faith. You're not sacrificing her."

Queen Bee nodded and continued smiling.

"Dustin," she said gently. "Why the hell would I kill my own daughter?"

Her statement shook him to his core. He gaped at her. "Your *daughter?*"

She nodded. "Yes, Faith Mills *is* my daughter. My married surname was Mills. Greme is my maiden surname. I reverted back to using it after my divorce."

While Dustin came to terms with what Queen Bee had just said, the old woman turned aside to his right and gestured.

"Okay, girls you can come out now," she said.

CHAPTER 84

"Hey, li'l sis, it's Dustin," Grace Mills said, as she stepped out through the archway in the Human Grove. "He's come to rescue you!"

If Dustin thought he was shocked by his discovery that Faith was Queen Bee's daughter, he was even more shocked when he saw Grace Mills' face.

Oh crap! They're identical twins?

Because, now that Grace Mills wasn't wearing either face paint or a flu mask, her face was indistinguishable from her sister's. In fact, the only way Dustin could currently tell them apart was because Grace's voice was lower in pitch that Faith's.

The two equally beautiful young women stood there smiling at him. Dustin looked confusedly back at them.

"They're twins?" he asked Queen Bee in shock.

While tenderly feeling her ass where Dustin had poked her with his gun, Queen Bee shook her head. "No, they're not. It's the result of the accident they had."

Dustin remembered the scene he'd seen, the vision he'd viewed.

He frowned. "How do you mean?"

"Well," Queen Bee explained, "after the operation, we needed a model to base Grace's new face on, as the plastic surgeons explained it would be impossible to restore her old face."

"So, they made me look like li'l sister here," Grace said. She laughed. "I don't even talk this deep normally. But I had to, so that you'll think we're two different people."

While saying this, her voice had reverted to an exact copy of Faith's voice.

Then Faith laughed. "I can talk low too." And Dustin realized that she'd spoken in that same low vocal register her sister had earlier used.

In fact, he suddenly realized he didn't know which of them was which anymore. Faith could be Grace and Grace could be Faith and . . .

And me? I'm just confused.

"What the hell is going on?" he asked Queen Bee. At some point during the sisters' explanation, he'd lowered his gun. Now, he stuck the gun in his pocket. All the fight had left him, now he just wanted answers. "Why would you arrange for me to date Faith?"

Queen Bee laughed. "Actually, Dustin, all this while you've been dating both of them at the same time." She nodded at his shocked expression. "Meaning of course, that you've been sleeping with both of them too, not just with Faith. Their supposed enmity was mere pretense to make their separation of identity more realistic."

Dustin reflected on this and now it made sense to him, how each time Grace visited, Faith acted differently after she'd left.

He glanced at them both and then looked back at their mother.

Of course, that explains it all. Although they look alike, they could never entirely match their different personalities. As to my never really suspecting anything, I'll put that down to my consuming so much Nif.

Even now, the mental clarity he'd gained from his two days of abstinence was being fast eroded by the psychotronic smell in here. The irresistible odor of the fruits threatened to take him over at any minute, to return him to his place in life, that of a mindless drone at the worm goddess's command. Only his desire for answers helped him hold out. However, his resistance grew weaker by the second; his mind felt like a chunk of cheese at which hungry mice ceaselessly nibbled away. It didn't matter how large the cheese portion was to begin with, sooner or later it would vanish.

"Alright, I think I get that," he told Queen Bee. "But why . . . why make such a fool of me? Did the goddess put you up to it?"

"Sort of," Queen Bee said, with a pleased, though not malicious, look on her face.

"So, what was the whole kidnapping charade about? Why have Grace pretend to abduct Faith? Why have me try to rescue them?"

"It was to prove that you truly loved me," one of sisters said.

Dustin looked at her. "Which one of you are you?"

She smiled back at him. "Okay, baby, sis and I have a few questions for you."

He nodded. By now the smell in the temple had eroded his objections, his mind was once more pliable clay in Boku Veeza's hands.

Question and answer had become one and the same. He knew that sometimes questions had no answers; at other times answers existed without questions prompting them. Most times there was neither question nor answer; neither query nor response was necessary. All that the faithful needed was Nightmare Fuel, the rainbow nectar of their loving worm goddess Boku Veeza.

Glory to Boku Veeza, she who is all in all!

The two young women stared at Dustin, their ocean-blue eyes filled with questions.

"I'm listening," Dustin told the sisters. "Ask away."

"Okay, which of us do you love?" the beautiful young woman on the left asked.

Dustin realized that he didn't know. They looked so gorgeously similar, spoke in the same delightful way.

And, all of this while, I've assumed they were one person anyway.

"Okay, maybe that's a difficult question," the beautiful young woman on the right said. "Here's a simpler one: which of us did you come here to rescue?"

Dustin frowned. He had the same problem of separating their identities. "It could have been either of you. No, that's easy to answer. Hey, who kidnapped who?"

"Maybe neither of us did," one blue-eyed beauty replied.

"Maybe we each kidnapped the other," the other blue-eyed beauty added.

The two young women now began turning around themselves, until Dustin no longer knew who'd initially been standing on the left and who'd been on the right. Finally, one of them was standing in front and the other behind.

"Okay, here's the simplest question of all for you, baby," the sister standing behind told Dustin, leaning her chin on her sister's left shoulder.

"Yeah, this one's *really* simple," her sister agreed. "Okay, sis, on three. One, two, three!"

The two of them slipped their black robes off, so that they were both naked. Next, the sister standing behind stepped sideways, so her body was as fully visible to Dustin as her sister's body was.

"Now, Dustin," the young woman in front asked. "Which one of us makes your cock harder during sex?"

"Oh, come on, darling, this should be an easy one," the young woman behind added. "Is it her . . . or me?"

Dustin stared from one perfect body to the other. His shoulders slumped in defeat.

"Did they fix their bodies too?" he whispered to Queen Bee in confusion.

"You know how jealous young women are of each other," their mother whispered back sympathetically. "Originally, Grace had better tits. But once she'd had her face fixed to look like Faith's, Faith then demanded to have her breasts fixed to look like Grace's . . . as compensation for sharing her 'patented good looks' with her."

"Okay, I give up," Dustin told the sisters. "You've successfully made your point, which is that I'm clearly in love with both of you, I came here to save both of you, and that I like you both equally in bed."

He turned back to Queen Bee. "But, what is this all about? Why did I need to fall in love with them both?"

Now the high priestess grinned broadly. "Oh, Dustin, how lucky you are. Truly, you're the most favored of Boku Veeza's worshippers."

"What? Why?"

"You've been given a second chance to become one of the guardians of Boku Veeza's sacred grove," Queen Bee explained. "Of course, you remember the conditions?"

He nodded. "One man, who loves two women equally, and the two women he loves." He groaned. "Oh shit. But I already had that attempt with Melissa and Jordan. I'm already disqualified."

Queen Bee shook her head. "Apparently not. Boku Veeza herself insisted that I make you a candidate again . . ." Queen Bee gestured over at her daughters, who both smiled sweetly back. "And that these two girls of mine be your guardian wives."

CHAPTER 85

Nightmare Fuel had reclaimed Dustin's soul and what was proposed made perfect sense to his filtered POV.

Everything was Boku Veeza; Boku Veeza was everything.

Dustin looked around the Human Grove, seeming to notice the six holiest worshippers for the first time. Once more he took in the ranks of the robed that surrounded the grove. The cult filled the temple. He felt the expectation that buzzed in their souls like bees.

This is the impossible made fully impossible; the imperfect made perfectly imperfect.

He stared around him, looking from face to face of those six kneeling armless 'holiest ones.' This was like taking a refresher course in how devastating agony could become. The faces of the six with trees growing out of their brains spoke of a pain far beyond human comprehension, a pain that made him jealous of them; because their pain also made them privy to the secrets of their goddess.

His former neighbor Doris Mills knelt directly opposite him. With her tree only half-grown in her brain, she was trapped in her own universe of agony, a cosmos of pain that would only grow worse, because in her own case, her tree's roots were coming out through her nose.

Doris was already suffering greatly. Three large roots had exploded out through her right nostril, completely shredding the flesh on that side of her nose into a bloody floral mess that dripped red. At the moment, just two slim root tendrils had emerged from her left nostril, but given time, they too would certainly first block off the nostril and then rip it wide open like a devil's flower, meaning that Doris Mills would have to breathe through her mouth for all of eternity.

But Dustin knew that Doris was very content with this, as were the rest of her brothers and sisters, a sextet unified by a horrific suffering, a shared hell with benefits that none but them could appreciate.

Great indeed are the horrors of Boku Veeza, Dustin thought.

They were all around him, the crimson truth about his universe was made clear in the blood that spilled from their pierced brains and dripped down their bodies and found its resting place in the deep ruts of the hexagram they knelt around.

He looked up their bleeding bodies, ascended the lines of pain in their faces, and rose up through the roots embedded in their brains like he was the sap of those huge trees in their heads. He felt himself rise into their trunks and fan out through their hefty branches and finally disperse as their leaves and their multicolored fruit. He exited as the trees' endless aroma that pierced the human brain like needles, that filled the mind like hypnosis, that overrode the will at will, that mastered the soul like death.

The fruit of the goddess ripened and fell. One such fruit fell near Dustin and rolled over to his feet.

He picked it up and bit into it. It tasted exactly like *Nif*. It was *Nif*. *Nif* was everything in here; both the secret of the goddess's lust for the pain of her worshippers and the justification of her being so evil.

Dustin ate the fruit and as he did so, he was filled with the memory of how he'd felt a few days ago when his mind had been sucked into the picture in Faith's house and he had watched the terrible beginning of the worm goddess's cult.

He remembered also how he'd felt being one of the guardians of this same grove. It had been fantastic. He wanted that feeling again, forever and ever and ever.

With this memory in his mind, he smiled at Queen Bee.

"I'm ready," he told her. "Let's do this again."

"Fantastic," the old priestess replied him.

"We'll get it right this time," Malarkey the clown assured Dustin as he and Tanana arrived in the sexagram, dragging their elderly female captive between them.

CHAPTER 86

"It's wonderful to see you again, Madison," Queen Bee told the old woman whom Tanana and the clown had brought into the grove. "One always likes to reconnect with old enemies."

Dustin now understood who the old woman was. She was Madison Smith, sister of the late Reverend Paul Smith who'd been abducted and killed by Boku Veeza's followers, and also the mother of Frederick Smith, who, masquerading as Freddy Reid (Reid being Madison's maiden surname) had successfully infiltrated Real Dreams and even become Bianca Sanchez's boyfriend before being found out and quartered for entertainment.

She was in those pictures of the Smith family that Woody showed me on his laptop. That's why I almost recognized her back there.

"You ain't gettin' away this time, old woman," Tanana told Madison with a grin on her face.

"Freddy's dead and soon you'll be meeting him in hell," Queen Bee told Madison.

Madison was gagged and so couldn't reply. Her eyes however spoke for her, revealing in turn her fear, then her sorrow on hearing her sole surviving son was no more, and then her anger and her desire for justice.

Malarkey laughed and forced the old woman to her knees before Queen Bee. "Or maybe, bitch, you'll meet Freddy in that shithole country called heaven," he added mockingly. "Personally, I'm delighted Uncle Lou got us all kicked out of there."

"Yeah," Tanana loudly agreed. "What a boring place. All we did all day long was tell the Old Guy how fantastic he was."

Their comments provoked great laughter from all those assembled in the temple.

Queen Bee clapped her hands. "Alright, quiet down, everyone, and let's get this done." She grinned down at the other old woman. "I'm certain that Madison here is in as much of a hurry to die and meet her God as I am to kill her and send her to Him."

This provoked even more laughter.

When the laughter subsided, Queen Bee turned to her daughters and instructed them: "Girls, get Dustin naked so that we can collect his semen in this infidel bitch's braincase and perform the marriage ceremony to bind you three in Boku Veeza's love."

Dustin sighed in delight as the two soft pairs of female hands hurriedly disrobed him.

Being rescued from my clothes is the perfect end to my rescue attempt.

His penis grew erect as they touched him, and by the time they'd gotten the last of his clothes off, his erection was full and strong. It was also pointing directly at Madison Smith, who pointedly looked away from it.

Queen Bee noticed the old Christian woman's revulsion and mocked her some more: "Maybe, after we've removed the top of your skull, Madison, we should make you suck Dustin off. Then you can watch him ejaculate in your skullcap."

Madison understandably looked horrified at this suggestion. She began working her mouth crazily, trying to remove her gag and say something.

"Don't do it, mom," one of the daughters said. "She might bite Dustin."

"Yeah, and we don't need another screw-up," Malarkey added. "I'm getting tired of the goddess turning down all the applicants. It's like she's looking for excuses to disqualify the candidates."

Tanana nodded. "Yeah, I agree. Sometimes it's like she's intentionally sabotaging our efforts on the slightest pretext. So, best not to give her any."

"Oh, alright," Queen Bee grudgingly agreed. Then she crouched down in front of Madison Smith, hooked her fingers under the kneeling Christian woman's chin and forced her face up. "So, bitch, you don't get to suck dick before dying. Your loss."

Queen Bee straightened up again. "Alright, Tanana, dick sucking and sperm collection duties return to you."

Then she nodded to the demon clown. "Malarkey, get the top of this bitch's head off. No need to be gentle about it, we don't need her brain intact afterwards."

Malarkey laughed as he danced towards Madison. "With pleasure, Queenie. You know I love the taste of infidel brain as much as the goddess does."

CHAPTER 87

Once again, Dustin witnessed the weird visual effect of Malarkey's mouth widening to an impossible extent. And of course, as his mouth got bigger, so too did additional teeth pop into place in it like links in a zipper being revealed by the separation of his flesh.

The additional teeth looked like metal hooks. Dustin knew they were sharp enough to cut bone; he'd watched them do so before.

Dustin found it impossible to describe the look on Madison's face as Malarkey bent down over her with those horrible teeth getting set to clamp down over her head and bite its top off. Her graying blonde hair wouldn't be any kind of an impediment to the demon's teeth cutting through her scalp and skull.

However, there was something in Madison's eyes, that warned Dustin of trouble to come. With her hands bound behind her, he didn't see what she could possibly do except die, but he just *knew* that something was about to go wrong now.

And then it did.

Somehow, right before Malarkey would have clamped his extended jaws over her head, Madison worked her mouth free of the gag.

Then she yelled at Malarkey: "Depart from me, you evil spirit, in the name of Jesus!"

And just like that—Dustin didn't see any divine lightning or any hammer of God strike in the temple—but just like that, Malarkey began melting away.

First, the evil clown shrieked like he was in intense pain. His head began smoking and his eyes popped from his skull, fell to the floor and sizzled into nothing. And then his extended mouth, with those twin rows of zippered metal teeth, also liquified and dripped down.

And then long tears appeared in Malarkey's clown costume, which to Dustin's surprise, was now revealed to be Malarkey's actual skin. The demon clown's weird flesh bubbled and smoked and dissolved and was soon nothing more than a puddle of tallow that discolored the floor of the temple.

While this was happening to Malarkey, everyone had different reactions.

Queen Bee looked horrified and worried. Dustin and the sisters looked surprised, and Tanana looked enraged.

Surprisingly (to Dustin at least), the rest of the worshippers in the temple shrank back in fear when Madison 'cursed' the clown, almost like they were trying to force themselves through the walls of the red chamber and escape from a terrifying unseen force.

Madison herself seemed surprised at what she'd just accomplished. But then she realized that she had an advantage here. If she could do it once, she could do it again. And to the other demon this time.

"You evil demoness," she began saying to Tanana, "I command you—"

Before Madison could finish her exorcism however, Queen Bee kicked her in the back of the head and put out her lights.

Madison fell forward and slammed her head in the middle of Malarkey's drying remains.

CHAPTER 88

"Give me a knife," Tanana growled angrily.

Queen Bee handed her a ritual dagger.

Tanana then pointed down at Madison. "Wake the Bible-thumping bitch up!"

Dustin wondered how this was supposed to be done, as Madison seemed to be out cold.

But it was accomplished easily enough. Faith and Grace pulled the old woman up onto her knees and then Queen Bee opened up Madison's mouth, opened up her own robe, and then pissed in Madison's mouth.

Once Madison Smith began choking on piss, she woke up fast.

"Leave her to me," Tanana said.

While Madison was still sputtering and spitting out urine, Tanana forced the old woman's mouth fully open and grabbed hold of her tongue. The hand with which she gripped Madison's tongue had transformed into something black and shiny, like an insect's foot, and the sharp claws at its tip dug deep into the soft pink tongue flesh, allowing the organ no retreat from its coming fate.

"So, Christian bitch, you like to perform exorcisms, huh?" Tanana told Madison. "Let's see how you curse us demons without a tongue."

Madison tried to get away, but Queen Bee got behind her, standing between her two daughters, and held her head firmly in place. Madison's tongue was already bleeding from the piercing of the claws with which Tanana held it, and now the demoness dragged it well out of her mouth and sliced it off.

Then, leaving Madison Smith with a mouth full of blood, she waved the tongue in the woman's face.

"Let me assure you that infidel tongues taste delish," she said.

While Madison stared at her in disbelief and tried to understand the agony that now filled her mouth, Tanana ate Madison's tongue.

Afterwards, the black demoness nodded to Queen Bee. "Let's conclude the marriage ritual."

"We still need to get the top of her head off," Queen Bee pointed out, after she, Faith, and Grace let go of Madison, who instantly slumped to the floor again.

Tanana shrugged. "So just do it the usual way."

Queen Bee turned towards the members of the congregation closest to the temple door. "Someone find an axe quickly and come chop off the top of this Christian bitch's head!" she ordered.

"Better hurry up before she chokes to death on her own blood!" one of the sisters joked, pointing down at where Madison now rolled in agony on the floor.

And Dustin, his head once more full of mysteries he'd never comprehend, watched all of this in a rapture of delight and with his penis stiff as a bone.

This is the right judgement for all defilers of Boku Veeza, he agreed. *I wish I could ejaculate on her corpse.*

CHAPTER 89

An axe was quickly found and brought. And then, Madison Smith, all of the fight drained out of her now that she had no tongue, was hauled upright again.

"We don't need her entire head," Queen Bee instructed the two muscular men who'd brought the axe. "Just the top of it."

"Ugggh! UgggH!" This was Madison's final attempt to protest, but all that resulted was a revolting oatmeal of blood clots spilling from her mouth.

One man held the old woman's body in place, and the other one held the axe.

"Hurry up, wilya?" Tanana told them. "I'm late for a Tinder date."

The men laughed and then nodded to themselves. Then, the man with the axe swung it at Madison's head.

That was it for Madison Smith. Her head sheared completely in two, with the part above her eyes dropping to the floor. Her two executioners then dragged her aside and dropped her like she was a bad habit.

Queen Bee waved the men away. They departed with the axe.

"I liked this better the way Malarkey did it," Tanana said, gesturing at the blood spilled everywhere. "Dude made a whole lot less mess."

Faith (or Grace) said: "Girlfriend, you're the one who cut out her tongue. That's where most of the bleeding came from."

After rolling her eyes at being reminded of this, Tanana then bent over and picked up the separated portion of Madison's braincase. She plucked out the portion of brain in the braincase, ate that, and then handed the emptied skullcap to Queen Bee. Whatever graying hair hadn't been trimmed by the axe now dangled down from the bony vessel, making it look like an animal turned upside down.

"Fantastic," the high priestess told everyone. "And now that I'm certain we've had this evening's share of entertainment, let's get on with what we're here for."

She pointed to Dustin and then nodded to Tanana. "Milk him."

CHAPTER 90

Being milked was very pleasant. Of course, Dustin would have preferred either Faith or Grace to have performed fellatio on him, but the ritual forbade either of them from touching him until the three of them had been transformed into Boku Veeza's guardians.

Still, Tanana did an excellent job, not the least because, even for a negress she had massive lips.

Finally, Tanana pulled her mouth off of Dustin's penis and masturbated him, skillfully capturing his semen in Madison Smith's bloody skullcap.

Then, while Dustin leaned on his two identical girlfriends to catch his breath, Tanana handed the skullcap to the high priestess.

Queen Been then nodded to her daughters. "Alright, girls, time to bleed you both."

Faith and Grace stepped forward eagerly. Queen Bee made incisions in their palms and collected their blood.

Next, holding the mixture of semen and blood over her head, she pronounced the spell that would bind her daughters to Dustin as a family unit.

Once she finished reciting the spell, Madison's skullcap vanished from her hands.

"You three are now married in the sight of Boku Veeza," Queen Bee announced. "Dustin, you may now kiss the brides!"

And Dustin kissed his two wives and looked forward to the final stage of the ritual.

CHAPTER 91

Because Dustin had been through this before, the ritual flowed past him like water. His one worry was that something would interrupt the flow of the stream like had happened last time.

But so far, so good. Queen Bee led her daughters—his wives—across the sexagram to a predetermined spot and told them to hold one another's hands.

Then she returned to his side and began chanting the spell that would transform the young women into female guardians. The congregation chanted along with her.

At the right moment, orange fire spurted from the eyes of the Human Grove and hit Faith and Grace Mills.

The sisters began burning. They screamed and burned and tried to escape from the orange flames. But the fire had formed a burning wall around them and there was no escape for them, only transformation into Boku Veeza's guardians.

But . . .

Dustin could see that the sisters' bodies were being altered in the midst of the flames, but altered into what? What they were becoming didn't look anything like the fantastic guardian females they were supposed to become.

And then the orange wall of fire winked out and everyone could see what it had just created.

"What the hell is that?" Dustin asked, as did those members of the congregation who could see in through the arches of the Human Grove.

Dustin looked at Queen Bee. The high priestess wasn't speaking at all. She was staring at what her daughters had become in horror, with her mouth open.

She looked at Dustin and he looked back at her, neither of them able to either believe or comprehend what they were seeing.

CHAPTER 92

What lay where the Mills sisters had stood looked like a mess of burger patty. It was simply an orange mass of meat. It dripped juices, and Dustin saw fingers and toes poking out of it at points.

Staring closer at it, he made out a single blue eye in its top surface.

He thought the mess on the floor was dead, but then the blue eye blinked.

No one had yet moved. All those present in the temple were frozen by the sense of horror that the burger-like mass of flesh naturally created. The mess contracted and expanded like it was breathing.

"It's alive," Tanana told Queen Bee. "But what the hell is it?"

Queen Bee made no reply. She had tears in her eyes.

Finally, Queen Bee walked forward and crouched beside the orange mess and prodded it with a finger.

At her touch, the orange bulk mewled loudly, "Stop, mom, that hurts!" and Dustin knew he was hearing Faith and Grace's mingled voices in that single cry.

Queen Bee slumped and fainted.

And as she hit the floor, the temple began fading from around Dustin again.

Oops, not again, he thought as everyone except Queen Bee and Tanana vanished from around him.

CHAPTER 93

When their location stabilized again, Dustin discovered that the three of them were in Boku Veeza's chamber.

He also saw that the revolting orange mass of quivering flesh that had recently been the gorgeous Faith and Grace Mills had made the journey too.

Worryingly, the girl's remains now lay atop the worm goddess's feeding mound.

"Hello, Dustin," Boku Veeza said.

He waved up at her. "Hi."

Oh yeah, now we're all in for it. We've done something wrong, and now the goddess is gonna eat us all.

"No, I'm not going to eat you all," Boku Veeza replied in his mind.

While speaking, she was smiling at him. Her smile puzzled him. Just like when she'd told him that an excessive exposure to her person destroyed human brain cells, she seemed almost embarrassed.

Queen Bee was just coming out of her faint. On realizing where they were, she almost fainted again, but Tanana kept her awake and pulled her to a sitting position with her back against one of the casks that the goddess's husband Michael was busy filling.

Most of that guy's brain cells must've died by now, Dustin thought. *Dude don't even seem to notice we're in here.*

Dustin looked back at Queen Bee. The high priestess was staring up at Boku Veeza with hatred on her face.

"What the fuck, you worm-bitch?" Queen Bee asked, pointing over at the blob of orange meat. "What have you just done to my girls?"

"They are my most beloved worshippers now," Boku Veeza replied with a smile totally unlike that which she'd just given Dustin. Where her smile for him had seemed uncertain, this one was cold and imperial, the smile of a supreme being who was sure of her position. The worm goddess squirmed about on her silver throne. "Soon, I will eat both of them," she said, "and they will be part of me forever."

"Don't let her eat us, mom!" the mess of meat screamed. "Save us!"

"Shut up!" Boku Veeza warned the meat.

The orange mass fell silent, but began squirming as if trying to get away. The fingers and toes on its surface became extremely active, but seemingly they were all on its upper side, which was clearly the wrong side of its body for locomotion. As it were, the wiggling digits could only gain purchase on the air.

Dustin frowned at the nauseating sight.

Yes, here at Real Dreams craziness is the norm, but there is such a thing as too much crazy.

"Hey, you can't eat them, or even leave them like that," he told Boku Veeza. "They're my wives and I love them both."

"Thou shall love no other goddess but me," Boku Veeza thundered, so loud that Dustin and Queen Bee had to cover their ears.

"Yeah, yeah, that's easy for you to say," Dustin said when the echoes of the goddess's voice had subsided, "but you can't keep killing my wives. This is the second time that you've screwed up my relationships. What do you expect me to do afterward? Smile and praise you?"

Boku Veeza looked angrily down at him. He glared just as angrily back up at her, daring her to do something.

"Listen here, *you're* the one who set this guardian thing up," he went on. "And now, you're the one who's fucking up your own setup. Try to be consistent: either you want a trio of guardians, or you don't. If you simply want a human three-course meal occasionally, just damn well say so."

The expression on Boku Veeza's face was chilling. "Your ice is thin, human. Don't slide on it."

But Dustin didn't care anymore. Fed by his anguish on seeing what had happened to Faith and Grace, and the memory of what had happened to Melissa and Jordan before them, an intense rage had broken through his *Nif* haze.

"Hey, I don't give a shit if the ice breaks and I fall through it. I've figured out that the worst you can do is eat me."

"And afterwards make you part of her anus for all eternity," Tanana whispered. "Seriously, man, don't push her too hard."

Dustin looked down at Queen Bee, who was once more weeping. Then he looked back up at the worm goddess, who'd now begun uncoiling herself from her throne.

"You're making me hungry," Boku Veeza threatened, as her brown bulk squirmed and twisted. "And I see only one possible thing here to eat."

"Don't eat us! Please!" the orange meat shrieked in that single voice that was actually two separate voices.

"Please don't eat my daughters!" Queen Bee pleaded with tears running down her cheeks.

Boku Veeza paused a short distance from the meat. She smiled coldly and triumphantly at Dustin. "See?" she said. "Your high priestess understands and accepts her puny place in my scheme of things, even if you don't. What do you say now?"

Dustin didn't know how he knew, but he could tell she was bluffing. For some reason, Boku Veeza didn't wish to offend him.

What the hell?

He decided to call her bluff. The smell of her in here was the air, but he managed to resist her elixir's attempt to rule his mind.

"What I say, honey," he told Boku Veeza, "is that you return both Faith and Grace Mills back to their human forms, and then you and I can discuss whatever it is that you really brought us here to talk about."

The look the goddess gave him then, assured him that she was merely two drops of saliva away from eating him.

"What? You . . . you . . . d-d-dare order me-me-me a-about?" she stuttered at him.

"Dude, I'm a warnin' ya," Tanana whispered to him.

"Don't worry, I got this," Dustin whispered back. "There's more to all of this than meets the eye. She wants something from me and she knows she won't get it if she screws me over."

Boku Veeza swelled up like she would burst, her humongous coils and segments exuding odor like pleasant farts. But then she settled down again.

"Alright, I won't eat them yet," she told Dustin, with an expression on her Native American face like she wanted to scalp him. "Now we can talk."

He shook his head. "Uh uh. No talk yet. Restore them both back to their human form *before* we talk. You've no reason or right to treat your own loyal followers like they're your shit."

Boku Veeza looked like she would explode into a rage again, but then she nodded. "Alright."

The next moment there was a flash of orange light and both Faith and Grace Mills were back as themselves on the goddess's feeding mound.

Both beautiful young women shrieked in fear, leapt down, and instantly ran over to grasp Dustin.

"Baby, baby, baby! Oh, thank God! She was going to eat us like we're infidels!"

"Step away from Dustin!" Boku Veeza told the sisters. "I said—step away from him!"

They stared up at her in fright, uncertain what to do. After all, Dustin was the one who'd just won them their freedom.

"Step away from Dustin," the goddess warned the two young women again. "He belongs to me now. He's my husband now, not yours anymore."

"What?" simultaneously exclaimed everyone in the goddess's chamber, with the exception of Boku Veeza's husband Michael.

"What?" Dustin repeated.

From atop her silver throne, Boku Veeza glared down at the Mills sisters: "I, your goddess Boku Veeza, am a very jealous goddess. Now get away from Dustin, you two young fools, or you go back to being hamburger meat again."

The sisters hurriedly scrambled over to their mother's side.

"Da fuck is worm girl talkin' 'bout?" Tanana asked Dustin.

"Fuck me dead if I know," he replied.

CHAPTER 94

"I've come to understand my feelings for Dustin," Boku Veeza told everyone after Faith and Grace had helped Queen Bee back up to her feet. The goddess smiled to herself. "I've realized that I'm in love with Dustin. That is why I both like and dislike him; why I want to eat him and want to feed him at the same time."

Oh, shit! Dustin thought on hearing this. *She wants me? How unlucky can one guy be?*

Boku Veeza smiled down at the group of humans and demoness. "So that's why I disrupted the ritual to make the grove's guardians. I decided that the person I love must not be with my priestess's two daughters. He's mine and mine alone. Do any of you have a problem with this?"

No one said anything. But then Tanana raised her hand.

"Yes, what is your objection, demoness?" Boku Veeza asked her.

"So, alright, I get it that you love Dustin and all that," Tanana said, "but you're already fucking married." She gestured sideways at Michael, who, as if he was alone in here with his infernal 'wife,' was just returning from storing casks near the chamber entrance and was not paying the slightest attention to what they were doing or saying. "Do you really want *two* husbands? Won't that be like a conflict of emotions?"

Boku Veeza considered this like she'd not previously considered it. Then she nodded. "Good point."

Her next action was to extend her neck down towards them and suddenly snap her head sideways and engulf Michael in her mouth. She chewed for a few moments and then swallowed. Then she frowned down at them all.

"I'm no longer married," she told them. "Any other objections?" After speaking, she began trying to suck out a scrap of denim jacket that had become stuck between her lower incisors.

"Don't I have a choice in the matter?" Dustin asked Boku Veeza.

"No. If you don't love me like I love you, if you don't love me best of all, I will assume you love the priestess's daughters better than myself and I will consume them both."

Spoken out aloud, her voice was saccharine when she said this, but there was no mistaking the threat that her words conveyed to her listeners.

Dustin looked miserably at the Mills sisters. They both had tears in their eyes. "We love you, Dustin!" one of them said.

He looked at Queen Bee. Her eyes were pleading with him, begging him to accept to be the goddess's husband.

"Alright, I'll marry you," Dustin replied Boku Veeza.

He sighed. And now that he'd won one battle and then promptly lost another (now that he'd both saved the women he loved and immediately been forced to relinquish them), now he decided to simply let the smell of *Nif* in the goddess's chamber purge his worries and misery from his mind.

"I sure as hell don't envy ya, baby," Tanana told him.

The demoness sounded like she honestly sympathized with him.

"Now, everyone else depart and leave Dustin and I alone," Boku Veeza said.

With a look of immense gratitude to Dustin on her face, Queen Bee hurried her weeping daughters out of the goddess's chamber.

"I'm going too," Tanana said and quickly followed them.

"Now, Dustin my beloved," Boku Veeza said sweetly, when they were all alone in her chamber, "come close to me and let's get better acquainted. We will be in love for ever and ever and ever and ever and ever and ever. Isn't that a nice thing?"

"It's the most wonderful thing imaginable," Dustin replied as he walked over to her side and sat beside her on her throne.

Then the goddess worm spoke sweet nothings in his mind and dripped rainbow rivers of *Nif* all over him.

CHAPTER 95

The job of being Boku Veeza's husband was entirely repetitive.

All day long Dustin ladled rainbow worm milk into casks, then he watched Boku Veeza feast on infidel flesh, and then when she was quite full, she popped out one of those big wormy eggs for him to impregnate.

This was only fun part of it: the queer sex each time she popped an egg out. Dustin couldn't deny that he enjoyed that part of things. The eggs secreted something about his penis that made him feel he was one with the goddess.

For her part, the goddess definitely felt they were one whenever he had sex with her eggs. It was strange watching the worm-female shiver in orgasm, just like a human woman would do.

At first, Queen Bee regularly brought Dustin his meals in person. But after a while she stopped doing so at Dustin's own request, because Dustin discovered that he could survive on *Nif* alone.

Boku Veeza kept trying to get him to eat human flesh with her, but he continued resisting her efforts.

Now, Dustin never knew what time of day it was. Similarly, he no longer knew how long he'd even been living here with the worm goddess—had it been weeks, months, or even years or decades?

Most of the time, the sheer smell of *Nif* that surrounded the goddess had him high as a kite. Add to this the fact that Boku Veeza liked him to sleep next to her on her throne or wrapped up in her coils, and it was no surprise that Dustin's thoughts were generally about nothing else but his wife's glory.

In a short while, he'd more-or-less forgotten both Faith and Grace Mills. And possibly fearing for their lives if they showed the slightest further interest in him, both young women hadn't once shown their faces in the goddess's chamber since Boku Veeza had commandeered him for herself.

So, most times Dustin thought of nothing else except Boku Veeza.

However, sometimes, the *Nif* haze cleared from Dustin's brain just a little and then he did think of other things.

215

When this happened, he discovered that his worm-wife could care less what he thought about her.

She laughed in his mind when he thought she was disgusting and evil and a murderous bitch. She agreed completely with these impressions of her, and liked to be viewed that way.

She laughed too, when he thought she was ugly, because she knew this wasn't true. True, her annelid body was repulsive, but facially, she was as beautiful as the most attractive Real Dreams females.

Dustin discovered that what Boku Veeza liked most about his negative thoughts, was their sense of helplessness. Boku Veeza loved how weak Dustin felt, how powerless compared to her. She loved the feeling of futility that filled him on realizing that, hate her all he wanted, he couldn't move her any more than a wind can move a mountain.

At such times, Dustin was consumed by an overwhelming sense of terror; the terror that a human experiences when he encounters something so far beyond logical comprehension that he may just as well not exist when compared to it.

Boku Veeza loved this. She loved Dustin like this.

CHAPTER 96

But then, one day Dustin's thoughts veered to the rebellious. A simmering thought boiled over.

He remembered what had happened when Madison Smith had called on the name of Jesus. She'd successfully melted Malarkey down into clown pulp.

Hey, I wonder what will happen if I try something similar in—

But before he could complete the thought, Boku Veeza's unearthly voice filled his skull, cold and sharp as a knife.

"Dustin, darling," she said in saccharine-sweet tones of endearment. "I love you more than I have ever loved anyone else, as much as it is possible for a goddess to love a mere mortal. But, if you dare mention that hated name in here, if you dare mention that Jewish messiah you're thinking of now anywhere near me, I will eat you. Do you understand me clearly, darling? Do that and *I will* eat you."

"Yes," Dustin managed to say.

"You are mine forever. The other God can't ever have you."

Dustin nodded up at the giant woman-worm he was wedded to. "Of course, darling."

"Wonderful. Oh, Dustin, I love you so much. Come sit beside me. Come, come, come quickly!"

Powerless to resist, with his thoughts once more ceasing to be his own, Dustin went over and sat by her.

Surrounded by the intoxicating *Nif* smell of her, he began wondering how long it would be before his brain cells began dying too. That would be a great release.

A low IQ will be freedom from this heavenly hell. Only, it doesn't seem to be happening to me. My thoughts seem as clear as ever.

Then suddenly, a worrisome thought hit him:

Oh, my dear God, please no. I hope I'm not that one-in-a-zillion person who's immune to the brain-corroding effects of her Nightmare Fuel!

The loud goddess-laughter that filled his mind after he thought this seemed to confirm his suspicions.

"Am I?" he asked her. "Is that the real reason why you love me so much? Because I'm immune to your *Nif?*"

Boku Veeza laughed some more; he could hear the delight in her voice. "Maybe and maybe not," she replied. "It doesn't matter either way. Either way you'll stay mine forever and ever and ever and ever and ever and ever."

Yes. Either way, Dustin Mitchell was going to have a hell of a long time to find out.

The End.

ABOUT THE AUTHOR

Wol-vriey is Nigerian, and quite tall.

He believes there actually are things that go bump in the night.

He writes horror fiction—for adults only, please. And also some surrealist stuff.

Wol-vriey blogs at: *http://odditufarm.wordpress.com*

WOL-VRIEY
BIZARRO AND TRANSGRESSIVE FICTION

BOSTON POSH (BUD MALONE #1)

In 2028 AD, the USA is a nation ravaged by hungry dragons and dinosaurs. In Boston, Massachusetts, private eye Bud Malone is hired to rescue a kidnapped heiress. But nothing is as it seems.

Malone works to unravel a tangled web involving Boston Chinatown, a 200-year-old woman with a 9-year-old body, white robots, a human-liver-eating psychopath, a golem, a porcelain dragon, and a snake goddess with a crush on him. There's also a woman obsessed with chicken sex. Then Malone meets Posh Lane, a gorgeous call girl who's desperate to quit her pimp.

Romantic sparks ignite between Posh and Malone, but Posh's past suddenly catches up with her in a BIG way. To save Posh, Malone agrees to run a quest for Earth's new rulers, the Forks. But, Malone has no idea that agreeing to the Fork's odd request will send him on the weirdest trip he's ever been on in his life.

BOSTON CORPSE (BUD MALONE #2)

MAGIC CAN BE MURDER! - Drag queen Lucy Tang is back in Boston, and is hell-bent on settling her vindetta against casino owner Sookie Ling. And suddenly, Bud Malone, PI, has the case of his life to resolve.

When Boston's robot police force are baffled by a mind transfer case, they come to Malone for help. The one person who can likely help Malone out here is the witch Soledad Bathory. But Soledad seems to know a lot more than she's telling him. It's a case not made easier when Malone meets Soledad's beautiful cousin, Josephine 'Slave' Bailey. Slave has her own plans for Malone, most of which involve teaching him BDSM and making him her new Master.

Oh, and Rick Rogers owes Sookie Ling a whole lot of money, a gambling debt that's going to be literally Hell to pay!

BOSTON CORPSE - Not your average detective novel!

Burning Bulb

WOL-VRIEY
BIZARRO AND TRANSGRESSIVE FICTION

BOSTON LUST (BUD MALONE #3)

"Bless it, Father, for she has sinned."

Seven murdered gay women, all their bodies completely drained of blood. All also with large parts of their bodies dissolved away like acid has been pumped into their veins.

Bud Malone has to find the female vampire preying on Boston's lesbian population.

Then Malone meets the beautiful Trudi Carmen and the case gets even more tangled. Trudi needs Malone's help in recovering a ring that's gone missing. But how in the world is one little black ring related to either the dead women or their killer?

Resolving this case will lead Malone deep into Lucy Tang's legacy —The Abstracta. And then to the city of Genesis.

Boston Lust —Just when you thought Bean Town was safe to visit again.

HELL DANCER

Six people find themselves trapped in Detention, a nightmare realm where the demonic Schoolmaster is hell-bent on reforming them . . . until they die.

Porn superstar Venus Deluxe came to Springfield, MA to party, and next found her life hanging by a thread. One wrong answer will mean her death.

Suspended BPD detective Tanya Rockford was trying to stop one kind of violence, but found a terrifying another. With her and her companion's lives hanging in the balance, it's going to take all of her courage and resourcefulness to escape this hell she's stumbled into.

Porn stud Chad Cannon has made a career from his ten-inch penis. Here in Detention, however, it's his brains that matter. He'll soon be hoping all the pot he's smoked over the years hasn't completely messed up his memory.

The three students, Sherri, Jordan, and Mike? They were all just in the wrong place at the right time. Will anyone survive Detention?. The evil Schoolmaster doesn't plan on letting that happen . . . .

Burning Bulb
PUBLISHING

WOL-VRIEY
BIZARRO AND TRANSGRESSIVE FICTION

VAGINA MUNDI

Rachel Risk is a professional thief with super-strong hair that can stretch like tentacles to manipulate objects. Ashley Status has both a digitally augmented brain, and 'muscle-purses' in her arms and legs in which she stores inflatable objects—cars, guns, rocket launchers, etc.

When Raye is framed as the fall girl in a jewel robbery, the pair flee Chicago's vengeful robot gangsters and take refuge in the Hotel Bizarre, where the gorgeous 'vagina singer,' Femina, is performing for a week.

But the Hotel Bizarre is even stranger than its name suggests, and very soon Raye and Ash are involved in a deadly adventure, a struggle for survival the likes of which they'd never imagined possible with loads of deviant sex, drugs, music, and violence at every turn. And just what is the old woman in the skin desert really doing with all those cats glued to her walls?

VAGINA MUNDI—a Bizarro Hymn in praise of WOMAN!

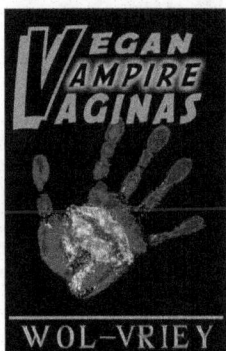

VEGAN VAMPIRE VAGINAS

The biggest bank heist in US history. And Tom Palmer can't remember pulling it off. And no, this isn't your standard case of amnesia. After a one-night-stand gone horribly wrong, Boston salesman Tom Palmer wakes up with a vagina implanted in his left hand. Then his day gets worse.

Tom is transported across space-time to a nightmare version of Boston, one where the Bizarro virus has transformed half the population into cannibals. Worst of all, Tom discovers that in this new Boston, he's the infamous gangster Pussypalm, wanted for robbing the Federal Reserve Bank of Boston a year ago. He also learns that the vagina in his hand is prophetic, i.e. it talks . . . after sex.

With 130 people left dead during his bank heist and six billion dollars missing, Tom knows he's living on borrowed time. It is in his best interests not to remember anything. Because once he does . .

Burning Bulb

WOL-VRIEY
BIZARRO AND TRANSGRESSIVE FICTION

VEGAN ZOMBIE APOCALYPSE

In the post-apocalypse worlderness, zombies rule the earth. They're allergic to meat, and brains literally make them explode. Zombies now eat blood potatoes, parasitic tubers grown in the flesh of humancows corralled in maximum security farms. Two fugitives meet in the ancient ruins of Texas. The first is Soil 15-f, a womancow who's escaped her farm a week before she's due to be killed and her blood potato crop harvested. The second fugitive is Able Kane, former head necros food technician, now sentenced to death for heresy. But Soil is no ordinary humancow.

Unknown to herself, she's the vegan zombie agricultural revolution, and the zombies desperately want her back. And the necros equally desperately want Able Kane dead. He's fled with a forbidden discovery which will reshape the world for the worse if used. And Able is just hardheaded/misguided enough to use it.

MELANIE NEMESIS CATCHPOLE

In Springfield, Massachusetts, Melanie Catchpole is hired to fetch back a magic teddy bear worth millions of dollars from a warehouse across town. Problem is, the warehouse is down in Springfield's O-Zone that totally weird sector of the city where Bizarro fell to Earth. The 'O' is a fairytale land, a place where dreams and nightmares literally live and breathe..

Worse still, the gingers—mutant cannibals—prowl the O. The gingers have already eaten everyone else Melanie's employers sent to get back the magic teddy bear.

Accompanied by the handsome but ruthless Doug Fisher (who she finds sexy but doesn't dare entrust her heart to), Melanie enters the O-Zone. Melanie and Doug are instantly caught up in an adventure they'd never have believed credible even if written as fiction . . . and Melanie's used to experiencing the very weird as the norm.

And now, additionally, there's a mystery to unravel: What does the dark, freezing-cold being called The Fixer want with Mary, the barkeep's daughter?

Burning Bulb
PUBLISHING

WOL-VRIEY
BIZARRO AND TRANSGRESSIVE FICTION

BIG TROUBLE IN LITTLE ASS

From Bizarro master storyteller Wol-vriey comes a truly weird western tale that will leave you awe-struck and on the edge of your seat...

In the town named Little Ass, tight-assed prostitute Rosa overhears a gunslinger's plans to assassinate rancher Edison Bennett. Once the badass Bennett learns of the plot, he ensures there'll be hell to pay for any attempt on his life!

Yes, it's going to take all of gunslinger Jude's shooting prowess, his eclectic collection of strange firearms, a trusty horse that requires an owners' manual, and the help of the lovely and invigorating Nell (who's EXTREMELY odd when the going gets weird), to survive the Bizarro hell that Edison Bennett unleashes in order to hold onto the land that he'd stolen from Madam Zizi.

BIZARRO 101 (A BASIC PRIMER)

Welcome to the strange place:

A collection of 37 flash fiction stories designed to introduce one to the Bizarro/New Weird Genre.

Weird, dreamy, nightmarish, absurd, sad, surreal, humorous . . . this collection of tales is all this and more.

***

"This primer is the very essence of any and all styles and types of Bizarro writing. Wol-vriey collects, distills, and bottles up these 37 tiny stories for your sensory enjoyment. This is an absolute must-read for anyone new to the genre, because it demonstrates the scope of what Bizarro is, and what it can be."
                    —Teresa Pollack, Bizarro commentator and blogger

Burning Bulb

WOL-VRIEY
BIZARRO AND TRANSGRESSIVE FICTION

Dr. Orgasm

Courtney Taylor is young, intelligent, beautiful, and successful. She also has a boyfriend who loves her deeply. The problem is, no matter what Courtney does, she can't climax during sex.

When Florence Rigid's communist forces destroy the city of Metaphor, Courtney and her friends Teresa, Highball, Miki, and Heather are cast into the midst of a quest to find the only person able to save the land of Innuendo—Dr. Carol Orgasm, wanted by the communists for developing the O-Pill, a wonder drug that grants women sexual ecstasy on demand.

The communists will do anything to get their hands on the O-Pill and prevent its reaching the millions of Innuendo's women. But Courtney desperately wants that pill too. And so it's now a race between Courtney and the communists to find Dr. Orgasm first.

And Courtney has no choice but to win this race. She must win it: For her own orgasm . . . and for the freedom of female sexuality everywhere.

PUSSY TRANSMISSION

Pussy Transmission were the most decadent Pop Art ensemble of the 90's. Led by the beautiful painter Isis Lynch, the trio revolutionized the art world. Then suddenly, without explanation, Pussy Transmission vanished into historical obscurity. Now, twenty years later, three women come to Lynch Place. Lily and Nina are journalists desperate to interview Isis Lynch. Raven, on the other hand, wants to find her boyfriend, who's gone missing inside Isis's house. Raven's worried—she's heard that Pussy Transmission broke up because Isis began dabbling in black magic . . . with devastating results. All three women will shortly wish they'd never left home. Particularly once the rats in Lynch Place start warning them that they're going to die . . . and Raven meets Betty Butcher, the bouncy supernatural psycho who's intent on chopping her into bits. Pussy Transmission, Baby! Just because . . .

Burning Bulb

WOL-VRIEY
BIZARRO AND TRANSGRESSIVE FICTION

GIRLS ARE NOT SMILING

Welcome To The Road Trip From Hell

Pagan is demon-possessed.

Lori is suicidal.

Britt is just terminally pissed off.

Meet three young Boston women on the run from the law, each with problems that will fuse into more than the sum of their individual parts, becoming a holocaust of sex and violence and terror, a literal rain of blood and horror and gore and evil.

And if that wasn't already bad enough, Pagan's pet demon is slowly transforming her into something both unspeakable and unholy. Truly, these girls aren't smiling.

BLUE NIGHTMARES

Consummate EVIL is coming. It is relentless and unavoidable. It is Blue.

Jessica Schreiber is seeing things. Very horrible things. Since arriving in Raynham for what should have been a relaxing vacation, she's been seeing *The Big Blue*.

Jessica is smelling things too—dead and rotting things that she can't see. She is sure those dead and rotting things are dead people. Lots of dead people.

Jessica's worst nightmares will soon become her reality. Her reality will soon become a terrifying nightmare.

The tentacled residents of the House of Death have a lot that they wish to show Jessica Schreiber. They have a lot that they wish to tell her. But will she survive long enough to learn their lessons?

Burning Bulb
PUBLISHING

WOL-VRIEY
BIZARRO AND TRANSGRESSIVE FICTION

BRAINCHEW

It was supposed to be a simple jewel heist, but it went badly wrong. Chuck got shot and died.

Lance hid his friend's corpse in the Pleasant Street Cemetery. But that was a big mistake—there was something undead, something extremely hungry . . . something eXXXtremely horrible, buried in the Pleasant Street Cemetery.

And Lance had just woken it up.

They called the monster Brainchew because it ate brains. Human brains. And it preferred those brains fresh from the heads . . . of the living.

And now it was awake again, Brainchew planned on feeding big-time tonight. Oh hell yes, it did.

BRAINCHEW 2: OUT OF THEIR HEADS

After Tiff Hooper recognizes Josh Penham, the man who abducted her and kept her in his basement and abused her, she brings her three friends to Raynham for a night of well-deserved revenge on him.

Only things don't go according to plan.

It is never a good idea to leave a corpse in Raynham's Pleasant Street Cemetery. You run the very real risk of awakening what lies underground there. And that thing—Brainchew—is more horrible and more evil than anything the average mind conceives of even in its worst nightmares.

Brainchew is back! And this time the monster is extra-hungry. But there are plenty of delicious human brains about tonight, and Brainchew intends to eat them all before dawn.

Burning Bulb

WOL-VRIEY
BIZARRO AND TRANSGRESSIVE FICTION

DARIA: AN EROTIC NIGHTMARE

Even the best laid women can go wrong.

Daria Simpson is HUNGRY. She's HUNGRY for sex and bloodshed and death.

Shelly Parker just wanted to have a threesome with her boyfriend Craig and her best friend Erica. Everything was shaping up nicely for their weekend of sexual fun and games, until they stopped at the creepy Crossway Diner and met Daria.

From the moment they met Daria, EVERYTHING went wrong for them; and it went wrong in the most horrific and terrifying of ways!

Daria: Paranormal service has been resumed.

WET BONES

Greg is about learning the hard way that you don't mess with Aunt Grace.

Nine completely fleshless skeletons recovered in the Massachusetts woods. Two detectives on the trail of a horrible, hungry monster.

Broken-hearted Allie Jackson has a date with a creature from Hell.

Things are about to get well out of hand for everyone, and in horrifying, terrifying ways they don't expect.

Burning Bulb
PUBLISHING

WOL-VRIEY
BIZARRO AND TRANSGRESSIVE FICTION

MR. UGLY

When a rotting corpse appears and starts butchering Raynham's youths, there's really only one question that needs answering:

Is this faceless and rotting monster Peter Howard, or isn't it?

Problem is, Peter Howard died 15 years ago. So how can he possibly be back from the dead and murdering people with such relentless and incredible brutality?

Peter's mother Malicia who's just been released from the lunatic asylum may have the answers to the crazy puzzle, but the two detectives investigating the deaths don't even know the right questions to ask her yet.

BRUTAL

Jane Winters is 28 years old.

She works as a checkout cashier in a department store. She's an attractive woman with a winning personality. She has both a photographic memory and an I.Q. of 189.

She's met the man of her dreams.

But she's also a cannibal with a unique and very scary mode of operation.

The group known as TULIP (The Urban Legend Investigation People) are out to either prove or disprove the legend of Insane Jane.

But have TULIP bitten off more than they can chew?

Burning Bulb

WOL-VRIEY
BIZARRO AND TRANSGRESSIVE FICTION

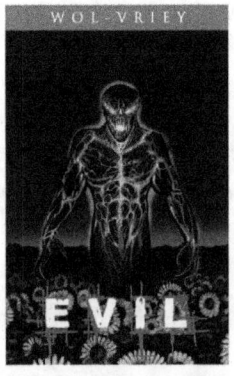

EVIL

The Evil began the week before Sylvia Stewart's 30th birthday.

Cathy Higgins died.

The Bargainer resurrected Cathy . . . for a price.

The price? Cathy's father Ronan had to plant some seeds for him.

But these were no ordinary seeds the Bargainer gave to Ronan Higgins. These were seeds from Hell: seeds which required human flesh as both soil and fertilizer.

And meanwhile, the unsuspecting Sylvia Stewart went ahead with the plans for her birthday party, which was to be held on Ronan Higgins' sunflower farm . . .

666

Ohio's State Route 666 stretches 14.7 miles between Zanesville and Dresden.

Most days, it's just a normal road with a funny name.

But for six minutes on the 6th of June each year, Route 666 becomes a gateway to somewhere else . . . a gateway to Hell.

Each year 13 unfortunates get trapped in the 666 underworld, with no way to get back home.

This year though, things are going to be very different. For one thing, there are currently a whole lot of turbulent human emotions at play in the underworld. And also . . . the psycho Al Gore is just about completing his collection of human heads.

And . . . what the hell is a church doing in Hell, of all places?

Burning Bulb

WOL-VRIEY
BIZARRO AND TRANSGRESSIVE FICTION

THE CLEAVERMAN

It began as a joke, a gag to pass the time that turned deadly. One rainy August night in Raynham, MA, nine friends jokingly invoke the evil phantom butcher called the Cleaverman.

These nine friends get a whole lot more than they ever bargained for. Because there's only one way to return the deadly Cleaverman back to the darkness he came from, and that is to solve his riddle, which starts: "Tell me the name of John Cleaverman's wife . . ."

And human beings being what we are, even with the Cleaverman out to butcher them all, our nine friends still manage to stir A WHOLE LOT of human misbehavior into the deadly mix.

At the rate they're going, it'll be a wonder if anyone survives THE CLEAVERMAN at all.

PERVERSE

When 21-year-old Heather Forrest accompanies three of her friends on a weekend trip up to Vermont, she has no idea what she's getting into.

Because, during a brief stop in the western Massachusetts woods, the girls get kidnapped and things go rapidly downhill from there. Soon Heather and her friends are fighting for their lives, fighting to survive the most perverted and impossible situation imaginable. And meanwhile, Hank Rollins is also in the woods, hunting the unholy monster that killed his wife and son . . . and he's hunting it with live human bait.

Oh yes, there will be blood. And there will be terror and buckets of gore also. And truly horrible atrocities will happen. Most definitely so.

Burning Bulb
PUBLISHING

WOL-VRIEY
BIZARRO AND TRANSGRESSIVE FICTION

THE VIRGIN

10 million dollars in prize money. 1000+ video cameras, lots of deadly weapons, 10 Suitors, 5 Virgins & 3 Hours . . . to keep your hymen intact.

Hailey Osborne wants to sell her virginity for a hundred thousand dollars. But then she's made an offer she really can't refuse: how about competing to win ten million dollars in a no-holds-barred underground game show, where all she has to do is remain a virgin?

There's just two problems:
1. Four other women also want that prize money.
2. There's ten suitors all contesting to take Hailey and the other virgins' precious hymens . . . by any means necessary . . .

But hey, it's just for 3 hours, right? How hard can it possibly be ? Hailey Osborne is about to find out.

THE BOOK OF ATROCITIES

Bestselling author Drake Melville has been missing for three years now. Drake vanished after publishing The Bleeding Oysters, an epic novel that set new standards for depictions of sleaze and depravity and human monstrosity in popular fiction. On vanishing, however, Drake Melville left a message for everyone, saying he'd 'left town' to go work on his follow-up novel The Book of Atrocities. The problem was, no one could find Drake. It seemed like he'd vanished off the face of the Earth. And now, three years later, Drake has just sent messages to his ex-wife Liz, his current (and abandoned) wife Melody, and his younger sister Chloe . . . asking them to meet him in Raynham, MA. Drake says he's now completed The Book of Atrocities and is ready to present it to the world. But there's a whole lot that Liz, Melody, and Chloe Melville don't know about Drake's Book of Atrocities. And unfortunately they're on their way to find out those excruciatingly painful truths. Because, see, Drake Melville is a VERY EVIL man with a VERY EVIL plan . . .

Burning Bulb

WOL-VRIEY
BIZARRO AND TRANSGRESSIVE FICTION

THE FINAL GIRL

Here there be monsters . . . because we made them.

At a secret location, 8 young women assemble to compete on the ultimate reality/game show—The Final Girl. The 8 contestants are: A young wife and her grown-up stepdaughter, a police detective, a prostitute, a nurse, a school teacher, and unemployed twin sisters.

The Final Girl is a no-holds-barred show beamed to an audience on the Dark Web, a show where murder is permitted and mutilation is encouraged.

The Rules:
1. Avoid being killed and eaten by the show's monsters and bogeymen.
2. Find the prize money—24 million dollars in cash.
3. Hold on to the money.

But only 1 woman can win. And to win The Final Girl reality show, that woman will need to be even more bloodthirsty and ruthless than the show's monsters.

Have a seat, everyone. The most dangerous game is about to begin!

WOMEN

John Miller must die . . . TONIGHT!

Megan Kemp initially went to the Penderson Mansion to collect a debt. But from the moment she stepped in there, getting back outside proved extremely difficult. And then what had merely been difficult for Megan suddenly turned deadly. Because something was going on in the Penderson Mansion that night. Five VERY ANGRY women had a score to settle, and no obstacle on earth would stop them. . . . And no one would get in their way and live to tell the tale either.

"John Miller must die," the women had decreed, and it looked like the forces of Hell would help them accomplish their deadly aim tonight.

But as the night progressed, Megan, who was now trapped in a deadly game of cat and mouse in the Penderson Mansion, found that despite her own troubles, her biggest question was: "What the hell did John Miller do to anger these five women this much?"

Beware, folks . . . sometimes things really do go too far!

Burning Bulb

WOL-VRIEY
BIZARRO AND TRANSGRESSIVE FICTION

RATIO OF BROOKES TO ASHLEYS

After being cursed by a dying woman, Mike Broadman's love life completely nosedives. One girlfriend cheats on him and the next one dies a very messy death.

Next, a psychic informs Mike that he's under an evil spell that will keep killing his girlfriends, and that the ONLY solution (the ONLY way that he'll ever have a happy love life again) is for him to only date women named either Brooke or Ashley from now on.

Mike tries to comply with this, but still, the deaths continue, and now they're becoming even more brutal and bloody. Mike now finds himself in a race against time. He needs to 'equalize the ratio of Brookes to Ashleys' before it's too late.

And then, just when it seems things can't get any crazier or deadlier for Mike, he meets 'Brash' — the twins Brooke and Ashley Lawrence . . .

And the body count keeps rising . . .

DELICIOUS ZOMBIE

The zombie apocalypse happened two years ago. Today, zombies are mankind's new cattle. The undead are headed like cows and killed and eaten by everyone. The reason for this atrocity? Eating zombie meat has been scientifically proven to reverse human aging. Therefore, anyone who eats the zombies will live forever. Nowadays there are no old people anywhere on Earth. Everyone is young and healthy. Even deadly diseases have regressed. "

Digestion is Salvation," the Church of Zombie preaches. But three people—scientist Ethan Hackman, ex CIA assassin Paula Neyman, and socialite Zoe Patterson—seek to change this madness that is modern life.

With a group of ruthless and sadistic bounty hunters hot on their trail as they attempt to save the world, will Ethan, Paula, and Zoe succeed in curing the zombies, or will the age of the 'Delicious Zombie' continue? One thing is for certain, however; there will be a HUGE amount of murder and mutilation, bloodshed, violence and gore before the knotty issue of the zombies' food status is resolved.

Burning Bulb

WOL-VRIEY
BIZARRO AND TRANSGRESSIVE FICTION

MOTEL GOTHIC

The Devil's Coin Game was a game for desperate men. And Dooks, Hicks, and Robby were three such men, men with nothing to lose, men prepared to gamble their lives away on the flip of a coin. The rules of the game were simple: one man would die, the other two would have their wishes granted by the devil. At midnight in the Sunflower Motel, the Devil's Coin Game will be played, and one of the players will not survive.

Elsewhere in the Sunflower Motel, two female assassins Mandy Cherry and Dewdrop arrive to murder someone. But things are guaranteed to go awry when the intended victim is a witch.

And on this same portentous night, Roman is about to have an unforgettable meeting with a prostitute named Christine. Christine Valona supposedly brings bad luck to all those who encounter her; but why is this, and who is she?

THE BACHELOR

One eligible bachelor, thirteen gorgeous young women, and a TV crew, on a remote Pacific island paradise. What could possibly go wrong? A lot!

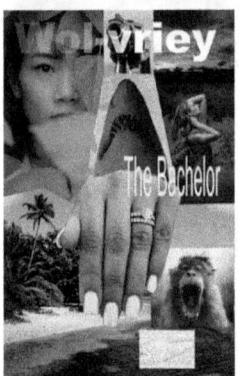

Tired of his refusal to get married and make her some grandchildren, American playboy Tyler Bradley is given a 90-day ultimatum by his wealthy mother to either get married or be disowned.

As a solution, Tyler's best friend, TV producer Disney Dizzford suggests that they hold a 'bachelor-seeking-love' themed reality show on Eternity Island, a remote island paradise off of the coast of Guatemala, which for some reason the Guatemalan government pretends doesn't exist. "When the black cloud comes," the strange old man warned, "monsters will emerge from the sea. When the black cloud covers the sky, all will die."

But nobody takes the old guy seriously, because of course this is the 21st century and there are no such things as sea monsters, right? That sort of stuff only happens in bad movies, right?

Wrong. The black cloud just arrived over Eternity Island . . .

Burning Bulb
PUBLISHING

WOL-VRIEY
BIZARRO AND TRANSGRESSIVE FICTION

MARRIAGE

Adam Norwood, suffering from an extreme photosensitivity skin condition, resides on a secluded island with his wife, Phoebe, and his possible wizard of a father-in-law, Lester. Despite outward appearances of a happy marriage, Adam's life is plagued by recurring nightmares in which Phoebe repeatedly kills him, driving him to the brink of insanity. To add to his woes, Hilary Burton, an alluring party guest on Goat Island, mistakenly identifies Adam as her former lover and is determined to win him back, setting the stage for a calamity that threatens the lives of everyone on the island.

Adam's condition and nightmarish visions pale in comparison to the impending peril he's about to face. The arrival of Hilary Burton unravels a sinister chain of events that may jeopardize the very existence of the island's residents, pushing Adam to discover a new and dire meaning of "bad" and "deadly."

THE MAN WHO KILLED HIS WIFE

Maryanne Wilson's death was definitely an accident. Her husband Bob had absolutely no intention of killing her.

But it was almost certain that a court of law would see things differently, particularly after Bob had sex with Maryanne's corpse . . . and that was why Bob Wilson decided not to call in the police, but to seek an alternative solution to the problem he'd gotten himself into . . . A solution which unfortunately only made matters a whole lot worse for him.

Everything began because Bob Wilson was working too hard and as a result was neglecting his loving wife, Maryanne.

And so, Maryanne asked their upstairs neighbor Jennifer for help.

Jennifer Haskins apparently knew a little magic, and so she cast a spell on Bob, one that would help Maryanne get laid on a more regular basis, like every night if she so desired.

What could possibly go wrong with a simple arrangement like that? Everything you can't possibly imagine . . .

Burning Bulb

WOL-VRIEY
BIZARRO AND TRANSGRESSIVE FICTION

LGBT: LUST, GORE, BLOODSHED, & TERROR

Hey, you want something completely effed up? Well, here it is! LUST: Lavelle, the lesbian porno actress whose dead lover comes back as a ghost to haunt her. GORE: Greg, the elderly gay man who decides to butcher his young, unfaithful husband and his husband's boyfriend. BLOODSHED: Bryn, the bisexual vampire endlessly seeking her soulmate, but who, somehow, always ends up killing her lovers. TERROR: Tammi, the disgraced transgender influencer who, unable to afford the cost of her Gender Affirmation Surgery, decides to become a 'complete woman' by magical means. These four people meet and interact at the Bonner's Corner nightclub, where their intersecting schemes and dreams will place them on a series of collision courses with each other that will lead to weird consequences for some and horrifying ends for others. Oh, and the witch named Rainbow. Why is Rainbow called 'Rainbow' anyway?

NIGHTMARE FUEL

After Dustin's girlfriend breaks up with him, his new neighbors introduce him to the Real Dreams club to help him get over the breakup. But the Real Dreams club is much stranger than it appears. While on the surface, Real Dreams appears to be a members-only sex club, everything at Real Dreams is fueled by the hallucinogenic drink called Nightmare Fuel, or Nif for short. Under Nif's strange influence, sex, torture, and murder are merely the tip of an iceberg of depravity, an insane debauched whirlwind that revolves around the worship of the worm goddess Boku Veeza. What exactly has Dustin gotten himself into? Because the longer he remains at the club, the crazier his life becomes. Dustin knows that the Real Dreams club members are keeping a huge secret from him. But can he learn what their secret is and save himself from the unsuspected and unholy terrors of . . . NIGHTMARE FUEL?

Burning Bulb
PUBLISHING

www.ingramcontent.com/pod-product-compliance
Lightning Source LLC
Chambersburg PA
CBHW071308250626
47159CB00004B/1348